SUSANNAH'S SECRET

Book #2 in Home at Last Trilogy

Jenny Wheeler

Published by Happy Families Ltd
Copyright © 2022 Jenny Wheeler

ISBN 978-1-99-116208-3 (Paperback)
ISBN 978-1-99-116207-6 (EBook)
ISBN 978-1-99-116206-9 (Kindle)

OF GOLD & BLOOD SERIES

Poisoned Legacy #1
Brother Betrayed #2
Double Jeopardy #3
Tangled Destiny–A Christmas Novella and Prequel #4
Unbridled Vengeance #5
Hope Redeemed–A Spanish Novella #6
Book Bundle Of Gold & Blood Series One, Books 1–3.
Book Bundle Of Gold & Blood, Series Two Books 1 & 4–Elanora's Story.
Tainted Fortune #7
Captive Heart–A Hawaiian Christmas Novella #8
Ancient Deception #9
Book Bundle Of Gold & Blood, Three Holiday Novellas (Books 4, 6 & 8)
Dangerous Desires #10

Home At Last Trilogy
Sadie's Vow #1
Susannah's Secret #2

The chief obstacle to a woman's success is that she can never have a
wife. Just reflect what a wife does for an artist.
–Anna Massey Lea Merritt–artist and writer, 1844–1930.

Prologue

She watched from the shadows of Portsmouth Square as the man she'd risked everything for strode to a rendezvous with his former fiancée and her best friend.

With every angry step, his body reverberated with impotent rage, his heels striking the San Francisco pavement with a decisive beat.

She'd made an audacious bid to promote his flagging artistic career, and instead of being grateful, he'd turned on her in fury and broken off their engagement.

I can do it on my own. I don't need your help. Or hers.

He'd leaned over her in the kitchen of their rented apartment, shouting. Spittle flecked her face as he bore down on her, his dark eyes red-rimmed, his handsome face pressed so close she had to fight the urge to grab it in both her hands and kiss him.

His volatility was one thing she'd always loved about him—until tonight. He'd always been like a prizefighter, brimming with energy, ready for action. But she'd never seen him lose his temper like he had less than an hour ago. And in all the years they'd been secret lovers, they'd never exchanged such bitter words.

That showdown in their suite at the St Francis Hotel, a stone's throw from where she stood in Washington Street, had changed things between them forever.

She could feel the vibrations of his anger traveling through the soles of his fine calf Balmoral boots, gushing over her like volcanic lava as she huddled in the meager cover of a waist-high iron picket fence. Small trees in Portsmouth Square, San Francisco's newest urban plaza, offered inadequate hiding places.

Blinded by his resentment, Gil wasn't listening for the footsteps of other pedestrians—or footpads—who might lurk in the streets on this midsummer's night, awaiting easy pickings.

And that's just as well.

She felt the knife knocking against her thigh in her skirt. The minute he'd thundered out of the apartment, she'd known where he was going. And she knew she had to stop him, come what may.

He was a total fool if he thought his reputation—and hers— would survive if he confessed all to Susannah.

She'd had to tell him what she'd done, to prepare him for the prize giving coming up the day after tomorrow.

But she didn't expect his first reaction: to run and blurt all to Susannah. He'd never stopped loving her rival, of that she was certain. Now she suspected he was making a desperate, calculated bid to reinstate their old love.

She felt for the knife again, reassured by its hidden weight.

She tiptoed into the street behind him, ignored by the rowdy late-night revellers on the far side of the park, past the lilac bushes with their shrivelled spring blossom.

There'd be no confession and no third engagement.

I'll kill him first.

One

Susannah put her empty plate down on the servery laden with a mouth-watering selection of breakfast options and wiped the back of her hand across her aching forehead.

She'd worked late last night, putting the finishing touches to the last work of her *Ebony David* series, and although the result had delighted her, she'd slept poorly when she'd returned home from her studio. She'd woken with a dull ache over her eyes.

And now, before she'd even swallowed down a mouthful of black coffee to revive her state of mind, someone was banging loudly on Elizabeth Westerhoven's finely carved front door.

Mrs. Roderiquez, the housekeeper, would answer it. Any minute now she'd be in the breakfast room with an inquiry, and it was just her luck no one else was up and about to handle it.

She picked up the empty plate again and stood poised, her eyes fluttering over the croissants and steamed spinach, the ham, eggs, cereal, fruit and oatcakes. A faint nausea grumbled deep in her gut as she waited with a half-cocked ear for the inquiry to come.

But when the breakfast room door opened, it was her young niece Cordelia who entered, followed closely by her uncle, the irritatingly attractive Jack Cabot.

A prickliness that raised the hair on her forearms replaced Susannah's nausea. She put her empty plate down with a heavy clunk. She wouldn't get breakfast at all at this rate, but maybe that was for the best.

"Susannah." Jack couldn't keep the hint of surprise out of his soothing baritone voice. "You're up early."

She replayed the unspoken insinuation in her head.

We all know you're a lazy cow who regularly sleeps in.

She flicked her eyes to Cordelia, as if by ignoring the comment she could permanently silence him.

"Morning, Cordelia," she said. "Tell me your plans for the day while you get some breakfast. What are you up to?"

Susannah glanced at her thirteen-year-old niece and a warm feeling spread inside her as she noted the girl's pink rounded cheeks and alert hazel eyes, set in a pixie face topped with long blonde hair. She was looking the picture of health.

When they'd arrived in San Francisco six months ago, she'd been pale, thin and drained of energy. Maybe some of her rejuvenation came from the fresh coastal air, but she had to admit her uncle's attentive care also played a key role in Cordelia's improved robustness.

She gave a curt tip of her head in Jack's direction. "Mornin' to you too, Jack."

He flicked her a cheeky grin, which said, *I know you can't stand me and you're putting on a good show for Cordelia's sake.* And he was right.

Cordelia flashed her an uncertain smile. "Uncle Jack said…" Before the young woman could finish her sentence, the door opened again and Mrs. Roderiquez stood there, her face crinkled with worry.

Her questioning eyes searched the room and rested on Susannah.

"There's a woman at the front door asking for you, Miss Susannah. Says her name is Mathilda. She seems rather upset." She added in a whisper, "I think she's been crying."

A questioning pause filled the spaces between the three of them—herself, Jack, and Cordelia. The latent hostility Jack had raised in her vanished.

"Crying?" She echoed the housekeeper's concern.

Jack stepped toward Cordelia and rested his arm around her waist, drawing her slightly closer to him.

"Cordelia and I will eat our breakfast in the kitchen to give you privacy," he said. "Come on, Blossom. What do you feel like this morning? Help yourself to what you want and Mrs. R can give us milk or coffee—whatever you like—out there." He gestured toward the kitchen from the breakfast room.

"That will be fine with you, Mrs. Roderiquez?"

She nodded, a quick smile of gratitude crossing her lips.

"Certainly, Mr. Jack, and I'll let the Countess know what's happening when she comes back in from her early morning walk."

She gazed at Susannah, her eyes raised in a question.

"Shall I bring her in? She'll be most pleased, I'm sure."

●●●●●●●●

Minutes later Tilly Morton trailed behind Mrs. Roderiquez into the breakfast room, anxious eyes searching Susannah out as soon as she stepped clear of the hallway.

She's nervous about how I'll react.

Susannah's eyebrows contracted in a frown even as she stepped forward to greet and reassure her friend.

We've been best friends for years. What is she anxious about?

Susannah pushed aside the question to focus on the moment. Her arms went around Mathilda's neck in a reassuring hug.

"Tilly! What are you doing in San Francisco? I didn't know you were visiting…"

Even as the words were out, she was second-guessing herself. Had Tilly told her she'd planned to visit, and she'd forgotten? Over the last few months, there has been a lot happening with Cordelia. Maybe she'd been too preoccupied to notice.

Mathilda pulled back from the embrace and gave a sheepish smile.

"Didn't I tell you? I'm sure I explained we'd be here. Gil and I. We've come for the opening night of the Bay Gold Expo."

"The Bay Gold?" The new San Francisco art award that Tilly—one of New York's best art agents—had entered one of her *Ebony David* works into.

It was Susannah's turn to pull back. She gazed intently into Tilly's face, watching to see if her expression revealed the deception she detected in her friend's voice. Why was Tilly lying to her?

"Yes! You're not the only one entered. A lot of my New York clients are putting their work forward this year, so I'm here to smooth the way for them."

Tilly fluttered her hands in a vague gesture. "You know. Make sure their works arrive on time and are submitted with the correct paperwork. That kind of thing."

For a few seconds, she seemed like the old Tilly. Confident. Directing. Determined. And then her brightened face crumpled, as if she suddenly recalled her reason for being there.

"But Susannah! You won't believe what's happened!" She buried her head in her hands. Susannah took her elbow gently and led her to the chair at the end of the breakfast table.

"Sit down, Tilly. Take it slowly. What are you trying to say?" She took the chair closest and positioned her body to gaze into Tilly's face.

Her friend's throat heaved with a dry sob. "It's Gil… I just can't believe it. He's dead, Susannah. Gil is dead. Someone stabbed him last night."

Her head dropped to her chest, and she stared at the empty plate in front of her, shoulders heaving.

"He went for a stroll after dinner and never came back." Her ragged breathing dissolved into wrenching sobs.

"Someone murdered him, Susannah! Gil's dead!"

Two

Murdered?

"What are you talking about? He can't be. There's some mistake."

A fleeting expression passed across Mathilda's face, like storm clouds chased by the wind. Stark fear in the first flash. And then a flickering satisfaction. Her lips pursed together as if she'd just tasted something sweet.

She gave a sudden shake of her head.

"No mistake, Susannah. I went to the police when he didn't return by midnight. They'd already found his body."

Susannah's temples throbbed. Her mind was a blank canvas. "When?" she cried. "When was this?"

"Last night. I told you. I couldn't do anything until this morning, but I've come straight from the police station to warn you."

"Warn me?" Susannah knew she was dumbly echoing everything Tilly said, but her brain wasn't working. She couldn't seem to vocalize anything except to repeat Tilly's words.

"Warn me about what?"

"Well, they'll want to talk to you, of course," Tilly said. The statement carried a hint of satisfaction.

There it is again. The implication that she's one step ahead.

"You two were engaged, and you didn't exactly part on good terms."

Susannah felt as if a dam was breaking inside of her. A fierce chest pain penetrated the numbness that had crept over her in the last few minutes, and she gasped.

She and Gil had circled each other for years before their final cataclysmic breakup six months ago.

But that didn't minimize the flood of loss that broke within her, part genuine grief, and part fear of the past they'd shared—and how it might look to an unsympathetic police officer.

"That was months ago," she cried, her voice rich with indignation. "And I haven't seen him since."

"Really." Mathilda's voice was heavy with disbelief, her skeptical pitch turning the inflection downwards. "I wonder then why they found his body just a few yards from your studio door?"

Susannah's head reared up at the clatter of footsteps in the doorway. Jack and Cordelia stood there with contented smiles. Her young niece skipped in without a care, eager to impart her latest news. Jack was taking her to the park or some such.

But she faltered, and the corner of her mouth drooped as she registered the charged tension that stretched between the two women. She stopped in her tracks, gazing from Susannah to Mathilda and then back to Jack, as if seeking direction.

"What studio door?" said Jack. "I didn't know you had a studio in San Francisco."

Susannah put her fingers to her throbbing temples.

"Jack," she choked. "Do you mind? I've had bad news and I can't handle an interruption right now." Jack's eyes locked on her face.

"Oh, I'm sorry, Susannah. "

He glanced at the sylph a few steps ahead of him, who'd been stretching on her tiptoes with excitement in the moments before she collapsed under Susannah's haunted eyes.

He drew a protective arm around his niece and Susannah felt the familiar resentment rise again. They were playing the same old scenario. Aunt Susannah was spoiling their fun all over again.

Three

"Susannah? What's happened?"

Susannah Carterton barely responded from where she sat, slumped forward at the uncleared breakfast table. She raised her head, as if coming out of a bad dream. Her eyes had a glassy sheen.

She's in shock.

An hour had passed since Jack had hustled Susannah's surprise visitor out and then passed Cordelia over to their host and his close friend, Elizabeth Westerhoven.

Cordelia cast an anxious glance back at the house as she'd left with Elizabeth, but the promise of a visit to Woodward's Gardens to view the peacocks and other aviary birds had quickly captured her attention.

Susannah hadn't said a word since the visitor had left.

He paused a few seconds, considering, then slipped soundlessly to the sideboard holding a silver tray and glass decanter. He poured a stiff brandy and brought it to her side.

"Drink this," he said. "I'll get more hot coffee to go with it." She stared back, barely registering his words.

When he returned a few minutes later and sat down opposite her, she hadn't touched the brandy glass. He reached tentatively across the table and placed his hand on her right wrist.

"You're in shock, Susannah," he whispered. "The coffee's coming. Meanwhile, you need a brandy to help you recover."

His touch seemed to rouse her. She flickered her almond eyes over his face and crept her hand toward the glass.

"Thank you, Jack. You don't need…" He squeezed her hand before dropping it.

"Shush. You're not in a position to judge."

He pulled his hand back. "Sip this and then tell me what's going on. I've never seen you in such a state."

Susannah sipped the brandy and after a few minutes straightened up and sighed.

"Thank you, Jack. You're being very kind." He waved her remark away. "For goodness' sake, Susannah. We're family. If you're upset, Cordelia is unhappy. If something's gone wrong, I might be able to help."

She gave a brief, bitter smile.

"Damage has already been done, I'm afraid. Someone I knew very well is dead. If Tilly is correct," she paused and took a huffing breath, "Tilly says he was murdered."

She glanced up and gazed into his face, her watery eyes glittering with unshed tears.

Jack allowed a few minutes before he followed up.

"And who, I pray, is Tilly? And who's died?"

"Tilly is Mathilda Morton. One of New York's top art agents and once my best friend. And the man who died? Gilbert Lusk. A New York artist I've worked with closely for years."

Jack's eyebrows hitched up.

"A New York artist? What's he doing in San Francisco?"

She shrugged, her shoulders rising in a helpless sadness.

"I'd like to know that too. I haven't spoken to him in six months.
"

"And this Tilly woman? Where does she fit in?"

"She was helping him manage his career. Getting his work exhibited in the right places, that kind of thing. She works for one of the leading galleries in Manhattan, so she has a lot of contacts."

"And I notice you said 'once' your best friend? What's that about?" Her face registered a flat resignation.

"Tilly had ambitions to be an artist herself when she was younger, but she's never carried through with them. She felt left out. Like I had advantages she didn't."

She shook herself, as if trying to shed a guilty burden.

"My family could give me support that hers couldn't. In the end, I think that came between us." She squeezed her shoulders up to her ears and let them relax with a long sigh.

"It took a long time, but gradually our closeness died. We became more like professional colleagues than friends."

She glanced up at him, her eyes challenging. "She was handling a painting of mine for entry in this big competition that's opening here this week. That's what our friendship has evolved to. A courteous, mutual respect, I guess is how you'd describe it."

"And what is she doing in San Francisco? Did you know she was here?"

Susannah's eyes slowly widened, as if she was only just registering her friend's presence here now.

"No... no. I don't remember her mentioning she was coming, and I think I would have recalled it. That big competition I mentioned is being judged here in a couple of days. She says she has clients apart from me she is here representing."

Jack felt that familiar tingle he often registered when something seemed off kilter.

"If you know one another so well, then why she didn't tell you she was coming? Ask to meet up?"

Her face clouded with a bewildered expression, as if she hadn't considered it before now.

"I suppose… I hadn't thought…"

She stared at him, her usual intelligence returning to her gold-flecked eyes, and she shook her head slowly.

"It is odd, Jack. Most odd."

"She knew about some studio that no one here knows about? What is this studio, anyway?" She shot him a rueful smile.

"I'm an artist, Jack. I haven't talked about it, but I've never pretended otherwise. It's what I do. I've sacrificed a lot of other things for my work."

He tipped his head in acknowledgment, but said nothing, encouraging her to continue.

She gave a drawn-out, weary sigh. "When I realized I was going to be caught up here settling Cordelia longer than I'd expected, I took a studio down the street from Portsmouth Place. It's a cavernous cheap place, just around the corner from the Art Students League in the old Probate Court building."

Jack was familiar with the ornate, high-ceilinged former courtrooms the students had divided into studios with burlap-covered screens. His friend, the talented watercolorist Lochie O'Riordan, maintained a space there.

It was the place where artists who didn't make the grade for admission to the San Francisco Art Association—with its old-school, male-only membership—met and collaborated.

Susannah's voice had muted, her face taken on a dreamy veil.

"I slip away there to paint whenever I'm not wanted elsewhere."

Jack fell silent as he considered what accompanying his niece Cordelia to San Francisco had entailed for her aunt. He hadn't particularly wanted her here. In fact, he'd resented her constant interference.

But six months ago, when Susannah was working comfortably in

New York, Cordelia's stepmother Sylvia died and then her brother—Cordelia's stepfather—had collapsed under the emotional stress.

A battle of wills ensued. He'd insisted they send Cordelia to him in San Francisco, and Susannah had accompanied her to ensure she received proper care from the guy she referred to as "the cowboy uncle."

For him, it had been the fulfilment of a lifelong dream to reconnect with the precious niece he'd lost when his sister died. But for Susannah, coming West had meant the disruption of her whole life.

His thoughts flicked back to the start of this conversation. Two words rang alarm bells. They were "died" and "murdered."

"Susannah. You said this painter friend was murdered? Is that correct? Do you know how?"

A loud rapping on the front door echoed down the hall, and Susannah looked up sharply, her eyes wide and panicked. She swallowed hard.

"No. No, I don't. I was so shocked I didn't get to ask Tilly about that. Isn't that odd?"

Jack's stomach rolled over.

Is it odd, Susannah? Or do you already know?

Mrs. Roderiquez appeared at the breakfast room door, her face pale and crinkled into worry lines.

"There's a policeman here to see you, Miss Susannah." She licked her lips nervously.

"He says it's urgent and it can't wait." Her words rang with apology. "Shall I show him in?"

Susannah's eyes locked with Jack's. "I guess we're both about to find out how your friend died," he said.

She lifted her hand to remonstrate, as if indicating he should leave.

"Forget it, Susannah. I'm staying. For Cordelia's sake, as much as yours."

Four

Police Captain Seamus Cassidy was narrow eyed and tight-lipped as he marched into Elizabeth Westerhoven's parlor with the impatient air of a cop expecting to make an immediate arrest.

His rolled-up shirtsleeves displayed muscular ginger-haired arms dotted with freckles. And as soon as he opened his mouth, his Irish brogue explained the flushed face with flinty black eyes gazing at her from under red-gold curls.

"Captain Seamus Cassidy," he announced, though Mrs. Roderiquez had given them his name only seconds before. He gestured to the man beside him, a pale-faced younger fellow with eyebrows so blond they were invisible. "This is Constable Wentwhistle."

His eyes roamed from Susannah to Jack with a restless, determined air, and Susannah was suddenly grateful to have Jack at her side.

"You're Susannah Carterton, I presume," he said, making a quick consult with his notepad. He fixed Jack's face accusingly. "And who are you?"

"Jack Mortimer Cabot, Esquire," he said. "A friend of Miss Carterton and the Countess Westerhoven." At the mention of Elizabeth's name, Captain Cassidy frowned.

"What's the Countess got to do with it?"

"Miss Carterton in a guest in the Countess's home." Cassidy glared.

"And the Countess has asked me to ensure Miss Carterton gets a fair hearing," Jack lied.

Cassidy pierced him with another pugilistic glare.

"Miss Carterton has just heard an acquaintance of hers has died, but that's all she knows of the matter," Jack added helpfully.

"And how does she know that?" asked the captain, a sour note curdling his voice.

"From the same person I understand you've already spoken to, Mathilda Morton. Miss Morton was here an hour ago."

Cassidy scowled. "Sit down, both of you. This is likely to take some time."

He fixed Susannah with his hard expression. "Miss Carterton, I have to ask you. Where were you last night between the hours of six and ten p.m.?"

Susannah's face drained of color. She stuttered. "Why do you ask? Is that the time they killed Gil?"

"Just answer the question, please," Cassidy barked.

"Let me see. I was at my studio on Washington Street. I went there at seven p.m., and worked for two hours, until nine p.m."

"Your studio?" Cassidy's voice came close to sneering. "And pray. What do you do in your studio?"

Susannah's face flushed red. "Why I paint, Captain Cassidy. I'm an artist. I'm sure Mathilda has already told you that, hasn't she?"

Jack jumped in. "Captain, Miss Carterton is more than willing to help your investigation, but I ask you to treat her with proper respect." He held the police captain's granite eyes for a long minute.

"She's a recognized New York artist."

There was a tense silence.

Jack continued. "Miss Carterton tells me the deceased was a close acquaintance of hers. Can you please advise us? How was he killed?"

Captain Cassidy's face took on a mulish cast.

"I'm afraid I cannot, Mr. Cabot. "Not until I've got an account of Miss Carterton's movements last night."

Susannah gripped the edge of the table and said, "I got a hack to Washington Street after we'd finished dinner here, arriving at a little before seven p.m.

"I worked there alone until nine p.m. I'd arranged for a hackman to return at nine p.m. to pick me up, but he didn't come. I locked up the studio and walked out to Montgomery Street to catch a ride home."

Captain Cassidy sniffed. "Home?"

"To here. Elizabeth Westerhoven's house. I have been staying with the Countess for the last six months."

"Did you see or hear anything unusual when you arrived or left?"

Susannah's face darkened, and her brow wrinkled. "Unusual? Like what?"

"Just answer the question, Miss Carterton. You've been there often enough to know."

Her face flushed a deeper red. "It was a normal Sunday evening, so far as I could tell. When I arrived, there were folks relaxing on the benches in Portsmouth Gardens, families sharing picnic teas, some street buskers playing Italian songs, children playing tag around the little trees. A gent taking his dog out for a walk. Nothing unusual."

"A dog? What sort of dog?"

Susannah shrugged. "A big white dog with smudges of camel and beige on his coat. I don't know dog breeds."

"Camel and beige?" the captain said, suspicion leaking from his voice.

Susannah sighed. "Brown. A big brown and white dog."

"How well did you know the victim?"

"Mr. Lusk? He's been a close artist friend for many years," she said.

Cassidy stared into her face questioningly, his eyes glittering black points, letting the silence draw out. Finally, when Susannah volunteered nothing else, he said, "I have to ask, Miss Carterton. How much of an artistic acquaintance?"

Susannah shrugged. "We worked on projects together. We gave one another encouragement."

Cassidy's face took on an inner glow, Jack thought. And although he couldn't say exactly why, Susannah's responses sounded paper thin.

"And what did you do then?"

"When?" said Susannah, sharp and flustered.

"When you got back to Mrs. Westerhoven's."

Cassidy's voice was low and laced with irony.

"I came inside and went to bed. What did you expect I'd do?"

Susannah flicked an uneasy glance in Jack's direction and then returned her glare to the aggressive captain, who'd allowed himself a sarcastic grin.

"I don't know what you'd do, Miss Carterton. That's why I'm asking. You didn't, for example, arrange a secret rendezvous with your former fiancé, then?"

Susannah's face turned a ghostly white.

"My… fiancé?" she stammered. "Who told you that?"

"Never mind who told me. Were you and Mr. Gilbert Lusk ever engaged to be married, Miss Carterton?" Once again, Susannah's eyes flicked to Jack.

"Yes. Yes, we were," she said.

"And what happened? Why aren't you Mrs. Lusk?"

Susannah looked to the ceiling, then the floor, as if seeking escape.

"It… it didn't work out, that's all. We had different interests…"

"So, it wasn't because Mr. Lusk took his affections elsewhere? To put it crudely, Miss Carterton, he didn't dump you for someone else? Another woman?"

Susannah's rounded eyes snapped back to the policeman's face. Her jaw dropped, and her cheeks turned an indignant beetroot red.

"It most certainly wasn't the case that he dumped me for someone else," she said hotly. "Quite the opposite. He pursued me for years, and I finally had to tell him it wouldn't work."

"So why didn't you tell us that right at the start, Miss Carterton? Why act as if you've got something to hide?"

Jack pushed himself to the back of his chair and surveyed the scene.

Cassidy looked like a cat with a mouse caught wriggling in his mouth. Susannah's face glistened, pale and anxious, her eyes darting all around.

She looks guilty as hell. Little Miss Rectitude. Always carping on about my messy past and unsuitable qualifications to be Cordelia's guardian.

Let her who is without sin cast the first stone and all that…

And yet… He saw deep into Susannah's misery and felt no triumph in it.

Five

What was I thinking?

Susannah combed her fingers through her hair with a distracted air after Cassidy departed, warning her before he went that she was not to leave San Francisco.

He already has me on the gallows—and who could blame him? I acted like a guilty person. I lied to him.

Jack had risen to see the captain out, and she raised panicked eyes to him as he stood in the parlor doorway and regarded her, brows concertinaed into querulous lines.

A flush of embarrassment rose up her neck as they stared at one another, each refusing to look away. Saying nothing.

Finally, he moved to the table and flung himself into a chair opposite, lounging back with his legs spread wide.

"What. Were. You. Thinking?" He massaged his temples as if he had a massive headache forming behind his deep forehead.

When she still held her silence, he added, "Or weren't you thinking? You realize he's even more convinced now than when he arrived that you killed this fellow? The fiancé." He spat out the last two words.

"Why is it so hard for you to face up to the truth? You're no ingenue. So, you've got a past. For Lordy's sake, Susannah. You always have to come across as Miss Perfect."

She stared at him, dumbstruck. Fury boiled over his classical features, giving him a fire-brand intensity which was even more compelling than his happy-boy-without-a-care-in-the-world act.

But why was he so angry? He'd never liked her. They both knew it, though he'd had the good manners not to come out and say it. His life would probably be a lot easier without her around to meddle in his plans for Cordelia.

"I thought you'd be happy. It's one way to get rid of me, anyway."

He catapulted up like an acrobat on a springboard, galvanized into action.

"You can just shove that ridiculous, self-pitying nonsense back down your throat."

He strode a couple of paces away from the table and swung around.

"Have you given any thought to how Cordelia will feel if you disappear? If you were gaoled or worse? Well, I can tell you. It would destroy her."

His words struck her as hard as if he'd wielded the butt of a gun at her midriff. She fell forwards gasping, grabbing at her chest for breath, tears flooding the back of her eyes.

"He caught me unawares, Jack," she cried out. "I was still in shock from hearing Gil was dead."

She put her hands to her face and tried to push back the tears.

"I know I made a mess of it. I'm sorry."

Salty water leaked through her fingers and down her cheeks.

"I'll make it up to her. I don't know how, but I will."

"Why didn't you admit he was your fiancé? That's probably the worst bit. He'll think you've got something to hide."

She kept her face in her hands, not daring to look at him.

If he sees my face, he'll guess I do have something to hide.

"What aren't you telling me?" he asked after a long silence. "I can't help you unless I know the full story. You owe it to all of us to come clean."

She finally let her hands drop away. She sat up and gazed straight at him.

"There's nothing to tell, Jack. We had an on-again-off-again courtship. If you could even call it a courtship. I wanted to put my art first. Before anything. He kept telling me we were stronger together.

"You know the old story… As it says in Ecclesiastes: *'Two are better than one, for if either of them falls, one can help the other up.'*"

She grimaced. "Gil was a firm believer in that. Especially the part about 'one helping the other up.'" She took a deep breath and tried to rein herself in, but some irrepressible force drove her tongue.

"The little handmaiden. That's how he saw me. I was there to lift him up. Not so much the other way round." Her mouth twisted into a caricature of a smile, and she swallowed down a familiar bitterness.

I'm turning into a sour, distrustful old woman. How very attractive.

She made a self-deprecating hand gesture and glanced away from him.

"Sorry. Getting on my hobby horse again."

Her eyes dropped to the floor, and she fell silent.

All he cares about is Cordelia. That's why he's here. He would run away if he knew the full story.

•••••••••

Jack recognized the trenches of deep despair in Susannah's face as her desperation flooded out. He'd been there himself often in the years after Cordelia disappeared and he'd wallowed in the half-life of Barbary Coast opium dens.

He'd known Susannah for six months, and for the first time he felt sympathy for her. She faced a double agony; of not being the person she wanted to be—a recognized artist—and the one society expected of her—a respectable married woman putting her husband and household ahead of everything else.

In her eyes she'd failed on both counts. Everyone knew women didn't have it in them to be serious artists. Men had the true creative fire. Women created babies. And she'd missed her chance with that option. In society's eyes, she was an old maid. And now she was a criminal as well.

"Susannah," he said carefully. "The nature of your relationship with Gil is none of the captain's business, except as it relates to motive.

"Was there anything between you that might lead you to want to kill him? That's all Cassidy needs to know. The rest is your personal business."

Frightened hazel eyes gazed at him a few seconds and slid away to the floor.

Not a good sign.

His heart thudded steadily on as he gave her time to respond, but when she remained silent, he made another attempt.

"Susannah?" he prompted, his voice soft and low. "Is the captain correct about what happened between you? That you were a 'scorned woman'?"

Her face flamed a fiery red as her eyes shot to his face, glittering with anger.

"That's not what happened," she spat, and took a heaving breath. "Quite the opposite occurred."

"Who else knows about this?"

Her outrage faltered, and she shook her head.

"How can they?" she said, her voice pitched high with indignation.

"It's an intensely private matter. Hardly a conversation you're going to chatter about."

He stared hard, trying to read the flickering shadows of contradiction in her eyes. She glared back, unrelenting.

"Have you talked to Mathilda about it? You said she was your best friend…"

Her gaze shifted to a painting above the fireplace, a Yosemite landscape in deep greens and browns.

"We haven't been intimate friends since I went to Paris and she stayed in New York." Her clipped voice signalled that as far as she was concerned, the discussion was closed.

He'd have to ask Mathilda if he wanted to know more.

Six

"If Aunt Susannah died, who would be my mother?"

Cordelia squinted up at Jack through slanting rays of bright sunshine, the air full of a warm, milky aroma.

His young niece leaned over wooden palings, her slim white hand clutching a handful of hay, offering it to a shy calf that stood on spindly long legs on the other side of the fence. At the back of the stall, the heifer calf's bulky black and white Friesian mother watched warily, her pink udder bulging.

They were visiting Jack's artist friend Lochie O'Riordan's Bernal Heights farm, and his surprise at Cordelia's out-of-the-blue question momentarily chipped away at his radiant glow inside.

Lochie's small menagerie was an unfailing source of enchantment for girls like Cordelia. Besides several calves, he had a sow nursing eight piglets and a flock of milking goats.

A placid old English sheepdog followed them, long tongue lolling out, the floppy fringe that fell over his eyes not impeding his pursuit of them, and Cordelia had been in seventh heaven.

Until this moment, Jack had thought her excitement at her first visit into San Francisco's rural suburbs had fully captured her attention and made her forget about the scene in the breakfast room.

He'd been unobtrusively monitoring her for any sign of upset after the appearance of the policeman yesterday, and this was the first indication she'd registered anxiety over the episode.

"Whatever makes you worry about Aunt Susannah?" he asked, injecting his response with as much light-hearted surprise as he could muster. "Nothing's going to happen to her."

Cordelia bored into him with alert emerald eyes he well knew missed nothing.

"But what if something did happen?" she replied, her jaw set in a stubborn lock, never taking her eyes off him.

"Well, if something terrible happened, then I guess Countess Elizabeth could be your pretend mother. And I will always be here for you, Cordelia. You know that."

The stubborn expression softened, and she flicked him a quick smile.

"The Countess is too old," Cordelia said. "She's more like a grandmother."

Too old.

She's only a couple of years older than me, thought Jack with a pang, but he couldn't help smiling. The world through children's eyes.

If Elizabeth is too old, what does that make me?

"Your aunt is in fine health. She's going to be with us for many years to come."

She turned back to the pen, where the unweaned calf was sniffing at the hay. Jack suspected, in fact he knew, that the infant was too young to eat hay. She still feasted on her mother's milk. Perhaps that's what had unconsciously sparked Cordelia's inquiry.

"So why did the policeman come yesterday?" she asked, her eyes firmly fixed on the animals before her. Avoiding direct eye contact, just like her aunt. Did that mean if she didn't like the answer, she could pretend she didn't hear it?

In Susannah's case, that might be exactly why she hadn't wanted to meet his gaze.

"Because one of your aunt's friends died, and the policeman wanted to ask her about him."

He sensed the stiffening in her thin shoulders, clothed in a crimson corduroy pinafore frock over a cream blouse. He brought his hand to the back of her neck and gently stroked the tension away.

"Did you ever meet her friend Gil Lusk?"

The delicate skin under his soft hands immediately tensed.

"Not really," she said.

"Not really? What does that mean?" He laughed.

"He came to dinner one night, when I was in bed."

"Oh, I see. A grown-ups dinner, was it?"

Cordelia's father had adopted her out—Jack thought of it as "sold" because the ratbag gambler had exchanged her for money—to an older New York couple after Jack's sister Tammy died of a sudden fever.

When her stepmother Sylvia had died a year ago, her stepfather struggled with depression, and Jack had leapt in and requested she come and live with him.

"Not a dinner party," she corrected him. "Papa Tom was away on business. It was just Susannah and the man."

She turned reluctantly, her eyes narrowing in the shimmering sunlight. She'd put on a healthy growth spurt since arriving in the West, but she suddenly looked once more like the pale, fragile child who'd arrived by train six months ago.

Her New York doctor had warned her frailty might suggest tuberculosis, but Jack refused to acknowledge that threat. He searched her face, crushing down the tension tightening in his chest.

"Papa Tom. He wasn't there with Gil?"

She shook her head sharply, and reached out to pat the sheepdog's head, as if seeking comfort.

"No." She drew in a quick breath. "I didn't like him. That man. He was scary."

"I thought you said you didn't meet him," Jack reminded her.

"I didn't," she blurted. Too quickly, he thought.

"Why was he scary?"

She turned back to the enclosure, but not before Jack saw a guilty cloud darken her eyes.

She'd spied on them, he guessed. He saw it all in his mind's eye. A little girl who couldn't sleep. Perhaps she'd had a bad dream.

Maybe she'd tiptoed downstairs looking for comfort and unwittingly seen something she knew she shouldn't. Or maybe she was simply curious and stole down to take a peek. To satisfy herself Susannah was still there.

He took her by the shoulders and turned her to face him.

"So what happened, Angel? Did that man Gil upset Aunt Susannah?"

Her eyes widened in shock, as if he'd caught her in a lie.

"Nothing. Nothing happened. Aunt Susannah said nothing happened."

Her breath was coming fast and shallow, and her peaky little face had settled into perplexed lines. He gathered her into his arms. "It's okay, sweetheart. You're not in trouble. You can tell me."

She swallowed hard, as if trying to digest the lie, and her lips set in a straight hard line.

He glanced at the calf. "I think that little calf wants some of his mother cow's milk. He's not quite ready for hay yet. Let's go back to Nan Waters and see what she's prepared for lunch."

Nan was Lochie's sturdy housekeeper, and Cordelia had relaxed in her motherly presence from the moment they'd met.

As he took her hand to lead her back to Lochie's house, he could feel the stress drain out of her slender body. First Susannah, in denial. Now the child knows something she can't talk about and feels she must lie about to protect her aunt.

He clutched the child's hand even tighter.

This is not good. And I need to find out the full story before Captain Cassidy does.

Seven

They were exploring the yard while Lochie completed a portrait sitting. As they wandered back into the house, he heard Lochie call out to Nan: "All clear now, Nan. Dot's getting tidied up and then she'll have lunch with us before I drive her to the train."

As they stepped inside the weatherboard cottage surrounded by farmland, Jack drew Cordelia to his side and pointed at the dazzling watercolours that filled every inch of the living-room walls.

"See all those gorgeous paintings of flowers and animals and ladies gathering flowers? My friend Lochie did all those. His mother was a wonderful artist, and he takes after her. And we're going to meet him any minute now."

Cordelia flashed him a sparkling smile. She loved drawing and spent hours sketching pictures of dogs they saw in the park.

Before they'd got seated in the places Nan showed them to, Lochie burst through the fringed silk curtain that separated his studio from the main living area, his arms extended in a warm welcome.

"Jack! It's been too long since I saw you." He clasped Jack's shoulders and squeezed affectionately before turning to Cordelia. "And I see you've brought a beautiful maiden to visit as well."

Lochie was California born and bred, but both of his parents were

Irish, and his voice carried a faint musical lilt of the Emerald Isle in its cadence.

Cordelia smiled in shy pleasure. "This is my niece Cordelia," explained Jack. "She's come all the way from New York to see how she likes this side of the country."

"And what do you think so far, Cordelia?" Lochie stood back from her, considering her with a kindly artist's eye. "Do we meet with your approval?"

Cordelia glanced at Lochie with an almost coquettish slant in her eyes and said, "I love your animals. Especially the calf and the dog."

"I see," said Lochie teasingly. "The animals pass, but the humans have still got a way to go. What's wrong with you, Jack?"

Jack was wondering how much longer Cordelia could be seen as a child. She was on the cusp of womanhood. He was pondering the question when the silk curtains parted and a flaxen-haired lass much the same age as Cordelia poked her head through.

This must be Dot, the artist's model Lochie had referred to.

She eyed Cordelia, as if drawn to her, and Lochie immediately took his cue from her attention.

"Ahh, Dot," he said. "Or more properly, Dorothy, but you prefer Dot, don't you?" She glanced at Lochie and took two quick light steps into the room. Jack saw immediately a winsome grace in her face that carried through to her light butterfly movements.

"Dot's been working with me on my latest series," said Lochie. "It's quite a departure from what I've been doing, and she'd been wonderfully patient with me.

"Dot, this is Cordelia," he gestured to the girl, "and Jack. Jack is a close friend and business partner, and Cordelia is his niece, visiting from New York."

"I'll probably be staying," Cordelia suddenly piped up. "If Aunt Susannah lets me."

She gazed in open admiration at Dot. "Do you enjoy working with an artist? I'd love to do that."

Lochie glanced at Jack in surprise and took over as host. "Your aunt might not be so keen on that idea," he said with a quick smile.

"Come on, let's get you seated. Dot, I think it would be an excellent idea if you sat next to Cordelia and left Jack and me to talk boring men's business."

Nan served them a chicken and leek pie that Cordelia enjoyed so much she agreed to a second slice. While Jack and Lochie caught up on the news about their mutual commercial interests—Lochie's father Raizney Grigor had appointed Jack as Lochie's mentor to coach him through his first few years of managing his inherited estate—the girls chattered happily together.

Whenever Jack could, he eavesdropped on their conversation. It seemed to revolve around Lochie's animals, and Dot knew a surprising amount about them.

In the pause between the first course and a light dessert, Jack introduced his second motive for this visit. To pick up on the art world gossip mill.

He knew Lochie paid for a small studio in the Art Students League building, where he occasionally hung out to keep in touch with fellow artists in town.

He deliberately waited for a lull in the conversation as he pitched his next question.

"What's going on in the San Francisco art world at present, Lochie? Anything exciting?" He adopted a casual tone, as if prompted by idle curiosity, but he caught a glint in Lochie's green eyes that made him suspect he'd already guessed why he was asking.

Lochie glanced at Dot. "You know better than me," he said. "What's the old man up to?"

He turned to Jack. "Dot works for Aloysius Mandelow, who's the bigwig in San Francisco's art world. I can only get her as a model when he doesn't need her."

The girl shrugged lightly. "They're all a twitter about the big art show that's opening tomorrow. It's meant to be for West Coast artists, to encourage local talent, but the word is artists from lots of other places are entering.

"Some of the locals don't like that. They want to keep the money that the rich guys here spend on art for local painters."

Lochie nodded appreciatively. "That's interesting," he said, the admiring tone plain in his voice. "I can understand their point of view. But it also means the prestige of the thing grows. Isn't that good for everyone? Then the winner isn't coming from one little pumpkin patch."

Dot smiled. "That's why the Doc's happy. He's boss of a bigger pumpkin patch."

"The Doc?" asked Jack.

Dot's porcelain complexion pinkened and her eyes shifted uneasily to Lochie.

Lochie took over: "Aloysius. He's a professor of art at the local academy. He's Dr. Aloysius..." He braced his shoulders in a barely discernible reflex that Jack noted with growing interest.

"He's the president of the San Francisco Artists Society. They're one of the main sponsors of the show, and so the kudos trickles down to them when big-name artists enter. He's also one of the chief judges."

He glanced to Cordelia and noticed she was biting her lip; her face was paling even as Dot's continued to redden.

A sudden thought occurred to him. "Aunt Susannah's got one entered in that show, Cordelia. She mentioned it yesterday. Has she said anything?"

Cordelia shrugged, but said nothing. Her pinched face was closed. Dot cast an inquiring glance toward Cordelia.

"Your aunt's an artist? What's her name?"

"Carterton," Cordelia whispered. "Susannah Carterton," as if reluctant to disclose the name.

Dot's eyes widened and flicked a significant look to Lochie, her eyes alight with some new understanding.

She licked her lips and started uncertainly. "There's a lot of gossip that some New York artist has won the grand prize. They haven't announced the winner yet. Maybe they haven't even decided yet. But there's a lot of talk."

Lochie clasped his hands to his chest and Jack saw his fingers were marked with flecks of crimson and dark green paint.

"There's a wild rumor going round about that fellow who was stabbed in the street. That he was an entrant," he said. "Maybe even the winner. That's one crazy suggestion, anyway."

He shrugged. "It's supposed to be a big secret. No one can know for sure. It's probably all arty gossip."

"Are you saying his death was something to do with the competition?" asked Jack. "Like some local got angry or something?"

Lochie made a helpless hand gesture.

"Who knows? He might have got drunk in a bar and got into an argument, you mean? Maybe called a local a hick? Just speculating. Silly things happen when guys drink."

"He wasn't killed in a bar, though," Jack said. "They killed him in the street."

"Yes, I know. Not far down the street from our building, actually. I hear Doc has already talked to the police. Is that right, Dot?"

The young woman moved restlessly in her chair, as if sitting at the table was becoming increasingly uncomfortable.

At that moment, Nan bustled in with a fluffy beaten dessert. "Peach flummery," she announced proudly. "From our own orchard and cows."

Dot flashed her a grateful smile.

"The League building," Jack asked. "That's near Washington Street, isn't it?"

Lochie dipped his head to Nan as if to say, 'Serve it out, Nan,' and then turned back to Jack.

"The League is on the corner of Montgomery and Washington. That fellow—what was his name—Lusk? They found him half a block down from the corner. Not far at all. The police are asking if anyone heard or saw any fights."

"And had they?" Jack peered from Dot to Lochie. Lochie shook his head. "Not that I've heard," he said. "Did you hear anything, Dot?"

Her eyes flickered to Cordelia, who was gazing at her dish of peach flummery with downcast eyes.

"Doc thinks it's nothing to do with the contest. He thinks it's more likely to be a lover's quarrel. The guy was two-timing or something. That's what he thinks."

Jack was watching Cordelia's somber face as she stared into her dish.

She joggled her chair away from the table.

"I'm full, I'm sorry," she said without looking at Nan. "I'm going to see the calf again." She turned and stumbled out, leaving them gaping.

"First time I've known anyone to turn down Nan's peach flummery," said Lochie with a wry sideways grin to Jack.

"What's going on with her?"

"I'm sorry," said Dot. "I shouldn't have said…"

Jack waved his hand in the air.

"My fault, Dot. Not yours. I kept pushing the subject, when I should have waited until she wasn't here."

"Thing is…" said Dot, leaning toward him, a quiet conspirator.

"That's not all Doc says. He says the woman they think killed that codger had a studio down the street from where he was kilt. Doc says he'd gone from visiting her when he got done."

She leaned in even closer and whispered:

"Do you think it could be Cordelia's aunt they're talking about?"

She glanced to the door.

"Poor kid if they are."

Poor kid indeed, thought Jack. Surely, she's not about to lose her third mother figure in a short and unhappy life?

Not if I can help it.

He rose from the table and glanced apologetically at Nan.

"I'd better see that Cordelia's all right," he said. "Sorry, Nan. I'll have to save tasting your peach flummery for another day."

Dot had risen with him, her face wracked with lines of worry.

"You won't let on to the Doc I told you anything? He'd get his mad up if he thought I'd been talking."

Jack glanced at Lochie in surprise.

"I don't recall you told me a thing," he said with a grin, turning back to Dot. "You've no worries on that score."

Eight

Six months earlier: New York

"First Paris and now San Francisco."

Gil Lusk was smiling, and his voice carried a teasing lightness, but his eyes glittered with a malice that set Susannah's nerves jangling.

He'd reached over to refill her glass with her brother's excellent French Bordeaux, and he set the bottle back down with a dull clunk that sounded final.

He paused theatrically and raised one of his bold, dark eyebrows. Funny. She'd once thought that little trick of his alluring. Now it made her stomach clench.

"You're always running away from me, Susannah. And just when I thought you'd seen sense and we could get back together again… You've been home in New York less than a year…. And now you're off again?"

His voice was edged with that whiny, spoiled rich boy plaintiveness he'd never grown out of.

He'd always been like this—an enticing double layer cake laced with something unpleasant—the cream layer between the sweet sponge adulterated with vinegar.

Sooo attractive, with his craggy masculinity and that shock of dark hair over the strong eyebrows. Get up close though, and it wasn't too long before you tasted something sour and unexpected.

They sat at one end of Thomas's walnut dinner table that seated eight in an otherwise empty brownstone near Central Park—empty, except for her niece and Thomas's adopted daughter Cordelia, who was asleep upstairs.

Thomas was away on business. She'd sent the staff home. This was a private dinner with an old fiancé.

She pushed some of the roast chicken Thomas's cook Ma Botica had prepared for her dinner onto a fork and attempted to swallow it, but suddenly she didn't have room for another bite.

She ballooned inside with an anxiety that tingled to the ends of her fingers.

"Gil, you know I've no choice in this. Since Sylvia died, this isn't a good place for Cordelia. I'm watching her fade away day by day."

She fingered the stem of her crystal wineglass with its crimson load.

"Tom's deep in his cups. You know that. And the uncle in California is determined to have her go there. He feels they stole her from him when her father adopted her out. He wants her back."

She paused and lifted the glass and sipped, her slow, deliberate motions calming the tension inside.

"The family are apparently good people, thoroughbred stock. Came over with the Mayfair types. It's not fair to keep her from them, not when Tom's like he is."

Gil had been socking back his Bordeaux, and he reached to re-fill his own glass, his mouth set in an irritable grimace. "I know all that. You don't have to tell me. I'm not dense."

His face rippled with impatience. "But why do you have to go too? Put her on a train with her governess. Hire a nun to accompany her, if you must.

"I don't understand why you're hurrying off to the other side of the country with her. She's not your responsibility, for goodness' sake."

She's not your daughter and she never will be.

She let out an enormous sigh. The old argument. The one they'd been having since they first met over a canvas and brushes ten years ago.

He'd always wanted her for himself, from the day they'd met. As his muse, his companion, his wife, the mother of his children. But not as an artist practicing her own craft; just one who used her sure eye and innate sense of color for inspiring and admiring his work.

This was why she'd run away to Paris. To escape him and further her career away from his suffocating attention. Was this what other women called love?

"Gil, I'm fully aware of my status as the spinster aunt. Thanks for reminding me. But I'm not letting that child go off to some unknown California cowboy alone.

"She's been through too much in her young life already. I'd never forgive myself if it turned out to be a disaster and I wasn't there to rescue her."

Gil tossed his head in the air testily and then raked his hand through his shiny locks, combing them back from his forehead.

"You can't help yourself, can you? Always rescuing waifs and strays when you could have a perfectly respectable home of your own. It's not too late…"

She suddenly stood and pushed herself back from the table. Her legs had developed a will of their own. She leaned over him. The only time she could do that was when he was sitting and she standing.

"We've been over this, Gil," she said huskily. "Please don't start on it again. Subject closed. I came back for Sylvia and Cordelia. Otherwise, I'd still be in Paris."

Her beloved Paris, where she'd done the best work of her career, work still unseen by any public. Where she'd had the freedom to explore and follow her creative drive wherever it led.

She'd never have left Paris if there hadn't been the family emergency back here, brought on by Sylvia's fatal illness.

She thought of a frigid Paris hospital room, a starchy sheeted bed, and a young woman, her face drained of living color, with a mewling newborn locked in her arms.

She'd walked out on one abandoned child. She wouldn't do it a second time.

Nine

Cordelia woke with a start. She opened her eyes and stared at the white ceiling, with the wreath of carved leaves that circled the hanging light in the middle of her bedroom.

They'd set ajar the door of her room as usual, to allow in a faint glow of light from the upstairs hallway. She liked it that way. She didn't feel so alone if the door was open and she could sense other people moving around the house.

She scrunched up her eyes and tried to remember the dream that had woken her up. She was running away from something, but try as hard as she could, she couldn't remember what.

All she could recall was the panic rising like a tide within her and something drawing closer. Whether that thing caused the panic or was rescuing her from it, she didn't know.

She glanced to the doorway, trying to judge by the strength of the light what time it was. None of the bluey light that came from Ma Botica's bedroom further up the hall was visible.

That could mean Ma B had already gone to bed and turned her lights off, or that she was still in the kitchen washing dishes after Aunt Susannah's dinner.

But the pale gold light that spilled from the hall and the

downstairs foyer? It fell onto her pretty Oriental carpet, with its glowing red, purple and green scrolling patterns that reminded her of India.

And that meant that Aunt Susannah was still awake downstairs, maybe reading a book or sketching some of her designs in the library.

She lay flat on her back in the ambient light and shivered as she let her thoughts wander. She was being sent away again, just like last time when her mother died, though she could hardly remember her mother now.

First her mother Tammy, and now her adopted mother Sylvia, had died. They hadn't allowed her to go to Tammy's funeral, and her new parents never mentioned her, but she'd gone to Sylvia's funeral and she didn't think it helped much.

She was still alone, except for her aunt, and Susannah was away at her studio a lot. She'd let her go there with her a few times after Sylvia died and before the funeral, and she'd loved the funny smell of the paint that tickled her nose.

She'd wanted to see Susannah's paintings, but she'd kept a cloth over the big one in the middle of the room. She'd said it wasn't suitable for her. But why not? If it was all right for her aunt to paint it, why wasn't it all right for her to see it?

She was turning her back to the door and cuddling Fluffy Dog, her favorite toy, her eyes feeling heavy, when an angry voice woke her up again.

"Come back here." A loud, angry man's voice, coming from downstairs. The sound of hurried footsteps. Light steps. A woman walking fast.

"I said, come back here." The man was shouting, sounding angrier than before.

Then a mere whisper. "Gil, I beg you. Don't make a scene. You'll wake Cordelia."

"Cordelia, Cordelia… That's all I hear these days. What about me?"

The woman's voice was definitely her aunt's. At the mention of her own name, she'd frozen, hugging Fluffy Dog tightly to her chest. Before she even knew what she was doing, she'd slipped out of bed and moved to the open doorway.

Her aunt's voice grew louder now, partly because Cordelia was closer and partly because she could tell she was getting grumpy.

"You, Gil Lusk, are a mature adult. Cordelia is a vulnerable child."

Gil somebody? Who's he? Not one of Father's friends that I've heard of. And what does vulnerable mean? She tiptoed down the hall. She kept her doggie friend close because her insides were shivering.

Then she heard the crash of breaking glass and Cordelia knew for sure her aunt and the man were in the dining room. She crouched behind the balustrade, staring through the bars into the dining room.

"Ten years. Ten years I've been waiting for you to see sense." The man again. Her aunt's voice came through strongly now. She wasn't whispering anymore.

"Gil, you need to go home. You're drunk. You're not in any state to have this conversation."

"Drunk, am I?"

Another sound of breaking glass. Cordelia trembled. The man was throwing things. Probably glasses at the wall.

"Get out." Susannah was screeching now, like when an evil wind whipped around the garden. "And don't come back until you can behave like a gentleman."

"I'll give you a gentleman. Someone needs to teach you a lesson."

Cordelia froze as the two of them, her aunt and a big man with black hair, came into view. Her aunt was backing away from him, attempting to escape. And the man? He had one of Thomas's carving knives in his hand and he raised it above Susannah's head.

Susannah's mouth was wide open in a big O. She was terrified—Cordelia could see it, even smell it. She cringed further into the carpet but still couldn't look away. The man kept advancing on her aunt.

Run! Cordelia wanted to scream out the warning, but fear had clamped her throat shut. She couldn't make a sound, just like in her earlier dream, she remembered in a rush. She'd been running and trying to call for help, but no voice would come out.

Susannah seemed to suddenly come to her senses. She raised a silver candlestick she held in one hand and smashed it over the black-haired man's shoulder in a slashing movement.

He howled and dropped the knife. It rolled on the floor right in the doorway. An ivory handle, carved with her papa Carterton's coat of arms. Two crossed swords that meant Never Give Up.

Something like that, anyway. Her father—stepfather—had told her all about it, a family story. The man who'd been threatening Susannah scuttled forward, bending to scoop the knife up, and Susannah brought the candlestick down across his back.

He crashed to the floor, falling to his knees over the long blade, panting like the dogs Cordelia saw fighting in the park. Susannah stood behind him, the candlestick still raised threateningly.

"I said get out," she said in a voice that made Cordelia feel cold on the inside.

"One more move and I'll call the night watch."

The man named Gil rose slowly, like a gorilla at the zoo, from all fours to his full height. His teeth glowed like the monkeys at feeding time in the zoo.

"You pathetic old bag. The night watchman."

He opened his mouth and laughed, and slobber ran down over his chin.

"What can he do?"

Cordelia tried to make herself invisible on the stairs, scrunching down into a wobbly ball.

He's horrible. He's going to kill Susannah.

She didn't see what happened next, because she was too scared to watch.

"Get out!" Her aunt was screaming now, and there was a terrifying thudding sound. The man howled again. She heard a dragging noise down the hall to the front door.

When she dared to look again, blood trailed on the floor. Her aunt staggered back into view, the candlestick dangling from one hand. Cordelia whimpered. She couldn't help it, and Susannah stared across to the bottom of the stairs.

"Cordelia." She dropped the candlestick and rushed to where Cordelia crouched, desperately trying to make herself as small as she could.

"What are you doing here?"

Suddenly, her frozen voice returned. She burst into sobs, tears springing from her eyes.

"I couldn't sleep," she said. "I thought he was going to kill you."

Susannah swept her arms around her, clasping her to her waist.

"Darling, darling girl," she said, stroking her hair as Cordelia sobbed into her aunt's soft velvet jacket. "It takes more than that madman to put me down."

They stood like that for what seemed like an age, with her aunt calming her, cooing soothing nonsense words like "Everything's all right. Don't worry. It was nothing."

All lies, of course, but they made her feel better for a while.

And then finally, Susannah walked her upstairs, put her back to bed, hugged her once more, stroked her hair as she lay back against the pillows, and said: "Nothing happened here tonight. And you saw nothing. Understand?"

Cordelia nodded.

And when she got up the next morning, the blood was all gone. If the horrible man had broken any glasses, there was no sign of them. And Cordelia wondered if it had all been another bad dream.

Ten

It had taken a couple of hours, but once Jack had gleaned from Dot where Aloysius Mandelow's studio was, he loitered in the street outside—casing the place like a burglar. The person he'd been waiting for turned up a couple of hours later.

He'd made a quick recollection of what this Mathilda woman looked like in the brief moments he'd seen her in Elizabeth's breakfast room, so he knew what he was waiting for.

An hourglass figure, and a pretty face just on the wrong side of thirty. He noticed calculating lines around her mouth and dark rings that showed through thick makeup around her eyes. Her years in the New York art scene had taken their toll on her in ways that Susannah had avoided.

He pictured Susannah in his mind's eye, comparing the two women as Mathilda—Miss Morton—alighted from a hansom cab and paid the driver before entering the doorway that led to Dr. Aloysius Mandelow's fourth-floor penthouse office and studio.

Susannah's sunshine-colored hair gleamed, her hazel eyes sparkled with a youthful vitality that was attractive and endearing when she wasn't being the annoying self-appointed guardian of what Cordelia was allowed to do.

With a rush of affection, he understood how different it was for women and men coming to adulthood—with men being given far more leniency to test their wings and receive social forgiveness if they messed up occasionally.

So much of what Susannah stood for came from her own hard experience. He guessed, though he'd never taken the time to inquire, that she was simply trying to spare Cordelia from some of the shaming and humiliation she'd borne along the way.

She might seem pedantic at times, but she retained a fresh enthusiasm and vibrant indignation that showed she'd never given up and fallen into weary cynicism.

Nor had she capitulated into a marriage of convenience with someone like Gilbert Lusk. The more he thought about it, the more surprising that was. Lusk was from a good family, had a private income, and could have protected her from much of the disapproval she attracted as a single woman serious about art.

She could have hidden behind him and continued her work, shielded from nosey society matrons. He wondered why she hadn't agreed to that remedy.

Maybe her onetime best friend "Tilly" would enlighten him. He crossed the street and wended his way upstairs to Aloysius Mandelow's office.

Lochie had agreed to introduce him to the good doctor as "an investor"—originally from New York—and looking to buy art on behalf of his recently married sister who was setting up house.

Mandelow's eyes glinted at the prospect of a wealthy patron, and he'd been more than pleased to go out to coffee with him and Lochie earlier in the day. So when he presented himself once in Mandelow's office, he couldn't have been more delighted.

"Mr. Cabot," he said, standing up from behind his desk and crossing the floor to shake his hand. "Nice to see you again so soon.

I was just telling Miss Morton here all about you."

"Oh?" Jack said, turning his most devilishly handsome smile on Mathilda. He allowed for a studied pause and then exclaimed, "Why, I believe I've already seen you, though I wasn't fortunate enough to be introduced.

"Weren't you at Countess Elizabeth Westerhoven's house a day or two ago? Calling on Susanna Carterton? Now let me see, didn't Miss Carterton say you were very close friends—best friends, I believe?"

Mathilda Morton's cheeks blushed at that. Aloysius Mandelow stood like an MC at a picnic. "Miss Morton, let me introduce Jack Cabot, of the Pennsylvania Cabots—"

Jack rarely leaned on his blue blood ancestry, but he'd considered it justified to boast of his Founding Father bloodlines in a good cause. Mathilda Morton's eyes widened. She was impressed, Jack thought. Interesting…

"I'm afraid this unfortunate death has put quite Miss Carterton out of sorts," Jack continued, blinking innocent eyes as if to show he'd no idea why she'd been so affected.

"Was the unfortunate victim a friend of yours too?"

The blush faded instantly, and her countenance reassembled in doleful lines.

"He was," she whispered, as if speaking at a normal volume would be disrespectful.

She cast a sly glance in Aloysius's direction.

"Miss Carterton and the victim were more than good friends, so I'm not surprised she's pulling out her widow's weeds."

Mathilda Morton shifted uneasily from one foot to the other, concerned perhaps that he'd think her a gossip.

"Oh, really?"

Jack felt a pang in his chest. Susannah, a woman of integrity, would hate to know Mathilda could sink so instantly to malice.

"You're not surprised? Why so?"

He raised his eyebrows to Aloysius, who still stood between them like a circus ringmaster.

"Miss Carterton is my niece Cordelia's aunt, so I'm interested in any information that will help protect Cordelia from scandal."

Mathilda's lips twitched in delighted surprise.

"Really? You're Cordelia's uncle? I understand when the girl first went to live with Thomas and Sylvia, she barely talked of anyone but her beloved uncle Jack. It nearly drove them mad. It seems there was nothing Uncle Jack couldn't do. He was a complete magician."

He shook his head. "Ah, what a shame times change," he said, while enjoying a warm inner glow her words had prompted. "I could listen to that kind of praise all day."

He glanced at Dr. Aloysius. "I'm very tempted to steal your visitor away for a coffee, if I have your permission," he said. "Could we return in, say, half an hour?"

He turned to Mathilda. "That's if you're agreeable?"

He knew the query was a mere formality. The flash of jealousy he'd seen in Mathilda's eyes when he first mentioned Susannah's name told him more clearly than anything that here was a woman who coveted everything Susannah had and she didn't. He suspected Gilbert Lusk was high on that list.

Eleven

The Café de Paris was conveniently situated across the street from Mandelow's quarters, and Jack was soon settled at a table with Mathilda Morton awaiting the delivery of their refreshments—café au lait for her, and a strong long black for him.

From the first moments they'd emerged onto busy Montgomery Street, Mathilda had grasped his arm with a predatory talon, using the excuse that she needed protection crossing the street. She'd aroused his defensive instincts, but he didn't underestimate the calculation that flashed beneath her practiced coquetry.

Mathilda Morton had a steel trap of a mind to match the grip of her long buffed fingernails.

He waited for their coffee to be served before he got down to the conversation he was really interested in. What had gone on between Susannah and the dead man?

"You hinted a few minutes ago there was more than a simple friendship between Miss Carterton and Gil Lusk?" He flashed her a wry smile.

"Naturally, I'm interested in what you meant there. I don't want any unexpected surprises unsettling Cordelia." He followed up the smile with a light shrug of his broad shoulders.

"You know how it is, I'm sure. She's settling down nicely here in California, but she's coming up to that age when she could get unpredictable. I want to protect her as much as possible from unpleasant rumors."

He took a testing sip of his coffee and murmured his approval. "Miss Carterton—Susannah—has been an upright role model for the girl, so I was surprised that something more complicated might be afoot?"

Mathilda Morton watched his face with an eagle eye as he did his best to portray the bumbling, clueless male who was completely out of his depth in "woman's business." He read the satisfied smile that crossed Mathilda's face.

She's fallen for it. She's about to oh so reluctantly deliver the bad news, and while she does it, implicate Susannah in this man's death.

Mathilda delicately dabbed at the corners of her mouth with her serviette, keen to remove any traces of milky coffee froth. Rather like the cat that's got the cream, he thought, and waited, leaving an expectant silence for her to fill.

"I'd hate to say anything that would ruin your picture of Susannah's rather proper exterior," she said, casting a sly look his way.

I bet you would.

She let the statement hang suggestively between them. He flashed her another bright smile.

"I know this can't be easy for you, but I would be beholden to you if you're able to help me," he said. "Cordelia is the most important thing in my life. She's had such a rough start, with my sister dying and everything."

He shot his most expressive appeal and waited yet again.

Softly softly catchee monkee, as they say down on the Bay docks.

"I understand. I'd never break a friend's confidence. Not usually. But I understand. These are unusual circumstances and a child's happiness could be at stake."

"Quite," said Jack, and gazed into her gray-blue eyes. She'd been attractive once, but the greedy shiftiness he saw in her face diminished any beauty that might once have shone there.

She licked her lips, as if anticipating something sweet.

"Gil Lusk was an artist whose star was very much on the rise. He and Susannah had a tortured past, sadly. She set her sights on him and wouldn't let go.

"They came close to marrying twice, but Gil backed off both times because Susannah was so possessive. She wanted to be the artist, and she resented his success."

She glanced over as the café—which had been quiet when they'd arrived, filled with the early lunch crowd, junior clerks from the banks and sharebrokers happy to sit over coffee and croissants and talk shop with their kind.

Jack hooked his mouth into a sympathetic little moue.

"I know this is difficult when you've been such close friends, but please continue. What happened?"

The hint of a tear sparkled in her right eye, and Mathilda dabbed at it discreetly.

"In the last couple of years, I've taken over managing Gil's career and he'd been making a big splash in the New York scene."

She hesitated. "We entered his latest work in this big art show Dr. Mandelow is judging, the Bay Gold, and it wouldn't surprise me if he does well here, too. Gil and I were becoming closer and closer…"

Her eyes flickered across the unfolding café scene as if she was reluctant to continue. Jack waited in silence.

"When Susannah came back from Paris last year, she was fed up. I think she was jealous of the entire scene. That Gil had forged ahead without her. That we were close."

"I'm seeing a pattern here," Jack said encouragingly.

She smiled understandingly.

"It was awful," she said, dabbing her eyes again.

"We'd been such wonderful friends. Then she and Gil had this explosive row. She got violent and hit him with a hefty silver candlestick. Left him with a nasty cut across his neck. She was lucky he didn't make a fuss."

Jack's heart lurched as the embellishments continued.

If she's telling this tale to that tricky police captain…

"I must have been awful for you," he said. "Caught in the middle like that."

She nodded, the tension in her face relaxing.

"It's so nice you understand," she said. "It was dreadful. We'd been friends for so long. For it to end like this…"

Jack sat up straighter in his chair. "Like this? You don't mean you think Susannah actually had a hand in Gil's death?"

She stared down at her shiny, claw-like nails for a long minute.

"Of course not. No, no. She couldn't have. We only arrived in San Francisco a few days ago, and we've been very busy helping Aloysius."

Her eyes glanced around furtively, fearful of being overheard.

"It's the weirdest thing. I know Susannah has a studio here in town. It's probably the worst kept secret. She doesn't want it to be known in case it damages her reputation… She's always been so very aware of being a Carterton…"

The malice laced in her voice was becoming more evident with every word.

"And dear Gil… His body… they found him…" She was snuffling and beginning sentences without being able to finish them, the perfect picture of a woman in distress.

"It was only a few doors away from Susannah's studio. Lying there, stabbed to death."

She was whispering now.

"I can't help asking myself. Is that a coincidence or what?"

Twelve

Susannah was lingering over breakfast when the short-tempered Irish police captain returned, even more pugnacious than he'd been the first time.

He shouldered his way into the breakfast room as if expecting opposition. His ebullient confidence frightened her, and she half rose from her chair in alarm, before he fixed her with a suspicious glare and instructed, "Sit down, Miss Carterton. I've got more questions for you."

The air gushed out of her chest like someone had punched her in the stomach, and she clutched her hand to her ribs in a futile gesture of protection.

He sounded triumphant. What else had he discovered since he was here last?

Constable Wentwhistle, the silent offsider, trailed into the room behind him, an object wrapped in cloth held under his right arm.

"Give that here, Wentwhistle."

Seamus Cassidy cleared the space in front of her of dirty cups left behind by the rest of the family. He pushed aside earthenware pots of marmalade and honey for the toast and slipped into a chair beside her, his right shoulder uncomfortably close to nudging hers.

A random thought popped out of nowhere: Is this how they intimidate suspects?

I'm such an innocent. I've never been in trouble with the police before.

"Am I in trouble?" She'd voiced the question that rang loud in her head without even realizing it.

Cassidy gave her an unpleasant smirk.

"Well, you tell me, Miss Carterton. Have you done anything that would warrant you being in trouble?"

She pushed back her chair, the legs screeching on the parquet floor. It might appear to be the reaction of a guilty person, but she desperately needed the breathing space.

What is going on here? I've got nothing to be frightened about. Absolutely nothing.

And still her heart raced. Cassidy turned to Constable Wentwhistle, his hand stretched toward him in a mute gesture, and the junior officer handed over the wrapped item he'd been carrying.

"I'm going to ask you if you recognize this item," the captain said, "and I'd advise you to ponder before you answer."

Shivers ran down both her legs, and she smoothed her hands down her skirt to ease her anxiety.

Is this happening?

She gripped hard on the wooden arms of her chair to stop herself from slipping into dizziness. The policeman's voice was suddenly a distant sound, and she pinched up her face with concentration to hear what he was saying.

He was unwrapping the item they'd brought, and his mouth was moving, but she'd drifted too far away to hear his words. She momentarily was somewhere safe, a long way away from danger, her ears buzzing and her head filled with a woolly sensation.

And then, like a pricked balloon, she crashed back to reality.

Cassidy's voice was loud and demanding, the deafness gone.

"Have you seen this knife before?" His gaze was so intense, she had the sudden notion he was looking clear into her soul. She shook her head, panicked into denial.

"Answer me, Miss Carterton. Speak up. I'm not a lip reader."

She realized her mouth was opening and closing like a fish in an aquarium, with no sound coming out.

"No. No. I've never seen it before."

He must have taken it. That terrible night when he threatened me. He took the knife.

The same ivory handle. The Carterton crest on the hilt. From the heirloom cutlery set passed down through the generations.

"Think carefully now, Miss Carterton."

Cassidy's manner had changed from belligerent to something else. What? Through the turmoil in her head, she searched for the answer. Congratulatory? Smug? Superior?

He knows where it's come from. He's worked it out.

She gathered up the last vestige of her inner strength, straightened her crumbling body in her chair and asked, as bold and brassy as she could muster.

"You're making a big song and dance about this object, Captain. Where does it come from? May I ask?"

"Why, Miss Carterton, I'd have thought you might have already guessed the answer to that." His smile was phony and feline.

She shook her head, although her face was flushing red with shame and despair.

"We found this knife lodged in Mr. Lusk's chest. I'm certain the doc who's doing the autopsy will find it caused his death. You've vehemently denied ever seeing it before, so I'll have to move on to Miss Morton and check with her. I wonder if she will shed any more light on the matter."

Thirteen

"I'm telling you, Susannah. That woman is toxic. She may have been a friend once, but you shouldn't trust her with anything now."

Jack was pacing up and down Elizabeth's peaceful study, warning Susannah about Mathilda Morton, without coming out and admitting he'd trapped her into having coffee with him.

"If she knows anything about your life you'd rather keep private, then consider it already widely circulated. She'll be blabbing away to that policeman. I know it."

Susannah scrunched her eyebrows in disbelief.

"How do you know that? You've hardly met the woman." She plopped down on plumped-up sofa cushions with a relieved sigh and reached for the coffee already poured for them.

He'd sought her out in Elizabeth's enchanting white and green study, and he was doing his best to warn her of the lay of the land. But she wasn't having any of it.

Always preferring to occupy the moral high ground, Susannah found it difficult to accept that Mathilda was doing her best to cast Susannah as Gil's most likely killer.

Why she was doing that, he hadn't yet worked out.

"She wouldn't do that to me," she protested. "We've known one another since we were nine years old. She's one of my oldest companions."

"I suspect she's jealous of you."

"Jealous? Don't be daft. She's entering my work into this Bay Gold show that's opening tomorrow. I entrusted that to her because I know her."

"And what about her and Gil? Was there anything between them?"

Susannah laughed, the first time he'd seen her looking amused since she'd heard of Gil's death.

"Oh, certainly," she said. "They got engaged six months ago. She's welcome to him."

She looked at him over her raised coffee cup, her eyes sparkling with mischief.

"I don't… didn't want him."

"But what if he still wanted you, and Mathilda hated you for it?"

"Hate me? You think she hates me?"

He could tell by the sudden paling of her complexion that he'd hit a nerve.

"I do," Jack said. "And I'm wondering why."

She stared at her hands, tucked into her lap, and then shook her head.

"There's no reason for her to be jealous, or hate me. Whatever there was between Gil and me is over. It has been for a long time."

He pushed down an impulse to ask just what had been between them, but it was none of his business, was it?

He was only involved because he was defending Cordelia's interests.

"What exactly was between you anyway?" he found himself asking.

She gave him a strangely curious look, as if to silently ask, *What's it to you?*

"The police are going to regard it as key evidence," he said. "If I'm to protect Cordelia I need to know the story. The full story."

Her eyes flickered. "Oh yes. Cordelia. I was forgetting for a moment."

She exhaled a drawn-out, tired sigh.

"We were engaged." She made a little twist with her lips, as if tasting something unpleasant. "Twice. Engaged twice, if you want the full story."

She reached out and poured herself another cup of what was now undoubtedly cold coffee.

"Do you want me to order…?"

"No. It's okay. It's just to distract myself from the unpalatable truth. I fell for the temptation of a romance even though I knew deep down it would never work."

"And what temptation exactly did he offer?" he asked, his insides tightening uncomfortably at the vulnerability softening her usually determined face. He'd never seen this Susannah before. She was almost always the one in control.

"Oh, you know." She took a sip of the new coffee and screwed up her mouth. "You're right. It's gone bitter. A bit like me, I suppose." She gave a weak, self-conscious laugh.

"What temptation?" he repeated. More gently this time.

"Ohhh. The promise of a 'normal life,' I suppose." Her voice roughened, and she swallowed hard.

"Security, a family. A rest from fighting convention. I was sick of being labelled misguided."

She gave a hollow laugh. "First time round, I broke off our engagement and fled to Paris to study painting at the Académie Julian. They offer women painters a chance to do life studies, which none of the other academies allow. And you can't get taken seriously as an artist without having mastered life studies."

She flashed him a wry smile and fell silent for a minute.

"After a year of waiting for me to crawl home with my tail between my legs, Gil came after me to drag me home. I refused. We had another of our tempestuous bust-ups, and he went home threatening to get Thomas to cut my allowance."

She stood, as if barely aware she was doing it, and walked to the window and gazed out. Jack gave her plenty of time to collect herself. Then asked; "And did he? Thomas, I mean. Cut your allowance?"

Susannah turned back to him shaking her head, her face thoughtful.

"I never knew if Gil carried out his threat, but if he did, Thomas didn't act on it. But then, half a year later, Sylvia's illness forced me back anyway. Thomas wanted me there when Sylvia got too ill to manage the household. He'd been so good to me I couldn't refuse."

As she spoke the lines around her eyes became more harrowed. "I love Cordelia, don't get me wrong, but coming back was a hard thing for my work."

She let out a long sigh.

"And then in a weak moment I agreed to try again with Gil. I'd lost my dream of an artist's life anyway, so why not settle for second best?"

Her mouth twisted in another weary grimace. "Dumb, wasn't it? Almost as soon as I'd agreed, I knew it was wrong. I knew it wasn't going to happen."

"And how long ago was that?"

"Just before we came out here. By coming out here, I ran away again. That's how he saw it."

Jack sat very still and watched her as a succession of emotions crossed her face, like clouds blown by a stiff wind. Sorrow. Embarrassment. Yearning. Fear. And finally, guilt.

They held the silence for a long time, and finally Jack spoke.

"What have you got to be afraid of, Susannah?" he asked, his voice tender. "How did you and Gil part? Did you recognize that knife the cop arrived with half an hour ago?"

He spread his hands wide in a gesture of surrender. "Forgive me for asking, but Captain Cassidy is digging around like a pig rooting for truffles. And you can bet he'll be asking your friend Mathilda about it anytime soon.

"He asked you if you recognized that knife, and you said you'd never seen it before. Was that the truth?"

She searched his face with haunted eyes.

"No, I'm afraid it wasn't."

"And does your friend Mathilda know that?"

She didn't avoid his gaze. She simply nodded and said "Yes, she does."

He let the words hang in the air between them, and then he rose to his feet.

"In that case, Susannah, we'd better hire you a lawyer, because we've got a problem."

"We?" she said. "I know your main concern is Cordelia, Jack. You don't have to worry about me."

He shook his head, suddenly irritated.

"What happens to you affects Cordelia, Susannah. You can't avoid it."

"Then I'll go away," she said, hoarse with desperation. "I never wanted to bring her harm."

"Susannah," he said, his voice edged with exasperation. "There's no running this time. Try that and Cassidy will immediately interpret it as an admission of guilt. Besides, Cordelia would be devastated."

She hesitated, licking her cracked, dry lips. Her face was pasty pale and Jack saw a thread of sweat beads across her forehead.

"I didn't kill Gil, Jack," Susannah whispered. "I promise you. That's the truth."

She gave an urgent shake of her head.

"I didn't kill him. God's honor. But I did meet him."

Jack's heart was in his mouth. He stared at her, speechless, and then he croaked out his worst fears.

"That night? The night he died? You met him?"

Incredulous, knocked sideways by her confession, he waited for her to correct it, to say that wasn't what she'd meant at all. But she didn't. She gazed at him, tears trickling down her cheeks, and slowly nodded her assent.

"Then you'll need a lawyer," he said. "You needed him yesterday."

Fourteen

Long after everyone else had retired to bed, Susannah sat at her dressing table in the cozy peach-wall papered bedroom at Elizabeth Westerhoven's house, staring at herself in the mirror, her mind like ink-blobbed blotting paper.

She didn't recognize the hunted acorn-colored eyes that gazed back from the gilded mirror. Their lively gold glint was gone, and as she ran her palm lightly down one cheek and then the other, she took no pleasure in touching her wilted skin.

The events of the day—Jack's suggestion that Tilly had turned Judas on her especially—numbed her. A mocking refrain repeated like a nursery rhyme in her head.

So fancy nancy? Where are all your glorious dreams now?

She was facing the possibility of arrest in a murder investigation. A few weeks ago she'd dismissed Jack as a spoiled playboy. Now she was relying on him to get her off murder charges.

She ran her long fingers along the deep grooves on her forehead.

You're a sorry sight, old girl.

The drooping petals were about to fall off the rose, and she could see no comforting signs of mature buds to compensate for losing youth's dew.

Look at those dark circles. You haven't been a fresh-faced girl for a long time, her inner self whispered.

Where did the years go? And what have I accomplished in them?

You're getting baggy around your jawline.

And you're in danger of hanging for a murder you didn't commit.

For killing a man you once believed you loved enough to marry.

She stared at herself and mouthed the question silently, as if not able to believe it herself. *How did it come to this?*

And how am I going to get out of it?

The confrontation with Jack a few hours ago rolled ceaselessly around in her head, like a play she had a leading role in, but for which she'd not fully learned her lines.

He'd been so gentle, so supportive.

He's only being nice to protect Cordelia. Remember that. Don't make a fool of yourself a second time.

Still, she was incredibly grateful to have someone like Jack on her side. And, because he'd mixed in such spotty circles, he had all sorts of acquaintances he could call on, people she'd never have imagined she'd need.

He was already hard at work, calling favors in at every turn. Anything to clear her of this disaster. First, he'd arranged for a lawyer, whom she'd meet first thing tomorrow.

Then he'd got some murky private investigator out casting around for eyewitnesses the night Gil died. If they could drum up evidence to clear her, she wasn't too proud to accept, even if he had a limp and a glass eye.

"That cop Cassidy thinks he's found the guilty party," Jack told her. "He won't bother to look further afield."

He'd flashed her the lopsided grin she was coming to treasure.

The one great thing you could say about Jack: He didn't mind getting on the wrong side of society, and he was impervious to the gossip—probably deserved—which besmirched his reputation in high places.

Equally, that meant he could appreciate men—and women—from any quarter of life. He didn't waste time judging them on their social standing. If they were cordial and companionable, he'd befriend them.

He'd gazed at her with an intensity that rang through her, alerting every sense.

"If we can raise enough doubts to muddy the waters…" Another quick grin as he turned to leave her. "That will be a good start."

Fifteen

The lawyer Jack had roped in to defend her interests shared the same blue blood antecedents as Jack. They grew up together, Jack indicated, and her brother Thomas would have approved.

With his bespoke tailoring and faintly English accent, Gerald "Mad Dog" Peters looked every inch the high-born barrister he was. Flushed with pride at having landed his services at such short notice, Jack had warned her to show immediate and enthusiastic gratitude when she was introduced.

"None of your high lady posturing today, Princess," he warned her over breakfast.

Her eyebrows shot up in indignation. "High lady posturing? What are you talking about?"

"You mightn't be aware of it," Jack cautioned. "But you can come across as Miss High and Mighty if you think someone isn't measuring up. And Gerald is easy to underestimate.

"He may look like a King Charles Spaniel, but believe me, he's got the instincts of a street fighting pit bull. And if we're going to get out of this mess, you'll need an English pit bull."

When he introduced them half an hour later, Susannah saw immediately what Jack was talking about.

Peters was tall and slim, with curly ginger hair, an immaculately trimmed beard and a "new" style single-breasted frock coat with a velvet collar. Gerald was a dandy, but not to be taken lightly.

Fashionable dresser he might be, but he was a street fighter if he needed to be, one who was known as "Mad Dog" Peters around the courts of law.

"Gerry" Peters—as Jack called him—was renowned for his steely cross-examinations and his "win at any cost" approach. He'd stoop to anything—bribery, browbeating threats, blackmail, or violently partisan speeches—to see his clients cleared, and for once Susannah wasn't too proud to object.

She thanked her lucky stars that her strictly proper sister-in-law wasn't alive to hear she'd had to stoop to using "Mad Dog's" services, though she hoped if Thomas ever heard of it, she'd excuse her because Gerald's father had once been a Supreme Court judge.

After a few minutes of polite, "getting to know you" conversation during which he displayed a remarkably well-informed knowledge of the arts scene in both New York and San Francisco, Peter moved on to telling her exactly how much deep muck she'd got herself in.

The assistant he'd brought with him, a slightly built red-headed youth who had not said a word beyond "Good Morning," stepped up when asked and assembled a small blackboard on a trestle stand. He silently handed his boss a long piece of chalk and Peters turned to write three numbers on it.

1, 2, 3. With a horizontal line drawn out from each. In a deep, gravelly voice that got more animated the longer he talked, he outlined in excruciating detail all the reasons she should be seriously concerned about her situation.

He tapped his chalk on the board and picked them off on long tapered fingers that looked like they belonged to a concert pianist.

"One. You're his former fiancé, with not one but two broken

engagements. The police love the 'woman scorned' scenario. A jealous lover? Case closed."

"But that's not how it was," Susannah protested, half rising to her feet in her anger. "He was the one who wanted to keep it going, not me." "Mad Dog" Peters lifted one eyebrow with senorita drama and remained silent.

"Two. You had a 'secret' studio very close to where the victim was stabbed. Obviously, you'd been conducting secret assignations there. Perhaps you even staged something to make him jealous."

Susannah shot to her feet.

"That's ridiculous. There were no assignations. I didn't want him to be jealous. Quite the opposite."

"Sit down, Miss Carterton," Peters said in a snappy voice. "The worst is yet to come." He's a King Charles spaniel, she thought with infantile glee.

"And three. And here it comes, ladies and gentlemen. The murder weapon found buried in poor Gil's chest has been identified by a witness as belonging to Miss Carterton. It even bears her family crest of arms."

"Stop. What?" Susannah shivered in the icy chill that took hold, a big freeze out of place in the stuffy room.

Gerry Peters gave her a triumphant grin, and spoke louder and slower, as if she was a halfwit or decrepit and deaf. "I said: The murder weapon is a Carterton heirloom. You didn't know that?"

She avoided full disclosure by asking, "Identified by who?"

Jack flicked her a glance that said plainer than words could, *I can't believe you're still continuing with this charade.*

Mr. Peters put down the blackboard pointer and folded his arms across his chest.

"Jack warned me you were not giving us full transparency, Miss Carterton. Now is the time to change that. If you want me to represent you, there will be no more secrets. Do you understand?"

He fixed her with beady brown eyes that she'd thought of as belonging to a soppy lap dog ten minutes before, but there was nothing soppy about them now.

She was the recalcitrant pupil, caught in the headmistress's glare. And she'd never felt as bad about anything in her life.

Jack broke in. "You told that police captain you'd never seen that knife before."

A hot embarrassment supplanted the icy shock of moments before. They'd caught her out in a condemning lie.

Why did I say that? Am I the one who's crazy?

She licked her lips nervously.

"It's Tilly, isn't it? She's the one telling tales out of school."

"You've set her up by lying."

The tears leaped up behind her eyes then, and she squeezed them shut to stop herself from crying. She felt sick with shame.

"You're right," she mumbled. She levelled her gaze, first with Jack, and then the Peters man. She fixed him in a direct line.

"I apologize. I don't know what I was thinking. He caught me off guard…"

She gazed around her wildly, but understood there was no escape.

"You were right, Jack. You warned me about Tilly, and I ignored your advice. Please don't abandon me now."

She swallowed a lump in her throat and gazed at Peters.

He allowed a long silence to flow between them, till she felt prickly with doubt.

"So what happens now?" she choked out.

"Now, Miss Carterton, you sit down and tell us exactly what happened. On the night Gil Lusk took that knife from your brother's house. And then when he came to see you the night he died."

He flashed a conspiratorial look at Jack. "Depending on how

satisfied I am with your accounts of those two occasions, I'll decide if I want you to remain my client or not. Your life may well depend on it, so get talking."

Sixteen

The cream of the San Francisco art world circulated under glittering chandeliers in the Lick House dining room at 41 Montgomery Street, one of the finest addresses in the city, modelled by its owner James Lick, one of the city's richest men, on a room he'd seen at the Palace of Versailles thirty years before.

And to match the grandeur of the setting, most of the "big names" of the San Francisco art world were here, as well as the patrons, the railroad and silver millionaires who decorated their mansions with art.

Mining magnate George Hearst, Paris-born financier and banker Francoise Pioche, wheat broker Isaac Friedlander, who at six foot seven inches tall stood head and shoulders above everyone else in the crowded dining hall—they were all there to snap up paintings that appealed to their taste, as well as to witness any drama that might ensue.

Susannah had done her best to rise to the occasion and look like she hadn't a care in the world, gowned up in emerald green satin number with a stand-up neckline which highlighted her smooth, elegant neck and corn-silk hair.

Close to her side, Jack was the picture of sartorial elegance in a black tie and impeccably tailored formal jacket with satin lapels.

I've never properly valued the way this man can fit in anywhere. Susannah marvelled at her short-sightedness as she surveyed the room and decided Jack was the most attractive man present.

I was so busy castigating him for his unsavory connections, and now I'm in dire need of them if I'm going to keep my freedom.

Earlier that day Jack had told her he'd hired one of his old Barbary Coast mates, Sam Malarkey, well versed in downtown groggeries, to make it his mission to comb the taverns and bars for street gossip about Gil's death.

Meanwhile, Jack was going back to Lochie's model Dot for a second attempt at dredging up art world gossip.

With Jack at her side, she was warm and protected. In the surrounding hubbub, he leaned close to her ear and asked, "How are you feeling now?"

He guessed she'd wanted nothing more than to crawl into bed and turn her back on the world. But Peters insisted she face up to the arty crowd and put on a good show acting as if nothing was wrong.

"Appearance is half the battle," he told her. "You've entered a work in this the Bay Gold contest. You've got to get out there and strut your stuff. Look like you expect to win. And if you don't win, don't let them see you care."

She leaned up and whispered to Jack, "Much better for having you here. Thank you for insisting on coming. It would be twice as hard without you."

His eyes flashed with understanding. "Elizabeth, Dolphie and Sadie should be here any minute. That will boost the team." He took her elbow and guided her toward an extensive set of tables holding refreshments.

"Let's grab something to drink and find somewhere to sit down. Then tell me all about this entry of yours. It will be quite something if you win amid all this uproar."

The painting. She smelled the linseed oil tang of her Paris studio, saw in her mind's eye the beautiful dark supine form of Ezra, his exquisite sculpted body like an ebony version of Michelangelo's *David*.

He formed the framework to her revolutionary critique of art world conventions, designed to keep women artists locked out by making live modeling an essential part of the requirements for a "serious" artist, while preventing women from taking part in live model sessions.

In Paris, far from the grandfathers and gatekeepers, she'd set up her own live studio sessions, and turned the convention on its head by using a male model rather than a female one.

It had freed her from aping the accepted canon. And the work she produced was the best she'd ever done. She knew it in her heart. Free to pursue her vision, she'd done a dozen paintings suitable to be shown in one complete exhibition, and she'd entered one of those pieces into the San Francisco show.

Whether or not she won a prize, the work would cause a sensation. She knew that.

Perhaps that's another reason I wanted to crawl away and hide, she mused as Jack collected two glasses of orange juice and she followed him to a corner to comfortable seating. It was a lot to take on at once.

I wasn't expecting Gil's death at the same time as I'm taking on the entire art establishment.

Once they'd got themselves seated, Jack turned to her, his intense blue eyes sparkling.

"Before we go any further, let me compliment you on how you look tonight, Susannah. You're serene in your world. Peters will be delighted."

He hesitated. "And that green does wonderful things for your eyes. You should wear that color more often."

A trill of amusement bubbled up from inside, and she laughed. "I treasure that, coming from you, Jack. I haven't been a gracious person these last few months, and I'm feeling guilty about it. You've weighed in on my side after I've been a right royal pain."

It was his turn to laugh. "Don't worry about it. Susannah. I know you only had Cordelia's best interests at heart."

His face turned somber. "And I'm beginning to understand how much you've sacrificed to be here with her. You've put a hot career on hold, haven't you, to act as her guardian in San Francisco?

"When you would have preferred to be painting, you've been chaperoning your young niece-by-adoption. Now, tell me about your entry in this show. What can we expect to see when your work is unveiled tonight?"

Seventeen

Paris 1869

Ezra Hartzell had the patience of a saint. If the last two weeks of concentrated work hadn't been enough for him to lose his cool, this morning's session had proved it.

Susannah Carterton gave out a deep, contented sigh, put down her charcoal sketching pencil on the easel shelf in front of her, and flexed her tightened shoulder and neck muscles.

With this morning's intense session, she'd completed the preliminary studies for the monumental series she planned, but enough was enough. They all needed a break.

She stood and stretched, a sense of satisfaction warming her from inside as she wiped her graphite-blackened fingers on the green and gray plaid artist's smock over her elegantly simple chambray day dress.

"Get dressed, Ezra, and we'll all go out for coffee."

She gestured to the opened doorway which gave entry into the rest of her apartment in the charming 9th arrondissement square where most of her neighbors were creative types—writers, musicians, and other artists.

Montmartre, the buzzing epicentre of the artists' community, was a hop and a step away, and she, Ezra and Fleur regularly frequented cafés like Rat Mort where innovators and Bohemians gathered to flirt, swap gossip, and discover the next model for their work.

The "Dead Rat" was where she'd met Ezra and Fleur when she'd arrived in Paris six months ago.

As she rotated to survey the room, she savored the sense of belonging she'd so quickly gained in her Parisian home, taking in the gilded mirror over the fireplace, the cold grate hidden at this time of year by the pretty needlepoint fire screen she'd discovered in one of the many neighboring second-hand shops.

On the mantelpiece sat a bowl of lilacs she'd clipped from the portico outside her front door that morning. Reminded of their presence, she drank in the scent of the flowers' pleasantly cloying sweetness.

Her dearest friend, Fleur de Havilland, an art student like her and Ezra at the private Académie Julian, gave her a sparkling challenge as their eyes met.

"Happy with how it's going?" Fleur's peaches and cream complexion dimpled with the question, so typical of her cheeky, incorrigible temperament.

The Julian was a respected art school that—unlike the snobby Ecole des Beaux Arts—accepted women and foreigners.

They hadn't been required, as Beaux Arts students were, to pass a vicious French language examination, and the Julian—unlike their rival—allowed women to undertake tuition in nude studies.

Susannah shrugged, but she knew her face gave away her joyful release. Paris had been like getting out of prison. She slung an arm around her friend's shoulder.

"Ready for one of the Dead Rat's pastries? I think we deserve a treat for all our work today!"

Fleur giggled. "You're obviously pleased with the way it's going, and I don't blame you." She gestured to Susannah's nearly completed sketch.

"This series is going to shake the rafters. I can't wait to see it."

Ezra tapped on the doorjamb as he returned, clad in a crisp white shirt and workman's trousers.

Even dressed in the unassuming garb of a French laborer, he was eye-catching: a tall, muscular Adonis with a chiseled jaw, dark intelligent eyes and a natural grace of movement that reminded Susannah of a big cat—a panther, she'd decided when she'd first met him.

A fellow American who'd escaped his homeland after the Civil War, despairing of seeing any reality in the so-called emancipation of his race, he was the perfect model for the series she planned to name *Ebony David*.

Nude studies of the female form were one thing. A woman artist painting a black man? That was confronting the boundaries of convention a step too far, Susannah knew, and she foamed with tension and delight whenever she considered how far out of line she was in attempting it.

She still hadn't decided if she would disguise her work by signing it with a generically male name…S.C.G perhaps, not showing gender. S.C.G would automatically be considered by the Paris Salon judges as male, of that she had no doubt.

Susannah responded, "How did you go this morning?"

She took a few steps toward Fleur's work, but her friend swiftly blocked the way.

"I did fine, Susannah, but you're so much better. Truly. Don't embarrass me by comparing."

Susannah protested: "I'm not…."

Fleur laughed and interrupted: "I know you're not. And of course, I do. You've got an unparalleled gift, Susannah. I'm proud to know you."

She couldn't have found a better model for the work than Ezra.

While Michelangelo's sculpture of David was a freestanding work in Carrara marble, she planned a series of oils as a clever commentary on the fashion for reclining female nudes.

Ezra's full-length, finely muscled back balanced along the line of one hip, the rounded buttocks draped in linen that fell away to display powerful thighs.

Her heart beat not with lust, but with aesthetic appreciation. She was delighted with how she'd positioned him to enhance the subtle beauty of his natural form.

She'd made her statement about women artists and the way they'd been fenced out of the major arts arenas. She linked arms, Fleur on one side, Ezra on the other, and they started for the door.

"I'm buying," she said. "You don't know what a blessing you are in my life. I've known nothing like it at home." Ezra shot her a challenging look.

"We'd barely be able to sit down at a respectable table together in Virginia," he said with a wry smile. "They say Lincoln died to free the slaves, but we are still having an awful hard time being treated like real men. You know it."

"I do, Ezra. Indeed, I do. You're much worse off at home than I am, and that's saying something."

She opened the front door to exit and stopped dead in her tracks. Standing the other side, his fist half raised to knock, was a man she knew only too well.

Her heart leaped to her throat.

"Gil," she said. "What are you doing here?"

"I've come to take you home," he said after a moment's hesitation, his voice booming and overconfident.

He eyed her companions, First Fleur. Then Ezra.

Under his cool survey, the merriment that bubbled inside her died away. She dropped her arms to her sides, and the closeness they'd shared moments ago evaporated.

She could see the cool contempt in his eyes as he looked them over.

"Looks like I'm not a minute too late," he said. "What damn fool idea are you chasing after now? I see Thomas has good reason to be worried about your reputation. He's sent me to bring you home."

Eighteen

"Thomas wants me to bring you home." Gil's words echoed in her mind, even as she rejected them.

"Gil, I've already told you. Paris is my home now. I'm an adult woman. I can make my own decisions about where I live. The Académie Julian is a wonderful school and I am learning so much—far more than I would be in New York."

It was several hours after Gil's bombshell announcement. They'd headed for the Dead Rat café as planned, and endured a tense session where she'd introduced him to Ezra and Fleur and attempted to explain about Paris and the art scene in which she was flourishing.

It had been a futile exercise, and as soon as it was remotely possible to leave without appearing downright rude, Fleur and Ezra had made their excuses and fled.

Their conversation limped along as they consumed a cassoulet which Susannah would have relished in different company. She'd lost her appetite, and she picked fitfully at the rich mix of bacon, duck, pork sausage and beans. She most fervently wished she could get rid of Gil and crash into an exhausted sleep.

But no such luck. He'd insisted on seeing her home, and then coming in to inspect her studio and observe the work she'd tried to describe to him to justify prolonging her stay.

One last try, she told herself.

I'll make a last attempt to convince him why it's important for me to stay on here. I'm creating work I could never do back home.

He's an artist himself. A good one. Surely, he'll understand?

They climbed the steps to the front door and walked through the lilac-draped portico. It was a still, warm Paris night, and the fluid notes of a Chopin Prelude floated in the air from the apartment on the opposite side of the square.

Susannah paused and looked up through the lilac boughs, to the river of stars wheeling overhead. She breathed in the heady sweetness of the drooping mauve blossoms.

A night for love, *pour amore*, she thought with a jolt of unease. She sensed Gil reaching for her shoulder to turn her toward him, and she plunged the key into the front door lock.

"Let me show you my studio." She half swallowed the words, her back firmly turned on him as she led the way inside, enjoying the entry's stored warmth from the sunny day and the relief of escaping Gil's impulse to reach out and kiss her.

They passed by the roll-armed chartreuse sofa, the blue and white Chinoiserie planter filled with white violets, the walnut veneer writing desk, all second-hand treasures she'd dug out from piles of less distinguished junk in the Montmartre markets, enjoying the sense of belonging as she led the way to the studio.

This is my home now, and I'm not going back.

Perhaps never, she vowed.

"You've got a nice place here," said Gil. "You always have had your own style."

She half turned, surprise lighting her face.

"You think so? I am very fortunate. I appreciate that."

She thought of Tilly. There was nothing she'd like better than for her to join her here, but she didn't have the means. Unlike hers, her family couldn't afford it.

"How's Tilly?" she asked Gil, painfully aware she hadn't yet replied to the letter she'd received weeks ago. "Do you see much of her?"

Gil's face was pale in the gaslight, and he frowned. "Of course I see her, Susannah. She's my agent." Susannah felt the air tense around them again. He was so jumpy.

"I know she's your agent. I just wondered how she was? Is she happy with life?"

Gil shrugged. "I suppose. Can't say I've asked. Why are we talking about Mathilda?"

Susannah saw the line between his eyebrows deepen, noticed the sullen undertow in his voice, and guessed there was more to this than he wanted to say.

She stepped into the studio space and breathed in the familiar aroma of oils, turps and mineral oil. Her pulse never failed to quicken at the promise it held of new work and excitement.

"I've been working on something different… a commentary, on what it means to be a woman in a man's art world."

The shadow in Gil's face she'd interpreted as sullenness seemed to dissolve into petulance. His bottom lip protruded, and his chocolate brown eyes narrowed.

"Because you have such a hard life, don't you, Susannah? All alone in Paris." She detected a faint sneer in the comment.

"What are you talking about, Gil? I've just said I appreciate that I'm fortunate. It doesn't change the fact that it's near impossible for a woman to be taken seriously as an artist. You know that."

His childish pique vanished. "I'm sorry, Susannah. You're right."

He turned slowly, taking in the room, the easels covered with white cloth so the work was hidden, the couch with a cast-off vermilion rug where Ezra posed.

"I'm bitchy because you so clearly don't miss me. You're doing more than fine without me. No man likes to be surplus to requirements."

She gave a shaky laugh. "It's not like that." She sounded nervous. And as she walked to her easel, she clenched and unclenched her hands.

Anything to change the topic, she thought. "I haven't told you about my latest idea, have I?"

"I don't know. What is it?"

The hint of petulance was back.

She pulled the covering clear of her stand, revealing the reclining study of nude Ezra.

"I'm doing a series of male nudes. Not just male, but African-American male. Ezra is exactly the one for it."

Her hand traced the sketched sinuous line of his hip.

"And it's got so many possibilities for underlying social commentary. I could add a small still life with domestic objects—the kind of thing the Old Masters sometimes included in female studies—to highlight the contradictions."

She turned to Gil, her heart light, her eyes on fire. Whenever she got to talk about her vision for this work, she got excited.

"Or maybe the opposite—typically male objects—a pipe. A fishing line. Either way, it works to challenge gender expectations. Not to mention the black-white thread."

She'd clasped her hands in front of her body as she spoke, like an excited child expecting Christmas tree gifts, and she turned to Gil in anticipation.

What do you think?

She was about to ask him the question, but as she caught the look on his face, her vocal cords froze.

He'd pursed his lips in a hard line, and his temples pulsed in a sign she knew well from past disagreements. He was about to fly into a purple rage.

She'd seen this sudden loss of temper once before, when she'd broken off their engagement and told him she was going to Paris to study.

She unclasped her hands and took a step away from her displayed work. She stared into his face and realized she was holding her breath.

They stood in a charged silence for what seemed like an eternity, and then he exploded.

"Are you mad? Do you want to destroy the last shreds of respectability you still hold on to? Not to mention what this work would do to Thomas and Sylvia and the kid."

He leaped to the easel and snatched up the sketch, rolling it up into a paper ball and throwing it across the room.

"Do you think they've gone to all that trouble to adopt that girl, to create a background for her that will allow her to be accepted into society, only to have her marriage prospects destroyed by her mad aunt?"

He gazed at her with contempt. "You might imagine you don't need a husband, but anyone with any sense understands women can't get anywhere without one. Are you determined to sentence Cordelia to the same fate you're heading for? A spinster reject?"

He shook his head. "I don't get you, Susannah. You've got a fine talent. You could paint pictures everyone loves—flowers and domestic portraits and things. And you have to choose naked Negroes."

He wheeled for the door.

"When I tell Thomas what you're up to, he'll cut your allowance, and I don't blame him. What will you do then?"

He paused at the doorway and stared back at her, his face shining in genuine confusion.

"I've tried to be patient with you, Susannah. You could have had a wonderful life with me if you hadn't insisted on wanting things you can't have. But you've truly blown it this time.

"And when you come crawling back home, I won't be waiting for you."

Nineteen

Fleur trailed one hand over the edge of one of Susannah's canvases with a faraway look in her eyes, while she wrapped the other lovingly around the rounded dome of her belly.

"Ezra will always be remembered in these paintings," she said in her lilting French, smiling to Susannah as she spoke.

"You've given him a place in art history, no matter what becomes of his own work."

Susannah searched her friend's face, a sense of unease creeping over her at the distanced, otherworldly cloud that seemed to envelop her.

"What are you talking about, *ma cherie*? Ezra's got years of fine work ahead of him. This slow period is just a patch he's going through. We all have them. He'll get back to work as soon as your baby's born and things settle down."

Fleur was gazing at the work in front of her, and Susannah wondered if she was even listening to what she'd just said.

"I love how you've captured him here. He looks so noble. So majestic in his autonomy. There's nothing of the slave about him." She turned to Susannah slowly, as if not trusting her burdened body to stay balanced.

"You've produced a provocative satire and a beautiful study."

She stared out the open window into the garden beyond. The lilac had finished flowering months ago. The more subtle fragrance of roses and lavender had supplanted its overpowering sweetness.

"I'll be remembered for our baby."

Remembered?

A shiver ran through Susannah. Someone's walking on my grave, she thought. That's what this makes me think of.

But it's not my grave we're talking about.

It was as if Fleur had a premonition of a forthcoming disaster.

"What are you talking about, sweet girl?" Susannah demanded with forced gaiety.

"You'll both be here for many more years, with more gorgeous bubbas thriving around you. Just watch."

Fleur stared into her face, as if she'd been hauled back from another world.

"I don't think so," she breathed.

And then with sharper urgency.

"Susannah, if anything happens to me, promise me you'll look after the baby. Ezra won't be able to do it. He's finding it hard enough to keep body and soul together now. Promise me."

She stepped forward and clutched Susannah's wrist with a panicky grip.

"Please, Susannah. Promise me."

"Nothing's going to happen to you," Susannah soothed. "You're worrying unnecessarily."

Fleur's hazel-green eyes flicked around the room, reflecting her inner turmoil, not settling anywhere.

"I'm scared, Susannah. Something bad is going to happen. Promise me."

Susannah stood and wrapped her dainty friend in her arms.

"Of course, Fleur. Of course. I promise. If something terrible happens, I promise. I'll look after your little one."

Sitting up in bed later that night, Susannah went over the scene with Fleur in her head yet again. She'd hardly had room for anything else since the disquieting conversation had taken place. Fleur was obviously upset, but she couldn't give Susannah any factual reason for her anxiety.

Since the corrosive encounter with Gil, she'd been waiting for the axe to fall. But there'd been no word from America. No angry letter from her brother announcing he was withdrawing the funds she needed to stay here. Had Gil even told him anything about their bitter fight?

She didn't know, and she certainly wasn't writing to ask.

Driven by a powerful urge to complete her work while she had the chance, she'd been treating every day as a gift. A treasure to be enjoyed right now in case they whipped it away from her tomorrow.

Her focus had been rewarded with the best work she'd ever done. She still didn't know how she wanted to present it to the world. But she was overwhelmingly grateful she'd had the chance to create it.

What if Fleur had a sixth sense about things? Her reassurances rang hollow even in her own ears, because childbirth was a perilous journey, and no one could guarantee the wished-for outcome—a blooming mother and a bouncing baby.

What if the unthinkable happened and Fleur couldn't look after her child?

Susannah hated herself for feeling a charged sense of anticipation. She'd surrendered any thought of having children herself. Her work came first and she couldn't even imagine herself married, let alone a mother. But if fate thrust a child into her empty arms?

It would be impossible to manage at home in New York. The scandal of raising a mulatto child would add an untenable extra dimension to an already controversial situation. From her brother's point of view, she could see that.

But if she was in Paris, thousands of miles away from the Manhattan gossips, with no one particularly interested in her lifestyle? She could come and go here with a freedom that would be unthinkable at home. She wouldn't have to face down gossip about whether the child was actually hers.

If she was in Paris, as long as her brother did not withdraw her allowance, she'd be able to manage with an adopted babe. And even if he withdrew funds, if she could sell her work, she still might manage on her own.

In New York? Not a chance.

••••••••

The doctor delivered Fleur of a strong healthy baby girl who had her father's long Olympian limbs and her mother's sweet rosebud mouth and hazel eyes. Susannah sat at Fleur's bedside and rejoiced for their good fortune.

"See?" she whispered in Fleur's ear. "Nothing to worry about. You have a gorgeous wee daughter, and many years to see her grow into a beautiful young woman."

She laughed teasingly. "The mite already looks like she's going to be an Amazonian warrior. She'll be hard to keep up with."

Fleur laughed along with her, but Susannah didn't miss the sharp, nervous edge to her mirth.

And her friend knew something no one else did, Susannah thought three weeks later, as she rocked the restless baby to sleep. The child they'd named Athena, after the goddess of wisdom, handcraft and strategy, one of the twelve Olympians.

Three days after her daughter's birth, Fleur fell unconscious with childbed fever, and she died six days later. By the time of her mother's death, Athena was already feeding from a wet nurse and sleeping in a bassinet tucked into one corner of Susannah's Montmartre studio.

Twenty
Three months later

SYLVIA DYING! STOP. PLEASE! STOP. COME HOME IMMEDIATELY STOP. CORDELIA NEEDS YOU STOP. DURAND WILL RELEASE FUNDS FOR YOUR FARE. STOP. YOUR EVER LOVING BROTHER STOP. THOMAS ENDS

Susannah's fingers trembled as she held the pale blue slip of paper out from her body, not wanting to read it again, refusing to acknowledge the devastation it carried in twenty-eight words.

She stared unseeing at the faint mechanical ink printout, all in block letters, that spelled the end of her life as she knew it.

Athena's rhythmic breathing in the crib beside her provided a sweet counterpoint to the susurration of the Brittany coast waves, sighing in and out of the yellow sanded cove in view beyond the windows.

Minutes before, she'd been watching in quiet delight at the Breton womenfolk on their hands and knees gathering cockles for dinner, their muted brown dresses highlighted by full-length blue and cream aprons and traditional cone-shaped white caps.

Children danced around them, buckets and spades in hand, collecting seashells and building sandcastles.

She'd been dreaming of the years to come, when Athena would be old enough to join them on the Brittany beach. Artists from the stuffy streets of Paris were increasingly flocking to northern sunshine at this time of year, leading French and American artists among them.

She was renting a simple beach cottage for herself, Athena, and the wet nurse, while Ezra was staying with a group of other American painters in an informal artist's colony a short distance away.

Now, she saw nothing of the idyllic coast before her. In her inner eye she was seeing her sister-in-law Sylvia, with her weary pale blue eyes that never quite shed an aura of fatigue, however much she tried to assert her strong, gentle spirit.

Her superfine papery olive skin showed every line, and although Susannah had noticed that Sylvia looked burdened down when they said their farewells eighteen months ago, she'd never expected her to die young.

She let out a long, mournful sigh that, with Athena's sleepy murmurs, mingled with the hiss of the waves.

Dignified and diplomatic, Sylvia had protected her repeatedly from social controversy. No one had been as supportive of her choice to pursue art as her brother's wife, even though she did it subtly, in a manner that didn't challenge social norms.

When she overheard disparaging remarks about Susannah's absence at her ladies' luncheons, she'd discreetly invite the gossips to afternoon tea and incidentally have one of Susannah's domestic studies on display. She'd laugh to Susannah that seeing her work never failed to silence her critics.

For a woman who didn't share Susannah's frustration at the restraints on female activity, and who also was not especially interested in the finer points of art critique, she'd been a bulwark of shelter.

And now she's dying?

Sinead, the Irish wet nurse, registered a gentle tap on the door and bustled in. "Is she awake yet?" she inquired. Her sparkling brown eyes sought Susannah's. "It's past her feed time."

Despite herself, Susannah smiled. "She's worn out by our walk this morning. She's still sleeping."

"I'll give her another thirty minutes and if she's not awake then, I'll wake her," the nursemaid said. She glanced at Susannah.

"Are you all right, miss? You look upset."

Susannah waved the telegram at shoulder height. "Bad news from home, I'm afraid. It's taking me time to digest it."

She rallied herself, made as if to stand, but she sank back down again, suddenly feeling overwhelmed.

"I need to send a messenger to Mr. Hartzell," she said with sudden conviction. "Is there anyone we know who could do that for me?"

She knew Sinead, with her naturally gregarious nature, had made a lot of friends amongst the artists and their hangers-on since they'd been here.

"Mr. Bacon's personal assistant, Joseph, was on the beach not long ago. He might be happy to help."

The esteemed American painter Henry Bacon had been one of the first to fall in love with the Brittany coast as an artist's retreat, and he'd welcomed Ezra to stay with him and a group of other Irish and American artists.

"Could you find him and ask?"

Susannah let out a whoosh of relief at not having to lift one foot herself. "I'll make sure I keep Athena happy if she wakes until you get back."

Twenty-one
San Francisco 1872

As Jack made his way across the Lick House dining room with Susannah's orange refill, he did a quick reconnoiter of the social scene. The key players in the Gilbert Lusk murder inquiry weren't hard to spot.

That aggressive police captain Seamus Cassidy did not try to camouflage himself. He stood out like a sore thumb, in the gray San Francisco police uniform, selected, they said, because a decade ago a darker color showed all the dirt from the unpaved streets.

He was hugging the perimeter of the room, boring suspicious eyes into anyone they alighted on. A high-society Bay Gold art show was not his natural habitat, Jack observed with a twitch of his lips.

Mathilda Morton was his pole opposite. If Cassidy looked like he'd rather be anywhere but here, Mathilda fitted the landscape as perfectly as a giraffe in a tall acacia tree.

She and Aloysius Mandelow circulated like linked planets in the same gravity field. As Jack moved with elegant grace, a glass in each hand, to return to Susannah, he noted neither moved far from the other, while both appeared to occupy their own force field.

Aloysius was in Mathilda's thrall. That seemed obvious and Jack could see why. In a scarlet satin off-the-shoulder number, Mathilda claimed a top place on the social totem pole. The response of those near her confirmed her attraction.

Men and women deferred to her, congratulating her on how lovely she looked. "We're all waiting with keen excitement for the coming revelation," said one particularly ingratiating academician, a tall, thin chap with a carefully trimmed, pointed gray beard and a nervous tick in one eye.

Jack recognized him as one of the leading Bohemian Club members, a man who was investing heavily in the art of the American West.

"Oh, really?" Mathilda said, a pleased pink blush creeping up her cheeks, softening the weariness in her face and taking ten years off her age. "It's all thanks to Aloysius." She gave a calculated hesitation and corrected her familiarity.

"Dr. Mandelow gets credit for tonight's success. He's the one who's drawn it all together." Aloysius Henry Mandelow positively glowed under her praise.

My suspicions were spot on, thought Jack, eavesdropping on the conversation as he passed by. She's caught him in her spell. And academic respect isn't the only draw.

Mathilda gave off a low hum of gloating satisfaction, he thought, like the sound you heard when bees discovered an almond orchard in full blossom, the honey flow ripe for harvesting.

She thinks she's won. And there's more coming yet.

●●●●●●●●

Susannah remained exactly where he'd left her. She had the detached air of someone who is physically present but in every other sense has vacated the scene, and the art show guests who circulated around her acknowledged that by giving her a wide berth.

That was odd, because of all the art world identities present, Susannah Carterton would be one of the most prominent. During her two years in Paris, she'd studied under leading names in the art world, and his inquiries had told him there was already a buzz developing about her vision and ambition.

When she glimpsed him, two glasses of orange juice about to be safely delivered, she rose from her chair and received one with a grateful sigh. She leaned over and muttered into his ear.

"I'm already persona non grata," she said. "Cassidy's already got me convicted and word's spreading fast." She glanced around, gesturing quietly with the hand that held her full orange glass. "They're frightened to come near in case they're sullied by the connection."

"That's ridiculous," he said, although he suspected she was correct in her assumptions. "They're intimidated, that's all. You're not exactly giving off approachable vibes, locked away in your own little world there."

A fleeting despair crossed her face. "Sorry, Jack. I've got rather a lot on my mind."

"They're going to be doing the unveiling soon," he said. "If there are any surprises coming, please tell me now."

She shook her head. "I'll be the last one to know," she said. "Tilly's been ahead of the game from the start, and I'm still playing catch-up."

He fixed her with a steely eye and nodded. "At last, you're seeing it my way. She's got Aloysius Mandelow around her little finger. I'm taking another look at him. But quick—any other secrets I should know about?"

Twenty-two

If only it were that easy.

Susannah returned Jack's gaze with a gurgle of laughter.

"What? Have I said something funny?"

She shook her head.

All her secrets? Not likely. But she'd do her best. She laughed again.

"Surely every woman's allowed some secrets," she said playfully. He deferred with an answering flirtatious grin.

"As long as they're not ones likely to get her in trouble with the law," he retorted. "Those I must know about."

She shook her head. "I don't have any of those. Pity Seamus Cassidy doesn't believe that." He took her arm. "Tell me anyway. And in the meantime, act like you're the reigning queen of San Francisco art. You deserve to be seen that way."

She thrilled again. "Jack," she said, her voice laden with guilty pleasure. "I'm nothing of the sort."

But the round they made of the room showed otherwise. Everywhere they strolled, local artists who'd recently returned from Paris, or others desperate to go there, wanted to share their experiences or ask her advice.

When thirty minutes had passed and they had not yet completed their first circumnavigation, Jack paused and gazed down at Susannah with admiration.

"For someone who considered themselves persona non grata, you sure have a lot of fans," he said teasingly. "They either want to compliment you on your work, compare notes, or ask your advice."

She laughed and should her head in denial, but her cheeks with pink with pleasure. "I guess you're right," she said. "But that's thanks to my brother Thomas. He's been remarkably generous with both the family money and his understanding."

Her thoughts flashed back to that last day on the sunny Breton coast, when his desperate telegram had arrived.

She'd been waiting for months for the axe to fall. For Gil to run back to America and stir up trouble with her family in revenge for her not being willing to fall into his plans for them to marry.

She'd never known whether Gil had that conversation with Thomas. Neither he nor Sylvia ever alluded to it, and she never knew if Gil had second thoughts or Thomas had chosen not to listen.

But when the axe fell, it came from an entirely different direction. And she couldn't refuse the request.

Twenty-three

By the time Ezra arrived on her doorstep under a thundercloud of anxiety, his tiny daughter lay fully fed and fast asleep again. He stood at the foot of her cradle and let out an enormous sigh of relief.

"She's not sick?" He turned to Susannah, his face lit from within in exhilarated relief.

"I thought… I thought when Joseph summoned me there must be some emergency."

Susannah took him gently by the elbow. "There is an emergency, Ezra. But not with Athena's health, thank the Lord. She is a bonny wee girl, as hale and happy as she's ever been. Come and sit down while I explain."

She led him to one of the two comfortable parlor chairs that, along with her easel and the baby's crib, she'd positioned in the studio. In a quiet voice, so as not to disturb Athena, she explained about the SOS telegraph she'd received from her brother.

"I can't ignore him," she said, her voice laced with anguish. "He's been so good to me, supporting me all this time, not complaining or criticizing my choices. Now he needs me, and so does Cordelia, his adopted daughter. Not to mention sweet Sylvia. I have to go home and do my share."

She raised her brows in a gesture that sought his understanding and acceptance. "You'd do the same in my position, I'm sure. The question is, can you take over Athena's care?"

Ezra gazed into her face, his eyes glittering with pain.

"Susannah, you know my situation. I can barely afford to feed myself. I can't care for a new baby as well. You know I'm getting somewhere in my career now."

A Biblical scene of Ezra's accepted in a Paris Salon exhibition had attracted positive comment, and there was talk of him traveling to Egypt to paint more of the same desert landscape as he'd portrayed in the praised work. Susannah knew this.

He stood, tense and soulful, gazing out of the window. The summer crowds were thinning from the promenade, and soon the trees would lose their first autumn leaves. He shook his head and stared back into her face.

"You know, I'm planning to paint in the Holy Land this winter. I can't do that and pay for her care while I'm away."

Susannah sensed there was more than the money involved. She hadn't missed the pain that flickered in his face whenever he looked at his baby daughter. She was already so like her mother, and she guessed, a constant reminder of his wife's death.

She rose slowly and stood shoulder to shoulder with her artist friend.

"I understand, Ezra. It's a terrible choice to be forced to make. Your career, or your child."

"It's no choice for me," said Ezra in a deeply strained rasp. "If I can't prove myself as an artist, then I'm nothing. I'd be worthless as a father and a man. This is something I am born to do." He gazed at her, deep channels of grief etched either side of his finely sculpted nose.

"The truth is, a woman will care for Athena better than I can."

He resumed his chair and buried his face in his hands. When he looked up, he had a resigned, faraway look in his eyes.

"I understand that woman can't be you, Susannah. You've been marvelous through this whole sad experience. I can't ask more of you. You have to go home. And it's out of the question that you take Athena with you. I understand that."

Even for a woman who'd pushed the boundaries of social convention as she had, returning as a single woman with a mulatto child was impossible.

Her brother's New York world—indeed even the less conventional world she inhabited—couldn't accept a babe like Athena. They'd assume she was the child of some liaison of Susannah's, for a start. She couldn't see Cordelia engulfed in the ensuing scandal.

She tried another approach. "What if we found a temporary foster home for her? With some loving, motherly sort of woman? I could even offer to pay the costs of her care for a while until you've got on your feet? Could we set up some provision like that?"

The hopeless fog in Ezra's eyes told her before he'd opened his mouth that he had no heart for committing to his daughter's long-term care.

He buried his face in his hands again. As if he hoped when he raised his eyes to the crib next time, it would be gone, and the baby with it.

"I can't do it," he cried in anguish. "Every time I look at that child, I'm reminded of Fleur. It's like losing her mother all over again."

He gazed down at his slender, long fingers. "I'm made to be an artist, Susannah. I believe a very fine one. I'm not set up to be a single father. Seriously, I'd rather we found her a good permanent home. That we put her out for adoption."

Susannah guessed with a thumping headache that when he said "we" he actually meant "you." He was looking to her to find a secure, loving adoptive family for Athena.

She walked over to the crib and gazed down at the tiny form, her angelic little mouth making occasional suckling sounds as she slept, and her heart split open.

Seeing Fleur die so suddenly, so unnecessarily, was hard enough. Now Ezra was asking her to break the promise she'd made to always look after her daughter?

"I'm returning to Paris tomorrow," she said. "I don't know the details of Sylvia's illness, but I don't think I've got much time before Thomas needs me back there."

She shook her head in despair. "She's such a darling, Ezra. And I promised Fleur I'd take care of her…" She caressed the quilt that covered the sleeping child, as if by her loving strokes she could protect her from future woe. Pain cut into the back of her throat, and she had difficulty in swallowing.

Ezra stood, his face a mask of stone, the color drained from his dark face.

"I trust you to do the best you can, Susannah. And if Fleur were here, I know she'd understand."

His footsteps were leaden as he crossed the room and let himself out.

I've sacrificed the hope of a family of my own to my painting, she thought. Ezra and I are not so unalike.

Athena stirred in her cot and cried out, a sweet mewling sound. Susannah's heart turned over with a painful thump.

She reached out and stroked the baby's head, and Athena's eyes flickered open. When she saw Susannah, her little body seemed to stretch with delight and she smiled.

Oh, baby girl. How am I ever going to give you up, knowing as I do you're my last chance at motherhood?

She ran her rough hand, chapped by the continuous washing of paint from her skin, across Athena's velvet-soft cheek.

Sleep some more little one, and when you wake, I'll be gone.

Twenty-four

"Ladies and gentlemen, your attention, please!" Dr. Aloysius Henry Mandelow stood on a podium and clapped his hands to demand the crowd's attention. It took a few minutes, but gradually the chatter quieted and then ceased altogether.

"We're all here together for one purpose, and one purpose only," Mandelow began, gazing around him with a superior smile.

"And that's to view the very finest of Art in the West and register our preferences before the judges make their final decision. We will take the popular vote into consideration when we award the big prize."

He consulted the notes in his hand, squinting through a monocle eye glass which Susannah considered ridiculously toffee mannered. Who did the fellow think he was?

"As I'm sure most of you are aware, in the next few minutes we are going to unveil the works we consider are of a quality to be included in an exhibition of the 'best of the best.'

"Please circulate and assess the works before you and then make your vote by registering with one of the sweet maids who is here for that exact purpose.

"One vote per person. We will keep your identities secret for the ballot, but we need to have your name registered so we don't have block voting to skew the outcome.

"And of course, you appreciate this is just one aspect of the judging. A panel of experienced art critics headed by myself will decide on the Grand Prize, with its substantial cash prize money, in the next forty-eight hours.

"We'll be naming the overall judges' winner the day after tomorrow, when we've tallied in the popular vote and added it to our deliberations."

He paused expectantly, as if awaiting a sign from Heaven. Susannah saw with a flash of comprehension that it wasn't a heavenly sign he was seeking, but confirmation from one of the aforementioned pretty maids.

A comely blonde at the back of the room clad in pink satin with a deep neckline bobbed a confirmation with a wave of her hand. Mandelow responded with a pleased smile.

"Ah… We've got the confirmation we were waiting for. Ladies and gentlemen, I declare the Bay Gold Art Expo officially open. You may proceed next door to the gallery and view the works on display.

"Unless otherwise indicated, they are all available for purchase, and if you see something you particularly desire, I urge you to get in quickly with your offer. I'm confident we'll sell a good proportion of the works we have on show tonight."

Susannah glanced up at Jack.

"There we are. Now you can go right on in and view my paintings for yourself."

"Wonderful," said Jack. "But I'm such a pleb when it comes to art. I definitely need you close by to interpret for me."

He waved his hand in the air as if he was a conductor putting an orchestra through its paces. "I very much value having a connoisseur of the arts to give us an interpretation of the works before us."

He added a slightly formal, plummy note to his voice as he spoke and Susannah burst into giggles. "You are incorrigible," she said. "But if you insist."

They linked arms as if entering onto a dance floor, and both of them smiling, followed the mob into the display gallery.

●●●●●●●●

"You entered more than one piece?"

Jack sounded momentarily surprised as they paused in front of a Susannah Carterton work in the style of Berthe Morisot, a contemporary Madonna-like study of a nursemaid in a blue smock, an angelic baby cradled in her arms.

It was the second of Susannah's paintings they'd seen. The first, a Brittany seaside study of women collecting cockles. had been brilliantly lit by summer sun and an ozone shimmer in the air. Jack loved it.

The baby study, by comparison, was a night-time piece. Candlelight shone on the faces of the woman and child, leaving the rest of the scene in a darkness that seemed foreboding.

"I didn't know you'd done any mother and baby portraits," Jack said, eyeing her with blatant curiosity. "Who are these people? I guess you painted them from life, not just from your imagination?"

She gazed at the painting and suddenly locked up inside. She did not want to talk about Sinead or baby Athena. The lump that rose in her throat whenever she remembered the day she'd said goodbye blocked her vocal cords. She glanced away and swallowed hard.

Jack eyed her keenly. "Are you all right, Susannah?" he asked, his voice sharp with alarm. She guessed he'd seen the glimmer of tears in the corner of her eyes.

She bent over and took a deep breath. A strangled laugh escaped, her failed attempt to make light of things. "I'm fine, Jack, just fine."

She cleared her throat. "Of course, I had to paint a mother and child to prove I can mix it with the Old Masters," she said, again attempting to laugh away her discomfort.

"And they're just paid models, like all my work," she lied. "The only live one was the beach study we saw earlier."

He regarded her with a querying spear of doubt, but let it go. "Uh-huh. I can't quite put my finger on it, but the beach scene seemed happy. This one? There's something sad about it, though I can't exactly say why…" He gave her another searching glance, but she remained silent.

"Is that it then?"

"Of Susannah Carterton's work? Yes, it is."

No reason to mention S. G. C. The less anyone knows of that, the better. Until the judging is done, anyway.

"But let's keep going. There's a few more left to complete everything."

The third to last painting was the one she'd been nervously waiting for all night. The *Ebony David.*

She gazed at the rich dark oils, at the way the light shone on Ezra's mahogany skin, giving it a King Saul sheen. She'd referenced an Old Master sovereignty and solemnity, mixing it with the light clarity of the new cutting- edge Parisians like Claude Monet.

Jack paused in front of the large canvas—four times the size of her other works.

"This is an imposing piece," he drawled, approval singing in his deep baritone. "It's kind of Old Master impressive and also New Master cheeky, if you know what I mean. It's hard to explain, but it does both things at the same time."

Susannah's spine tingled with pleasure. "Old Master impressive, and New Master cheeky," she echoed. "That's a great way to describe it. And tell me," she challenged, mischievous jokiness in every syllable, "what do you know about New Master cheekiness?"

Jack laughed. "Not much, until tonight, anyway," he said. "But it seems to me the artists displayed here who've studied in Paris—and I've met a few of them tonight—all have a freshness that the ones who've stayed behind don't have."

He leaned down and read the signature at the corner of the work.

"Well, I'll be damned," he said. "Proved wrong again. This one's by Gilbert L. Is that the same man? The late Gil Lusk? Your former fiancé?"

He swiveled toward Susannah. "I thought you said he never studied in Paris?"

Susannah stared at the signature, scared to believe her eyes.

Gilbert L?

For the second time tonight, she gagged as she tried to speak, and Jack gawked at her.

"Susannah… Are you all right?"

She fought for control, clearing her throat as if she'd swallowed a frog.

"Gilbert L? I guess it must be. The very same… And I agree… It's not the kind of picture I'd expect he'd paint."

Not in a million years.

But it's what could win a show like this, she thought with sudden clarity. And Mathilda is no fool. She knows that too.

Like the missing piece in a jigsaw puzzle, everything fell into place.

She's in love with him, and she's proved it to him by arranging for him to make his career by winning the Bay Gold Grand Prize.

"He's likely to win it with this work," she said, and her voice sounded like it came from somewhere underwater. "Pity he's not alive to enjoy it."

Twenty-five

Susannah stared at the *Ebony David* with a haunted look on her face, as if a terrible experience from her past had returned.

Jack took hold of her upper arm and gently shook it. "Susannah." No response.

"Susannah!" He spoke more loudly, in crisp phonetics that required action. Still nothing. He stood in front of her, gripping both shoulders.

"Susannah! Wake up!"

She rallied then and gaped into his face with a fraught expression.

"Are you all right? You look like you've seen a ghost."

Even then, she took a moment to pull herself together and let out a heaving sigh. "Oh Jack! Sorry. I was miles away."

She stepped back to escape his hold, and he responded by stepping away from her, giving her the space she so clearly wanted.

She laughed weakly. "I saw a ghost of sorts… Don't worry. Nothing serious. That painting. It took me back to something I thought I saw in Paris, but I'm mistaken. It's highly original, don't you think? I have seen nothing like it before."

Her voice, and the tinkling laugh that followed, sounded artificial and high pitched. Jack frowned.

"Are you sure you're all right? You don't sound like yourself." She flashed him a brief smile.

"I don't quite feel myself, either," she said. "I'm just tired, I think. There's been too much happening. I can't process it all." She turned away from the painting with what he interpreted as reluctance.

"I should get home. Tomorrow will be another big day, if Cassidy has his way. I'll have to be on my mettle to escape his questions."

They rode home in silence. A weary solemnity eclipsed the playful camaraderie they'd shared earlier in the evening.

"You've nothing to fear if you tell me the truth," Jack said as the hansom neared Pine Street.

A long silence hung out between them, and when she didn't respond he said, "You are telling me the truth, aren't you? The truth, the whole truth and nothing but the truth?"

He tried to make a joke of it, but they both knew he wasn't laughing.

She'd pulled the curtains down again. Something had happened back there.

She'd been delightful company for most of the night. Until the very end of the show when they came upon that stunning painting. Then she'd clammed up.

If she won't talk, I've no choice but to consult my other source of art gossip, he thought.

He'd seen Lochie and Dot circulating in the crowd, but they moved in quite different circles from him and Susannah, so their paths had hardly passed except to give each other a fleeting greeting.

That was good, he told himself. They've been talking to many of the people Susannah and I couldn't reach. He'd make it his business to visit them tomorrow and try to work out what was going down on that *Ebony David* painting.

Because as sure as he had hair on his head—and he was grateful that at thirty-eight he still had plenty of hair left—there was something about that work that had thrown Susannah off her game.

Twenty-six

Jack left it till late the next morning to wander into the Art Students League premises on the top floor of the old Probate Court building.

Art students, he knew, weren't early risers on a normal working day, let alone after a show like last night's extravaganza.

As he ran his hand across the burlap drapes which gave each cubicle minimal privacy, he smiled inwardly. Eavesdropping was part of the scene, and he expected to pick up an accurate buzz from last night. Indeed, he surmised it would be all anyone was talking about.

The silent empty spaces he peered into as he progressed into the heart of the League space bore out his suspicion that many of the artists would have a late start today.

A stale smell of late-night partying—the whiff of hard liquor and old tobacco—hung in the air and in some studios the detritus of late-night partying, overflowing ashtrays and empty bottles, still lay about.

But it gratified him to hear the drone of low male tones punctuated by the higher register of an excited female, as he approached the inner sanctum of Aloysius Mandelow's domain—the only room on the spacious floor to have solid masonry walls.

The heavy oak door was ajar, so he gave a cursory tap, pushed it further open and entered through the gap hugged by grooved columns, which soared up to the domed ceiling on either side.

The strong chocolate fragrance of Java coffee immediately assailed his senses. As he'd hoped and suspected, Mathilda Morgan and Professor Aloysius Mandelow were already on top of their day, celebrating last night's success with a morning brew.

They looked up as he entered, and Jack wondered if he imagined the fleeting smugness that crossed Mathilda's face before she plastered on a greeting smile.

"Jack Cabot," she crowed. "You're up early after a big night." She left a calculated pause and continued, "How did Susannah enjoy the occasion?"

He drilled her face for any other telltale sign of emotion, but she'd wiped any trace of her true feelings from view. She was all bland eagerness to please.

"Oh, I think she had a very pleasant time," he replied, equally vacuous. "In fact, I think last night was the most relaxed I've seen her in the six months I've known her."

She raised an arched eyebrow. "Really?" A tense edge to the word betrayed an inner pressure she was doing her best to keep hidden.

"Even about Gil's work? The *Ebony David*? What did she think of that painting?" He glanced at Aloysius and stretched out his hand to greet him before answering.

"Dr. Mandelow. Forgive my lack of manners. Good morning to you and congratulations on staging a most impressive show last night. It went off without a hitch, didn't it?"

Aloysius Mandelow's face creased into a beaming smile. "Glad to hear your opinion, Jack." he said. "I…" Glancing at Mathilda, he quickly corrected himself." We certainly thought so."

He pointed at his enormous desk, on which stood the silver coffeepot and several cups. "You are most welcome to join us for a morning coffee. Are you looking for anyone in particular?"

Jack shrugged loosely and gave him a quick grin. "Just felt like catching up on the after party goss…" He hesitated. "I'm hoping to catch up with Lochie sometime, but meanwhile, I'm delighted to join you and hear your views of last night's proceedings."

Mathilda had moved unasked to the coffeepot and poured him a cup. "Cream? Sugar?" she asked.

Jack shook his head. "Black as the River Styx," he said. "Like my soul." Her eyes flickered with amused appreciation as she passed him the cup.

Aloysius gestured to a chair next to his, on the opposite side of the desk from where Mathilda was sitting. "We certainly showed New York that we're their West Coast equal last night. Wouldn't you agree, Jack? Have you seen anything better in New York?"

Jack laughed. Seeing as I've never been to a New York art show, how in the heck am I supposed to know? he thought.

"Oh, definitely not," he said. "That's one thing that surprised Susannah, experienced as she is with the international scene. Just how high the standard was."

His eyes drifted to Mathilda, who'd settled with a disgruntled twist to her mouth.

Bring ignored doesn't sit well with her.

"Would you agree, Mathilda? I know you haven't had the exposure to Paris that Susannah has…" Her lips slipped into a grim line.

She hates it that Susannah has done so much she hasn't.

"But you know the New York scene better than anyone." She immediately brightened at the backhanded acknowledgment.

"Oh, I agree with Aloysius. Completely. It was a tremendous show. San Francisco is finally on the map in the international art scene."

She hesitated. "And it was fitting Gil's work got such a positive reception. It's just a shame he wasn't be here to see it."

"Oh? That painting? What was it—the one of the male nude—it attracted good comment?"

Aloysius broke in. "Oh, most definitely. It's a strong contender for the top prize, I'd think. We'll be making that final decision later today, when we've taken into consideration the popular vote.

"Of course, I can't comment any further than that, and we're consulting a panel of judges, but it has to be considered a front runner. It so cleverly addressed both the classical requirements and the avant garde. It's been a long time since I saw that done so masterfully."

"And I understand a handsome cash prize comes with it too? With Gil not here, who stands to receive that?" For the first time since he'd joined them, Aloysius tensed and his eyes darted to Mathilda and then the wall.

"I'm not sure. And of course, it's hypothetical at this point. He hasn't won it yet." His follow-up laugh rang with forced jollity. "We're going to have to consult his lawyer about his will. And if he hasn't got one, then I suppose it would go to his agent."

Aloysius's wandering eyes finally came to rest on Mathilda. Jack sipped his coffee and let the uncomfortable sense of something unspoken stalk the room.

And then he asked, already guessing the answer that was coming. "And who is his agent?"

Another long silence. Mathilda's fingers entwined in a white vine of apprehension. "I am," she said. "But there's nothing to be made of that. I represent many artists, including Susannah."

"Of course," Jack said with unctuous cordiality. "After all, you're the best in the business." She seemed to relax whatever she'd been holding in then. Her shoulders settled in a rested line and her head fell slightly forward on her previously stiffened neck.

"I'm so glad someone recognizes it," she said, through shrill laughter. "I'm sure you also appreciate I'd much rather have Gil alive than be collecting prize money on his behalf."

"Oh, I'm sure you would," Jack said smoothly. "Wouldn't we all?"

Twenty-seven

He was turning to leave, satisfied he had got as much out of Mathilda and Aloysius as he was likely to, when he heard footsteps in the hallway outside. Lochie and Dot entered at a bark of consent from the Doctor of Fine Arts.

"Mornin' Aloysius," said Lochie. He hesitated. "It is still morning, isn't it? Must be close to lunchtime…." He glanced around and acknowledged Mathilda and Jack with a perfunctory dip of his head. He whispered, "Morning to you too," before turning to Mandelow.

"Aloysius, I'm wondering if you require Dottie for anything over the next couple of hours? If not, I'd like to use her as a model for a study I'm working on and pay you the agreed amount for her time. Is that convenient?"

Aloysius tapped the edge of his desk thoughtfully. "That will be fine, Lochlan." To Dot: "But make sure you're back by 3:30. There are things I need done at home."

Dot bobbed, the dutiful servant. "Yes, Dr. Mandelow."

"I was just leaving," Jack said to the room. He addressed Lochie and Dot specifically. "I'll walk out with you."

Mandelow and Mathilda were already preparing for some other shared task. Mathilda had gone to a filing cabinet and was extracting files. The prof looked over the top of the monocle and picked up a pen at his right elbow.

"Thanks for the coffee," said Jack. "It was exactly as black as I like it."

As soon as they were out of hearing of Mandelow's office, he took hold of Lochie's arm.

"Can I take you both out for coffee for thirty minutes and pick your brains? Yours and Dot's," he said, glancing at the young girl at Lochlan's side.

"I don't want our conversation to be a public announcement if we can avoid it."

Dot grinned. "Not too much that's private around here," she said.

"As long as we're not too long," said Lochie. "I want to get that preliminary study done before Dot goes home with Aloysius."

"You go home with him? How come?" asked Jack.

"She's indentured to him. Arranged by the orphanage. They put them out to work at ten. Or even younger."

"Ahhh," said Jack. "I've got another friend that happened to." He thought of Isla, now well on her way to full literacy and having time to consider what she might like to do in life.

"It's a wicked system. I feel sorry for you, Dot." She licked her lips nervously.

"Dr. Mandelow's is a much nicer place to be than the orphanage," she said. "I never want to go back there."

"Pleased to hear it," Jack said. "Then let's get out of here. I don't want to hold you up any longer than necessary."

They seated themselves in a café a short distance down Montgomery Street and Jack set Lochlan in his sights, glancing aside to Dot now and then to include her in the conversation.

"I wanted to get your thoughts on last night," he said. "You talked to a completely different crowd from Susannah and me, and it's invaluable for me to understand what your friends and acquaintances thought about it all."

"About what, exactly?" said Lochie. "Wasn't it just another Madcap Artist's Ball when all is said and done?"

"Aloysius seems to think not. He considers San Fran is now on the international circuit for art. Do you think that's the case?"

Lochie glanced at Dot before answering. "We're probably not the best people to answer that, Jack. We're unashamedly parochial. I only want to paint what I love and know here in the Bay. I'm not interested in big prizes or international trade."

"Well, you should be," said Jack with mock solemnity. "Your work stands up against the best in any city, but I'm sure you already know that."

Lochie shrugged. "I don't want to be anywhere but here."

"And who would you pick for the big prize money? Any whispers out there on that?"

Dot had her head down, picking at her fingernails.

At the mention of prize money, she lifted it again.

"Many people are picking that male nude. The *Ebony David*." Jack whistled a reedy low note.

"And why is that? Because of the quality of the work, or it's notoriety value? It would certainly make news for San Francisco's first Grand Prize, wouldn't it? Winning Artist Murdered Two Days Before His Work Collects Big Prize?"

Lochie smirked. "Old Aloysius never misses a chance for scandalous promos… He's a master of them. But lots of people think the painting is worth the prize, anyway. What they don't understand is how Gilbert Lusk came to paint it."

"Why is that?" Lochie gave a light shrug.

"It isn't the sort of thing he's ever shown any inclination to do. He's been into reconstructions of Civil War battles.

"It seems like he avoided fighting himself, but now he wants to be seen as a strong military man. And none of the battles he depicts have any Black Americans in them. As far as Lusk is concerned, the Colored Infantry regiments didn't exist."

Jack regarded him with a level gaze. "He might have decided he had to change his tune?"

Lochie shook his head. "I didn't know the fellow. But some who do think it's strange."

Jack turned to Dot. "What about you, Dot? Have you heard Mandelow and Mathilda talking about this?" Dot paled under his light gaze and shrugged.

"Have I said something wrong, Dot? You don't have to be scared of me." She wordlessly shook her head and appealed to Lochie with eyes brimming with tears.

Lochie jumped in. "Aloysius has made it clear she's not to talk about anything relating to the show. He's set the fear of God in her, Jack, so best don't ask. She can't tell you, even if she knows."

Jack gazed at the fresh youthful face, and his heart burned in his chest. This could have been Cordelia if her life had taken a different path, if the family who'd adopted her had fewer scruples.

Dot's eyes were closed, and her face bore the imprint of painful secrets. When she ventured to look at him, her large blue eyes overflowed with tears.

"It's fine. Dot. Please, I don't want to upset you. Forget I ever asked."

Twenty-eight

Susannah fell into bed, grateful to have time alone to reflect on the thunderous revelation of the unveiling. And already certain she wouldn't get a wink of sleep.

Who perpetrated the fraud? Was it Gil who entered her painting under his own name? Or were they in cohorts, him and Mathilda, both with a grudge against her?

Whoever it was, they'd committed both a forgery—by erasing her pseudonym and replacing it with his name—and then entering it in a contest, swearing it was a truthful entry. Every entrant in Salon Shows had to sign a sworn statement that the work was all their own and executed by their own hand.

The thing that burned the most was that he'd scorned the painting when she'd shown it to him in Paris. He'd belittled her attempts to explain the philosophy behind it, and ridiculed her execution.

"You're completely out of touch with what people are buying," he'd jeered. "Who wants a naked slave on their wall, for goodness's sake? You're turning into more of a bluestocking every day, and it isn't attractive."

She'd entrusted the last details of the entry to Mathilda, because she'd left for San Francisco in a rush with Cordelia.

Could she bring herself to ask her former best friend the question that burned within her? Had Tilly been the one to mount this monumental betrayal, and if she was, did Gil know about it?

As she tossed and turned through the night, she came to the reluctant conclusion that whoever's idea it was, as one of New York's top agents, Mathilda must have known about it.

She'd either thought it all up herself and Gil wasn't even aware of it, or it had been Gil's idea, but she'd helped him execute it. Either way, Mathilda had to have known.

When she struggled out of bed the next day, hours later than she normally slept, with dark fatigue rings under her eyes, she felt like someone who'd been confronting a brick wall all night. She'd been trying to work out how to get over it, and still was no closer to an answer as the sun rose.

If I tell someone, they won't believe me, she thought. It's too bizarre to think someone would do this. And it would smack of desperation. They might accuse me of appropriating someone else's work.

The only people who'd ever seen the work—apart from her, Mathilda and Gil—were Fleur and Ezra. Fleur was dead, and Ezra was somewhere in Palestine painting holy wilderness.

She struggled downstairs to breakfast with a nauseous stomach and a thumping headache, enjoying a sense of reprieve when she discovered everyone else had already gone out on their daily business.

She'd have a coffee and nibble at some toast and then say she was feeling unwell and return to bed.

Her heart sank when Mrs. Roderiquez appeared at the breakfast room door with an anxious look on her face. She guessed before the dear woman opened her mouth what she was about to say.

"The police captain is here to see you again, Miss Susannah."

Susannah looked up from her piece of cold dry toast and suddenly could not contemplate swallowing another mouthful. Her mouth went dry and her tongue felt as if it was sticking to the roof of her mouth.

She cleared her throat and choked out the words. "Send him in, Mrs. R. And don't worry. There's nothing to fear from him."

Her tongue felt thick and disobedient around the words. Mrs. Roderiquez shot her a doubtful look and turned to usher Seamus Cassidy in.

Brave talk. If only I believed that, Susannah thought, as she stood to welcome the lawman to the table.

"Please sit down, Captain Cassidy. Would you like some coffee?"

The housekeeper hovered in the doorway, awaiting his response, and when he declined, she backed out and shut the door behind her.

Cassidy surveyed her with a calculating eye, and she was sure he had missed no detail of her dishevelled state.

"Had a hard night, have you, Miss Carterton? You don't look well." Anger boiled up within and she had to suppress the urge to retort tartly that it was ill-mannered to comment on a lady's appearance.

Ill-mannered and common.

Instead of speaking, she regarded him coolly and remained silent. They sat in that stalemate for a long minute, and then he leaned in to her.

"I'm here to report our progress on the case. I thought a woman who'd been engaged to the murdered man not once but twice…"

He bit into the word *twice* with grim relish. "Would appreciate an update. Particularly as I believe we're closing in on the offender. I expect to be making an arrest within a few days, if not sooner."

Her heart leaped into her throat, and she again found it impossible to get any words out. She sipped her coffee and nodded with what she hoped was an interested detachment.

His eyes searched her face for her reaction. She swallowed hard on the coffee and said, "That's good news, Captain Cassidy."

"Is it?" he said.

"Well, of course it is. We all want this dreadful business settled."

He pulled back in his chair but still eyed her like an eagle lining up prey.

"Tell me, Miss Cassidy. When was the last time you saw Mr. Lusk?"

Her pulse raced, and she couldn't stop herself from nervously licking her lips.

"Why, it would have been over six months ago. Back in New York. Before I came out to San Francisco. Gil came to a farewell dinner at my brother's house before we left."

"And you haven't seen him since then? You didn't see him in San Francisco during this current visit?" Her heart was thumping in her ears now, roaring to her to tell what she knew.

She pushed it back down and shook her head, setting her face with the most genuinely solemn look she could muster when her heart was ready to leap right out of her chest.

"Here? This time? Why no. I didn't even know Gil and Mathilda were here. We haven't been in touch for weeks."

"And when was the last time you spoke to Miss Morton?"

"Before this week, you mean? I haven't spoken to her since I left New York, but we exchanged a couple of letters."

That at least is true.

"Oh? And what were they about?"

"Art business, mainly. She was acting as my witness for entering works in the Bay Gold show."

"I see."

He swivelled in his chair and gazed around the room, as if he'd catch her out by noting some off-key detail in the decor. Then he turned his attention back to her.

"So, if I told you we'd located someone who'd swear they'd seen you and Gill Lusk meeting on the night he died, what would you say to that?"

Icy fingers clutched at her insides. Suddenly, she found it hard to breathe.

"I'd say they were mistaken. Badly mistaken."

"We found him less than half a block from your studio. I don't believe in coincidence, Miss Carterton."

Her tongue froze. She stared at the policeman, and a long silence dragged out between them that screamed GUILTY.

Susannah was a parched dog. She wanted to let her tongue hang out and pant frantically. She clenched her lips as she stalled for time.

Then the door flung wide open, and a rush of fresh air flooded the room. Jack stood in the entry, staring. In seconds he was across the room at her side.

"What is going on here? Captain Cassidy, I thought Miss Carruther's lawyer made it quite clear to you. He was to be present if you wished to question his client further."

He glanced down at Susannah. He was like a vague mist at her shoulder.

She pushed herself up from the table with both hands.

"I feel sick, Jack. I'm sorry. I'm unable to answer any further questions."

She backed away from the policeman and Jack and fled the room.

Cassidy picked up his briefcase and stood to leave.

"She's as guilty as sin," he snarled to Jack. "And you're a right fool if you don't recognize it. Don't worry. Lawyer or no lawyer, I'll be back. And next time, it will be with an arrest warrant. Tell her lawyer that."

Twenty-nine

Jack saw the bullying detective out and was returning to the breakfast room when he caught sight of Cordelia hovering at the bottom of the stairs, her arms hanging disconsolately at her side.

"What's wrong, possum?" he asked. "You're looking sad. What's making you unhappy?" She pulled a face at him that said, *I'm not a kid. Don't treat me like one.*

"Is Aunt Susannah all right?" she asked, pulling on the lobe of her right ear with her thumb and index finger. Fiddling with her ear. It was a sure sign she was upset, he'd learned in the six months she'd been staying here with him.

"Aunt Susannah's unwell and she's gone upstairs to rest. But she'll be fine. We had a late night, and she didn't sleep well, that's all."

"She won't die, will she?" The young woman's face was ashen, and when Jack examined her, he saw beads of perspiration dotted her forehead.

He took her in his arms and drew her close, stroking her long, flaxen hair.

"Aunt Susannah isn't going to die. Everything will turn out fine."
She pulled back and looked deep into his eyes.

"They said Mama Sylvia wasn't going to die, but she did," she said, her jaw jutting out mutinously. "I'm not a child anymore. I know bad things happen."

He circled her shoulder with one arm and led her gently back into the breakfast room. "Come in here, dearest Cordelia. Let's get you something to drink from Mrs. R and have a friendly talk. I know you got an awful shock when Sylvia died. She was good to you, wasn't she?"

Cordelia nodded, and the long strands that fell on either side of her ears swung around her face. She pushed it back with one hand.

"Sylvia had a very serious illness called tuberculosis," Jack explained. "Susannah doesn't have tuberculosis. She's upset about Gil's death, which is a natural thing to feel about a friend."

"It's all my fault," Cordelia wailed. "If we hadn't come to San Francisco, none of this would have happened."

Jack sat her down on the small sofa that faced out into the garden and cuddled her against him.

"Cordelia, that's not true. Susannah is in a sticky patch, but we're getting her out of it. And it's not your fault."

She pulled free of his embrace and gave an anguished cry. "It is true. That policeman. He just said Susannah met Gil the other night. He said he's got witnesses to prove it was her who killed him." And she broke into furious sobbing.

Witnesses? Has Cordelia been eavesdropping again?

He waited patiently for the girl's tears to dry up. He pulled a crisp white man's-size handkerchief from his shirt pocket and gave it to her to wipe her face. In the kitchen, Mrs. Roderiquez was delighted to serve up cool lemonade, which Cordelia sipped with speedy gratitude.

Jack took Cordelia out in the garden, where they sat on a bench seat under shady trees and sipped more lemonade. And then Jack understood.

Thirty

"We'll be checking the area for witnesses…" The memory of a red-nosed street peddler in a clown costume flooded her mind. Susannah could smell the violet fragrance from the basket he carried, overflowing with posies, and enough helium balloons tied to the basket handle to lift it skywards if it was left unattended.

She'd dropped onto her bed and fallen into an exhausted sleep. When she'd awoken, she'd had a raging thirst and no idea of the time. She dashed cold water on her face and teetered downstairs, frightened of what she might face there.

She'd ordered fresh coffee from the kitchen and blundered into the library to wait for its delivery. And ran straight into Jack.

"Oh, Jack." She groaned. "Is this an ambush?"

"Call it that if you want," Jack said. But there was none of his usual humor in his voice. He was all business.

"Tell me. What does that Irish cop want now? And why on earth did you talk to him without me or Gerry there?" He came at her in a burst of energy, but his tone was gentle. He'd guessed she was on the verge of tears.

She shook her head and said weakly, "He… he jumped me. He took me by surprise. I couldn't say no."

Jack registered his disbelief with a down-turned mouth. "Really? Miss Carterton being bulldozed by a common cop?" he teased. She took a deep breath, preparing to spill the bad news.

"He says he's got witnesses who saw me meeting with Gil on the night of his death."

Jack dropped into the chair beside her and said in a gentler voice; "We knew this was always going to be a danger. But how likely is it?"

She gazed up at him, and she knew her eyes betrayed her deep fear. "Almost definitely true. I forgot before, because I was so shocked to see Gil there. But as Cassidy was talking, it came back to me. A street vendor was hovering in the background, watching as Gil banged on my door."

"A vendor? What sort of vendor at that hour of night?"

"One of those guys who hangs around the square selling flowers and balloons."

The peddlers were a regular feature in Portsmouth Square on weekend afternoons when families and sweethearts gathered to picnic and swap stories and sweet kisses. The children loved the balloons, and eager beaus flattered their girls with endearments.

She'd seen the huckster several times when she'd been at her studio, and she remembered with a pinch in her gut that when she'd pushed Gil in the chest, someone had stepped out of the shadows and caught him.

Jack gave a long sigh. "And Mathilda will be happy to confirm that."

"Exactly. Cassidy's already heading off to seek her corroboration, I'm sure."

Jack jumped up. "Then I'll have to make sure Sam locates that vendor and has a good chat. At least we now know what we're up against."

"How's Cordelia?" she asked. "I hate to think what all this upset is doing to her."

"She's worried it's all her fault. She saw that fight in New York. But you know that because you've cautioned her to not mention it to anyone."

She blushed, but had the grace not to deny it.

"She's aware of a lot more than we've realized," he said, warning in his voice. "She's resorting to eavesdropping to keep up."

"Oh, Jack, I can't believe I've brought all this on her," Susannah wailed. "And to think I used to carp about you and your Chinatown haunts. That's nothing compared to this! No one will want to have anything to do with the niece of a murderer. She'll be the notorious deb."

Jack laughed. "Susannah, can I remind you? They haven't arrested you yet, and if we can help it, they won't."

He turned toward her. "I've just been having coffee with Lochie and Dot. Word is that Gil's painting is the frontrunner for the Grand Prize."

Of course it is.

A black hole opened deep in the pit of her stomach. What was she going to do about it? And when? If she raised the issue before the judging was complete, she could help the organizing committee avoid embarrassment.

What proof did she have to show she, not Gil, was the creator? And if word got back to Cassidy, he'd see it as an additional motive for a woman seeking revenge.

She could just see him now, with his sneering lips. *It was too much to bear, on top of him breaking off your engagement, was it, Miss Carterton? You couldn't tolerate the thought of your best friend marrying your former beau and them both claiming the Bay art prize?*

"You've missed out on the man and the art prize. Too much, was it? Come on. Confess now and it will be a lot easier for you."

And if she left it till after they made the announcement, then she'd have far less chance of being taken seriously. They would inevitably ask why she hadn't come forward immediately. Either way, she would raise bitter suspicions.

She stared into Jack's face. "They're right to award it the prize money. It's the most exciting work there by a country mile."

She was about to explain she had a studio full of works in the same series to prove her credentials, when there was a timid tap and Mrs. Roderiquez popped her head around the library door.

"A letter for you. Miss Susannah. Looks like from someone overseas." Her voice had an air of wonder, as if "international mail" was so amazing she could hardly believe it existed.

Susannah took the ivory white envelope, re-addressed to her in black ink in her brother's cursive script. A letter from France he was forwarding to her. Her fingers stiffened on the envelope, and her eyes flashed to Jack.

"I… I'll need to some privacy to read this," she said, stammering her foreboding. "Could we continue this conversation some other time?"

Jack frowned. "Why certainly. But don't leave it too long or it may be too late. Meantime, I'll get Sam on the tail of the balloon man."

Thirty-one

She fled to the garden with hot coffee and a plate of muffins, cheese and grapes. She settled back in her cushioned deck chair, her thumb poised to prise open the envelope, her heart racing in anticipation or dread—she couldn't identify which was the dominant emotion.

She contemplated the flowery script which looked like a woman's hand, addressed to her in New York, which was then struck out by her brother's much more masculine writing from his broad-nibbed Italic fountain pen.

The stamp was French, an earthy red study of Ceres, the Roman goddess of plants, fertility and motherly relationships, her Roman profile garlanded with wheat and grapes.

She guessed it was not from Ezra, and the opening words confirmed her suspicions.

"My Dear Mademoiselle," the missive began. Ezra would have begun with a more familiar greeting. *"My beloved Susannah,"* or something of the sort.

The excitement of only a few moments ago evaporated, replaced by dread. She had the urge to stop right there and refuse to read any further. Take time and regroup before continuing.

Her raised eyes settled on a family of fluttering hummingbirds in the nearby shrubs, fanning their tiny wings as they dipped slender purple throats into trumpet-like red flowers. They were emitting a range of strange little buzzing, clicking noises, ending in a long whistle.

How odd, she thought. They sound more like insects than birds. Despite her rising dread, her eyes sought the next sentence.

"It has been our godly duty and privilege this last nine months to feed and provide spiritual care and protection to Athena Hartzell, born by the grace of our Mother Mary, who you left in our care nearly a year ago.

"We consider it the outworking of our Christian purpose to see this beautiful child of God through to her first birthday."

Susannah's eyes blurred, so she couldn't read any further without clearing them. She dabbed at them and looked up to where the tiny birds frenetically went about their business.

Just like the nuns.

Her heart was like stone. She didn't want to read on. A dark tide of foreboding rose within her as she held the page closer to read through her tears.

"As we explained when we accepted Athena into our care, we cannot commit to keeping her for any longer than her first year.

"There are so many of these darling foundling children needing our loving help, it is, as we explained, our policy to raise them to be healthy babes and then either return them to their natural families or find them a permanent or foster home with good Christian families.

"Our letters to Athena's father at the address you provided have gone unanswered."'

Susannah swallowed the stone-like lump in her throat.

'It is with great sadness that we write to advise we can no longer maintain Athena's care here. We need her bed for newborns, who are in danger of not surviving.

'We are therefore reluctantly advising that unless you uplift Athena

into alternative care within the next three months, we will make new arrangements for her with a loving adoptive family.

'We hope you appreciate, Mademoiselle, that this was always the agreed arrangement, and we are not able to ignore what we told you when you brought her to us more than six months ago.'

Signed by Sister Claire, Sisters of St Joseph, Paris.

She put her head in her hands and wept.

Thirty Two

Jack looped his arm through Cordelia's and gave an enormous sigh of pleasure. Here he was, taking his beloved niece out on a downtown jaunt, something which a year ago was beyond his wildest dreams.

He sent another grateful prayer heaven wards for the Countess's efforts in tracking Cordelia down and approaching her adoptive parents. Without her, he'd never have found the girl again, never have discovered her stepmother was dead and her step father floundering in his parental role.

Shoppers crowded Montgomery Street, strolling in the sunshine, taking in the street scene, passing troops of gaily costumed women eyeing up their competition.

"Women in San Francisco seem freer than they do in New York," Cordelia observed with a wondering gaze. "There's something about the way they walk. They aren't looking over their shoulders, checking if their chaperone is still trailing them. They stride into the future. I like that."

She deftly dodged a peddler's dog cart filled with fresh oranges and flashed him a secretive conspirator's' grin.

"I know Aunt Susannah wants the best for me, but sometimes she can be a drag."

Jack tried to look stern as he faced down the smile, feeling guilty that he was doing exactly what Susannah often accused him of, taking the easy road, playing the good guy, and leaving all the hard work of parenting in absentia to her.

"She does want the best for you," he said through a light laugh, as Cordelia echoed the last words of his sentence in a parody of the schoolmarm's voice Susannah sometimes couldn't seem to help using.

Susannah's sudden upset retreat to the garden following the arrival of the international letter this morning had thrown a gloomy cloud over the entire house. He'd tracked down Cordelia and invited her out so she wouldn't once again assume responsibility for Susannah's down mood.

His earlier chat had convinced him they had to include Cordelia in what was going on. Trying to protect by keeping her in the dark just made her more anxious and insecure.

Whether or not Susannah would approve, he decided, he'd take Cordelia downtown to see the Bay Gold show. He'd introduce her to modern art, let her see Susannah's paintings, and give her a taste of downtown life on summer's afternoon.

You never know. If Lochie is in his studio on the way home, we might stop for coffee.

They'd enjoy an adventure and get to know one another better outside of the confines of Susannah's constant vigilance about Cordelia's reputation.

He bought them tickets to show, and they were soon wandering among the assembled works. It quickly became clear that Cordelia had already developed a discerning eye.

"You know a lot about art," he commented after she'd made a grown up observation about one of the paintings. "Did your aunt take you out to galleries in New York?"

She shook her head. "Not really. I studied art at Gardener's…"

Jack knew Gardener's School For Girls was one of New York's top private schools for girls at the time–Thomas had spared no expense on Cordelia's education.

"And was that fun?"

"It was OK. At least they took us out to see art shows in places like Knoedler's, learning more about theory."

Her face took on a thoughtful mist. "Aunt Susannah was usually off doing her own paintings."

"Knoedler's?" asked Jack, though he'd heard of the place.

"The biggest commercial art dealer in New York," explained Cordelia. "They had some of the new work from Europe. Where they have all the light showing through."

They'd paused in front the Bretagne beach scene that was one of Susannah's entries.

"Like this?" said Jack, gesturing at the work.

"Ohhh," said Cordelia, a concentrated glow of wonder spreading across her translucent complexion. "That's one of Susannah's. I know without even looking at the signature. I saw some sketches for it in her notebooks, but I've never seen the finished painting before. Isn't it wonderful?"

"In one of her notebooks?" Jack echoed. Cordelia took one of his hands in hers and gazed soulfully into his eyes.

"I stole a look at them. Is that so bad? I was curious about what she was working on, and she never talks about it. Sometimes I peek in her sketchbooks when she isn't around. Back home she left them in Papa's library sometimes."

Jack squeezed her hand affectionately. "Natural curiosity is a good thing," he said. "As long as you don't take it too far."

He paused and surveyed the room. The show was filling up again with interested patrons. All the works were for sale, and some already bore the red stickers announcing they'd been purchased.

"This show is proving to be pretty popular," he said. "Dr Mandelow will be pleased." Cordelia shot him an inquiring glance. "Who's he again?"

"He's the man who organized it. The big wig in the art world here." She nodded, instantly turning her attention back to Susannah's painting.

"Maybe someone will buy this one," she said. "Maybe Susannah could stay here and paint, and we wouldn't have to go back to New York at all."

"Would you like that?" asked Jack, aware of a sharp pain in his chest. He'd never considered that by bringing Cordelia out West, he'd disrupted so much of what she took for granted.

What if she's so attached to Susannah she doesn't want to stay here without her?

That would be like losing her all over again, but ten times worse. As they were speaking, they'd moved slowly on along the wall, and they paused again in front of the last few paintings, including the *Ebony David.*

Momentarily, he questioned whether a 13-year-old innocent should view a still life of a naked man, but then reassured himself. Only his beautiful back view and his facial profile were showing.

Susannah had composed it so carefully arranged cloth draped the rest of his body. And besides, if Cordelia was studying art, she must have seen some semi-nude studies already. Classical statutes and what not.

He turned to gauge her response and saw that confused lines rippled across Cordelia's usually tranquil face. "Is something wrong?" he said." You look confused."

"Is this… is that Gil's signature? Aunt Susannah's friend?"

Even the mention of his name had left her pale and tense.

"Yes. That's right. This seems to be the favorite to win the big prize. Everyone's talking about it. It's called the *Ebony David.* After

Michelangelo's David. Did you study that in class?"

She was barely listening to him. Her lovely face took on the bemused faraway look of someone who was being asked to take in too much information at one time.

"But… But… it can't be…"

She turned to him, her face twisted in bewilderment.

"Aunt Susannah… she has studies for this painting in her sketchbooks, too. Her Paris sketchbooks. They're exactly like this one. She'd even named it in one corner. The *Ebony David*. It's all there in her notebook."

Thirty-three

In her notebooks?

Jack stared into Cordelia's perplexed eyes, and momentarily, the surrounding room receded. There was just this precious girl, and a thundering fear, rising like rumbling storm clouds, already darkening the horizon.

Had Gil somehow stolen her painting? Had she discovered his fraud and challenged him over it? Even gone armed with the knife Cassidy had shown up with?

Or did he have something over her? Had he blackmailed her into playing along with his ruse? And if so, where did Mathilda fit into all of this? What might she be tittle-tattling to the Irish police captain at this very moment?

He took a gulp of air with the awful understanding that this gave Cassidy more reasons to blame Susannah. When he heard about it.

If he heard about it.

He replayed the police captain's accusations in his head.

First, he takes your fiancé. Then he takes your painting. He's stolen everything … your life. Who could blame you for wanting revenge?

"Jack… Jack." A young girl's voice called him back from his lost musings. Cordelia was standing up close, staring into his face.

He came back to reality with a thump, stepped back abruptly, and saw Cordelia's hands laced in front of her, and she was wringing them in deep distress.

"Oh. darling girl, I'm sorry. I lost myself for a moment there." He gathered his arm around her shoulders and turned her away from the imposing work.

"We've seen enough here. Let's find a coffee. Or maybe visit Lochie at his town studio, if he's there. Would you like that?"

She pierced him was a look which said, *You can't distract me that easily* and replied huffily, "I'd rather see him in the country."

"We can do that another day," he said. "He's working in town at the moment. Dot might be there." She perked up.

"Dot? I'd like to see her again."

"Let's go then."

He hesitated and glanced back at the *David.* The anonymous man it portrayed had a noble manliness that reached out from the canvas. His form carried a natural aura. He was a prince among men.

He thought of Lochie's casual observation the previous day.

As far as he was concerned, Black soldiers didn't exist, so I can't see him devoting all that time on a Black male nude.

He rallied himself to confront the present again.

"Let's find Dot. We'll talk about that painting another time."

Thirty-four

When they got to Lochie's, two things were immediately clear. First, the girls, Dot and Cordelia, were delighted to meet up again.

And Cordelia was nearly as excited to discover her new friend was looking after Dr. Mandelow's dog, a curly-haired, milk-chocolate-colored Irish Water Spaniel named Shannon, after the river where the dogs were said to have originated.

"Oh, he is gorgeous," she squealed, as he rose from his place, curled up on the floor, watching Dot with adoring eyes. "Can I cuddle him?"

Dot sat up straight, gave an apologizing shrug in Lochie's direction for disturbing the session, and smiled.

"Only if you approach him quietly. If you're too excited, he'll get all charged up. And you don't want to see a crazy Irish dog running around in circles in this small space!"

The young girls laughed, instantly at ease with one another.

"Tell you what," said Jack, seizing on a golden opportunity to get Lochie alone. "Why don't you take him out for a walk?

He pulled a couple of coins out of his pocket. "Buy yourselves ice creams while you're out."

As he'd been speaking, Cordelia had edged closer to Shannon and gingerly ran her hand from the top of his head and down his back.

"He's got a topknot," she giggled in delight. "Look at him! If it flops over his eyes, he won't be able to see to chase pigeons!"

Dot slipped off the couch, unbuttoning the housemaid's smock she was wearing as she moved toward a screen in the corner.

"Give me two shakes to get changed into my street clothes and we'll be off."

The girls left in a rush of youthful enthusiasm that filled the air with a honey-fragranced lightness.

"A housemaid's smock?" Jack said teasingly. "What's that about?" Lochie shrugged. "That's what the client wants. So that's what he gets."

Jack regarded him quizzically. "And who is the client, may I ask?"

"Normally, I'd say 'state secret'—but because it's you…"

They grinned at one another. Since Lochie's father Grigor had introduced Jack into his son's life as a guardian and business mentor a year ago, shortly before Grigor's death, they'd developed a deep trust.

Jack marvelled at Lochie's artistic talent, so like that of his mother's. And Lochie acknowledged he needed all the tutoring he could get while learning to manage the extensive estate Grigor had left him.

Jack dropped onto the couch Dot had just vacated and felt her lingering warm imprint. A long silence filled the room as Jack regarded the younger man expectantly. "It's Aloysius. But don't tell Dot. Even she doesn't know."

"Aloysius wants a portrait of his indentured servant dressed as a housemaid? Isn't that weird?"

Lochie shrugged dispassionately. "Each to his own, I guess."

"Lochie!" Jack yelped. "That's creepy to me. It's like me getting a portrait of Cordelia done as… Oh, I don't know—as one of Greek Sirens… It feels wrong. Defiled."

He lowered his voice. "He hasn't got a taste for young girls, does he?"

The fragrance of the Imperial Spa suddenly overwhelmed him. The luxurious baths attached to the Imperial Club had been one attraction in Sophia Morrigan's vice empire, which included the trafficking of young girls to brothels across the state.

His involvement in shutting Morrigan down had led to his acquaintance with Lochie's father and their subsequent business partnership.

He shuddered. Isla, the girl he'd met at Morrigan's establishment, had been destined for such a life before he'd intervened. He'd vowed to do everything in his power to crush the trade, which could also so easily have been Cordelia's story.

Lochie shook his head, though his normally pink face had paled.

"Nothing like that. At least, I don't think so. Word is he's got something going with that pushy woman from New York. The one that was here when you were here last time. What's her name?"

"Mathilda. Mathilda Morgan."

The snake head rises yet again.

"That's it," said Lochie, seemingly not picking up on his unease.

"Oh… So they're an item, are they? That's mighty handy when they are both on the judging committee for the Bay Gold Art Prize. I am right, aren't I?"

Lochie had been busy wiping the heads of his brushes clean and stowing them away as they talked. He gave his hands a final wipe and slumped into an armchair facing Jack.

"I think so." He nodded. "As I mentioned before, Aloysius prefers to keep his private life quiet, but the lady likes to boast when she's had a few at the bar."

"It all gets more and more complicated," Jack said with a sigh. "Tell me one other thing. Do you think they've decided on that prize? Have they already made up their minds to award it to that *Ebony David* work?"

Lochie's face split into an amazed smile. "Well darn me, Jack, you're just about as dammed intelligent as Shannon—and he's an extremely intelligent dog." He glanced around and hefted his chair closer.

"The walls have ears," he said. "But speculation on just that point has been ballooning. The whisperers reckon that fellow that died a few days ago already knew he'd won. He was preparing to spend the money. And they reckon that dame who lives at your place—Cordelia's aunt—knew it too and was pretty mad about it."

He dipped his mouth in an apologetic moue.

"Where's all this poisonous stuff coming from?" Jack's ears hammered with the pulse of rising blood. "And how could they possibly know?"

Lochie shrugged and sat back. "Don't ask me. I'm just repeating what's out there."

Jack shook his head.

"It's dangerous, Lochie. Rumors like these can destroy lives."

Lochie nodded, his face somber. "I know, Jack. If these stories reach the ears of that cop, I wouldn't like to be in Auntie's shoes."

Thirty-five

Dinner was over. Dot, Lochie and Cordelia were having a spirited card game on a small table at one end of the sitting room. Elizabeth's smoky blue Persian cat Persephone pretended to be asleep, stretched out on the sofa, while eying Shannon warily.

Shannon, a far less devious creature, lay on the floor, head on webbed paws, fixing the cat with a beady expectancy, as if ever hopeful she would stop sleeping and start playing.

Elizabeth, who'd been relaxing with needlepoint beside Persephone, stifled a yawn and announced she was retiring to bed early. Jack quietly poured two brandies and gestured to Susannah.

"There's something I want to show you before we follow Elizabeth to bed," he said. "I think you'll find it interesting."

Engrossed in their game, the card players barely registered their departure, but Susannah cast a doubtful glance in their direction as she followed Jack into the hall.

"What's all this?" she hissed in an indignant tone as she closed the sitting-room door behind them.

"Wait and see," he said and purposefully led her into the library. He gestured to the sofa. "Make yourself comfortable," he said and sat down opposite her.

She took a sip and eyed him balefully over the rim of her glass.

"Cut the mystery, Jack. I've had a very trying day."

"You and me both," he said sharply.

Her eyes snapped, picking up, he hoped, on his annoyance. She'd played him with one lie too many.

"I took Cordelia out for the afternoon, and made some more interesting discoveries about her young life," he said.

"Oh? Like what?"

"One thing, for starters. She sneaks a peek at your sketching journals when you're not around? She badly wants to know about your work, and it appears you're so busy creating you have little time to share it with her."

Susannah's face flushed hot pink, and she licked her lips.

They sat in a charged silence.

"She also eavesdrops to keep up if we don't include her in what's happening."

Susannah raised her eyebrows as if to say; *So what can I do about that?*

Jack shook his head in slow concern, as if she was a dull-witted child.

"And she knows a damn sight more about what's going on around here than I do." His voice carried a slow, deep irony. "It might be amusing if it wasn't so dammed serious."

"Jack," she said in a tired, bored drawl. "Don't overreact."

He paused, savoring his brandy, and pushed down the heat which was threatening to boil over inside him.

"When were you going to tell me that pile of dung who got himself murdered a few days ago stole your painting?"

Her face drained of all color, but her lips remained mutinously tight.

He took another slow sip of brandy.

"Are you never going to understand if we don't know the facts, we can't help you? You're not untouchable, Susannah, even if your father was one of the richest men in New York."

He let the silence drag on. Still, she did not speak, although he sensed from the tensing around her eyes that she was in inner turmoil.

"You realize—you fully understand—what will happen when our friendly police captain gets wind of this fraud? It's yet another motive, and perhaps the strongest yet, for you to kill this Lusk guy.

"First, he dumps you for another woman, and then he steals your prize painting. A piece the whole art world recognizes as revolutionary. His girlfriend arranges for it to win a major prize, and you're left with nothing but egg on your face.

"Did you already know about all of this before we attended that show last night? You looked at that painting with me and you didn't say a thing, though I thought you looked upset."

She banged her glass down on a side table and jumped to her feet.

"I did not know they'd done that. Had no idea," she said, her eyes sparking fury. "It flummoxed me as much as it has you. Gil saw that painting in my studio in Paris and he hated it. He mocked it. Said it was ridiculously ill-judged."

She jumped up and took a few steps away, as if wanting to escape, and then whirled to face him, her eyes flaring. "I could not believe my eyes when I saw his name on it, and that's the truth."

Jack sensed indeed he was getting the genuine story, perhaps for the first time since he'd begun the thankless task of trying to help her.

But as she stood before him, hands on her hips, her cheeks flaming, another creeping worm of suspicion wriggled into his brain.

He let her stare at him in suspense, not acknowledging the truth of her words. He inched closer until only a small gap separated them

Even with all her dissembling, he couldn't deny the strange pull he felt toward her.

He wanted to reach out, take her hand in his, and comfort her. He pushed that impulse down irritably and instead, he said curtly: "Swear to me, Susannah. Swear to me on Cordelia's life, that you didn't kill Gil Lusk.

"You've admitted you met him that night, and now we discover you had a powerful motive to be furious with him."

Her jaw tightened, but she visibly quailed like she'd been lashed.

"You can't swear it, can you?" he whispered.

"I did not kill him," she said, her voice breaking. "I swear it."

"And you've lied to me so many times already. Why should I believe you now?"

He knocked back the last of his brandy with an angry swallow. It tasted bitter in his mouth.

"You can bet that police captain is already getting all the dirt from your former best friend Mathilda. And he'll be around here first thing in the morning to ask you about it."

He flung his final furious dart. "Cordelia trusted you. You're the sun, moon and stars to her, even if you don't know it. And you're about to crash her entire world."

Thirty-six
Two Days Before the Bay Gold Show

Mathilda Morgan dropped her shopping basket in the hallway inside the front entry of the San Francisco hotel suite she shared with Gil Lusk and rubbed her sore wrist.

Bag hanging off her arm, she'd lugged a carefully selected range of delectable foods up the hill from downtown in anxious anticipation of the meal she planned for Gil tonight.

It had to be good. She wanted him primed and in his best mood for the announcement she was about to make.

She glanced down at the red mark on the underside of her wrist, where the heavy bag had left a mild abrasion, and gave it another soothing stroke.

I'm not a donkey or a cook, she told herself. And soon I won't have to pretend I'm either.

She shivered with excitement as she thought of the future ahead for her and her beloved.

She was already the top New York art agent, but soon she'd also be the wife of the most influential artist in America's most important center for art.

She closed her eyes and swayed dreamily as she pictured them holding court at art shows. She'd wear the latest Macy's fashions and Susannah Carterton would be a drab, might-have-been-but-never-quite-made-it spinster. Would she even bother to show up once she and Gil were the established couple of the New York art world? She'd probably shrink into the shadows, or even scuttle back to Paris.

She's always had that option, with Daddy's money behind her. Unlike me.

She glanced around the "suite" they occupied in the St. Francis. It was acceptable enough for a short-term stay, but she'd hardly describe it as a true "suite," with one bedroom, a small room for entertaining, and a tiny kitchenette.

The worn carpets, the sofas of anonymous generic design, and the smell of stale smoke from past guests lingering in the dusty air, all spoke of second-rate lodgings. The room felt like the maids shook their dusting cloths inside instead of out the windows, just to spite the mean owners.

When Gil is named as the big prize winner tomorrow, think of the prize money he'll get. We'll be in clover…

She clapped her hands together and bent down to pick up the three bags of food she'd carried home. She'd searched high and low for the things she knew he liked most.

She'd loaded up at the City of Paris deli with oysters done just as he liked them, raw in their shells with lemon juice. Add to that crispy browned roast chicken, green herb-filled salads and soft, runny cheese and fresh French bread, and they had the makings of a royal feast.

Complete the repast with his favorite Bordeaux red from the wine shop at the bottom of the hill, and she was confident he'd eating from her hand.

She glanced at the kitchen clock. Five thirty. He'd said he'd be home by six p.m. She began unwrapping parcels, serving up food on the limited range of dishes they had—that would be changing soon too—and smiled to herself as she worked.

Things were going to be different around here. And soon.

•••••••

When he finally staggered in, an hour later than she'd expected, his face flushed with the angry red blotching that showed up on his skin whenever he'd had one too many whiskeys, Mathilda got an instant headache.

Drinking one or two too many glasses of hard liquor and turning belligerent had become a pattern for Gil over the last few months. One she found difficult to deal with.

He was far less malleable in these moods, and less likely to enjoy his food. When he was like this, he usually just wanted to either keep on drinking or retreat and brood.

She pretended not to notice his state, stepping forward instead with a warm smile, her new dress in fashionable Mexican blue with double hems—the upper shorter and looped above the underlying one in a slightly darker shade, swishing around her. She'd felt especially optimistic as she'd prepared herself for this meeting.

But when he looked up, his heavy brows furrowed in an irritable V shape, his dark irises stony, she instantly knew she was overdressed and under-prepared for what was coming next.

"Where are *you* going?" he asked, the emphasis on the pronoun, the edges of his voice rough with annoyance.

"Me?" she replied, sounding vacant and hollow. "Nowhere. I thought we'd have a delightful meal together, that's all."

She gestured to the card table, laden with food. The amenities did not stretch to a dining table, so the flimsy baize-covered square was over-burdened with edibles.

Instantly, she questioned whether this was such a good idea. She recalled how easily riled he was by her attempts to create "togetherness" between them, brushing her aside whenever she attempted to talk about their future together.

In a drunken moment he'd proposed, and she'd accepted with alacrity, but he'd been reluctant to set any dates or discuss it since.

"What's there to celebrate?" His normally attractive baritone slurred.

"Let me take your coat, Gil," she said, advancing on him. "Get you settled." Before she could reach him, he took an unsteady step backwards.

"Never mind about the coat," he said, wrenching it off without her help and letting it fall to the floor before she could reach him. "Another drink wouldn't go amiss, though. Is there any brandy left from last night?"

She quelled inside at the thought of him pouring more firewater down his throat.

"You must be hungry," she said. She knew her smile would look anxious. "Why don't you sit down and I'll get you something special."

His eyes had a wary glaze, but he stepped up to the table and slumped onto one of the lightweight chairs. She was relieved to see it held him without collapsing.

"Look," she said, as if trying to get a toddler interested in vegetables. "Oysters. Just the way you like them. They had a fresh delivery today."

"What's going on?" he asked, suddenly more alert, less drunk. "You don't normally like to be bothered with preparing meals. You prefer to eat out or get someone in to cook."

She took a deep, patient breath. "We don't have a cook here, do we, Gil? And I wanted to have some private time with you. Just us. No noisy public dining room."

He regarded her for a long minute, and then picked up an oyster shell and prodded at it with a fork. The juice dribbled down his chin and onto his shirt front, and he dabbed at it impatiently.

"You'll never be Susannah," he barked. "You know that, don't you?" A knife pierced her chest, and she couldn't suppress a gasp of shock.

You never talk about Susannah. She's the forbidden topic.

"I... I don't know what you mean. I'm not trying to be Susannah." He smirked, and she could see the fog of the alcohol had dissipated. His eyes were as sharp as diamonds, and just as cutting.

"That's good then. Because you never will be."

"Gil, please. I'm the one you're marrying. I can do lots of things for you she can't."

His eyes flicked over her, his lip curled in what it dismayed her to acknowledge was distaste.

"Like what?" he said, a jeering sneer on his lips.

"Well, arrange for you to win the Bay Gold Prize for starters," she said, a strident, don't-you-dare-put-me-down tone creeping into her voice.

He stared. "You what?"

"I've organized it. I'm on the judging panel. You know that. And thanks to your desire for secrecy, no one knows we're going to be married. So. I've arranged it."

He tipped back on his chair, as if reeling from the news. "I assume this means you've been cozying up to some of the other judges? Now let me see... who is there?"

He had an infuriatingly smug grin on his face.

"I know." He put his hand up in the air, like a schoolkid raising his hand for the teacher's attention. "That slimy Dr. Aloysius. The one everyone knows only likes little girls, although whether he ever actually does anything with them, who knows? You've crept up on him and coaxed him into your back pocket."

The slurring returned with the last sentence. He looked in danger of falling off the flimsy chair, rocked by his own mirth. Then he sobered again.

"And what painting, I pray? What painting of mine justified the title of Best in Show?" He was treating the whole thing like some fantastical joke, and an icy dread gripped Mathilda's insides.

What can I tell him?

She stared at him, frozen. "I… Ahh… "She couldn't get the words out.

"Well?" he said, in horrible triumph.

He knows he's done nothing that could justify the Bay Gold prize. We both do.

"Tell me, if it's true. What painting?" He put a heavy emphasis on the words. "What painting?"

"The *Ebony David*," she said in a rush. "The *Ebony David*. That one." He reared up, bumping his big thighs under the table as he rose like a god of the seas, overturning it and sending an avalanche of food, dishes, glasses and cutlery to the floor.

"The WHAT?"

"I told you. The *Ebony David*."

Thirty-seven

"What have you done, you dumb bitch? Do you think people will believe I painted that thing? Even if I was capable of it? Which I'm not."

Suddenly, he wasn't drunk anymore. He was stone-cold sober, and the shard of pain in his eyes told her he was also mortally wounded.

"I loathe that thing. I saw it in Susannah's studio in Paris, while she was still working on it. We had a dreadful row over it."

He advanced on Mathilda, wringing his hands as he approached, as if seeking her neck.

"It symbolizes for me everything that took Susannah away from me. Paris… her damned insistence on her freedom… getting crazy ideas like painting a nude nigger…"

His face was a thunderous black cloud, steadily advancing on her. "If none of that had happened, we'd be together now," he cried out. "She'd be my muse and maybe I would paint something decent enough to win prizes."

He glanced around him. "No one else I know has her eye, her instinct for what works on canvas. No one."

He stared at her as if she was something the cat had dragged in.

"And certainly not you. Don't you understand? People who know their art will recognize that?"

He slumped down on the couch.

"How did you do it, anyway? Don't tell me. You painted my signature over Susannah's…"

She bit her lip and could feel her face flushing red in humiliation.

"You did? Oh, my… how original." He roared with snarky laughter and slapped one thigh with his beefy hand.

"Only you could be greedy and stupid enough to do something like that. Really, Mathilda?"

He stared, and she felt herself shrinking inside with every second he raked her with cold, assessing eyes.

"And what are you going to tell them when she protests that it's her painting?"

She glared back at him, wooden inside.

"She won't. She still loves you too much to humiliate you like that."

He stood upright. He was a good six inches taller than her, and suddenly she felt an overpowering fear.

Is he going to hit me?

"I doubt that very much," he said. "But have you considered my humiliation? By doing this, you're saying I'll never get there by myself. You think the only way I'll ever win is by executing a fraud on an ex-lover's coattails?"

He took a step toward the door. "I want nothing to do with this, you bilking harlot."

He turned and spat at her feet. "I'm going to tell Susannah, right now. Tell her everything. I may be a failure as an artist, but I'm not a cheat."

She scuttled across the floor, grabbing at his coat as he picked it up to put it back on.

"Gil, No. You can't. I did it all for you. What will happen…"

She broke off as he turned on her in a polar rage.

"What will happen to you?" He eyed her icily. "You didn't do this for me, Mathilda. You did it for yourself. 'Top art agent marries prize-winning artist.'"

He made invisible quote marks in the air with his index fingers.

"When this comes out, I doubt you'll have anyone wanting you to represent them. And as for 'us'—" Once again, he made the loathsome, mocking quotes in the air.

"There is no 'us,' Mathilda. There never was. And there certainly won't be now."

He pulled his coat on up over his shoulders, fixed the second to top button up, and turned and left.

Thirty-eight

He spent the next couple of hours in a gloomy tavern whose dim lighting and dull clientele of dock workers and sailors matched his mood. Alone at the back corner table, no one came near him, and he liked it that way. He stared into his glass and asked himself how his life had come to this.

Finally, when even he recognized he'd had enough to drink, he wandered out into the San Francisco gloaming and stumbled into the pretty green surrounds of Portsmouth Square.

The families who filled the park-like space during daylight had long gone. Those who were left behind were rather like him—lost souls with nowhere better to go, or young bloods intent on late-night rabble-rousing.

When he found himself a quiet corner on a wrought-iron bench, he pulled the last of his brandy from inside of his coat. He stared at the opened neck and considered. Did he want to get any more drunk than he was already?

He'd serious business to attend to tonight, and Susannah hated it when he'd been drinking. He thought back to the days when they were constant companions. He hardly drank at all then.

It's something I've got into in the last six months, since she's been gone.

He set the bottle down on the sealed path and stared at the hairy backs of his folded hands. They were big man's hands, with fingers like fat cigars. Not slender and long like the romantics imagined artist's hands. Still, he'd done some good work with them.

Good, yes. But not up to Susannah's best.

No. Not as good as Susannah's best.

He reached for his bottle and before he'd lifted it to his lips, he smelled a heavy patchouli perfume wafting from behind him. A young woman slid onto the seat beside him, her eyes ringed with kohl, lips painted dark red.

He didn't have to look twice to see she was a woman of the night. The makeup and her outfit—flashy pink and red full skirts and a plunging neckline, arms rattling with bangles—told him that.

He guessed she'd be no more than twenty-two, but her skin was flaky and dry and her flinty eyes were lined and weary.

"Hello," she said, her voice overly friendly. "You look lonely."

He couldn't help himself. He laughed in her face.

"As a pickup line, it's pathetic, sweetheart. But never mind. I'm not in the market for a pickup." Her mouth curved in a pout.

"Most of the jocks don't care about the pickup line," she huffed.

He smiled and looked at her more closely. Under the heavy makeup, she was thin and wasted. She was nothing more than an abandoned kid.

"I'm sure they don't, doll. Under all that face gunk, you're a pretty girl. But I'm not in the market for pretty girls tonight." She regarded him, a calculating glint in her eye.

"So, what are you in the market for?"

He laughed again. "You've got to work to eat, is that it? What's your name?" he asked.

"Me? I'm Polly to my clients."

"No. Not that name. Your real name." For a reason he didn't fully understand, it was suddenly important to talk to someone who wasn't pretending to be something else.

"Ohhh," she sighed. "My real name? It's so long since anyone used it, I've almost forgotten what it is."

"Try to remember. Just for me." He pulled a fist full of greenbacks out of his breast pocket, peeled off two, and held them in the air in front of her. Her brows went up in amazement and she eyed the paper hungrily.

Then her gaze fell to the street, and she seemed lost in thought for a long minute.

"Sunny," she sighed at last. "They baptised me Sunny Ann Rowlands. Only there's been nothing particularly Sunny about my life. I never heard the name from my mother's lips. She died before I was old enough to understand."

Another of life's throwaway children, he thought. Gil handed her two single dollars.

"Well, Sunny, let me tell you a story."

"Can I have some of that brandy while you do?" she asked, eying the bottle.

"Sure. I've had more than enough already."

OOOOOOOOOOOOOOOOOOOOOOOO

Telling another human being about his pain felt good, Gil thought when Sunny Ann stood up to go hunting after a group of young men who'd arrived on the other side of the Square.

"As you said, a girl's gotta eat," she said with a wry twist of her mouth as she departed, still clutching his bottle and wafting heavy perfume in her wake.

Her candid responses and pragmatic advice had helped him sort Mathilda's tangled mess into some logical order, and now he had some stepping-stones to follow. He sat there for another ten minutes, contemplating his next move.

The cool night air wrapped around him like a comforting shawl. His feet were heavy wooden lumps, reluctant to step forth on the mission he knew he must complete. He cursed Mathilda again under his breath for putting him in this situation.

Somewhere at his back, a night bird gave a mournful cry, echoing the slow beat of his heart.

Sunny Ann was a streetwalker with a conscience, he mused, with a flickering smile. More principles than Mathilda, anyway. She'd been forthright in her views of his recently terminated fiancée.

What a witch! Imagine. Doing that to her best friend!

He hadn't thought of it like that. He'd been so wrapped up in himself.

She'd even talked sense about Susannah: *You can't blame the wench. All us women. We just want our freedom.*

And on his dilemma: *Why don't you tell that bird she has to withdraw the painting before anyone else finds out? Simple. No damage done.*

He looked up at the silvering moon. It was simple, wasn't it? Just tell Mathilda to withdraw the entry. She could say the artist wasn't happy with it. He wanted to change it.

The only people who know it's been entered are the judges. Mathilda, Aloysius and one other. And me and Sunny.

And yet he couldn't get Susannah out of his mind. He thought of her, working away in her studio half a block away, just down the street from where he sat now.

What harm could it do to visit? See her. Tell her what had happened. She needed to know she shouldn't trust Mathilda any more, and he'd explain he was going to insist it was withdrawn.

You never know. She might be grateful.

He stood, reassured that this was the best course. He couldn't face going back to that hateful "suite" right now, anyway.

Thirty-nine

Captain Cassidy had made another breakfast call at Elizabeth Westerhoven's, but this time Susannah—with Jack's backing—was canny enough to insist she would not speak to him without her lawyer present.

That's how they all came to be sitting around the dining table at the Pine Street house at midday, when Cassidy strode into the room with an infuriatingly confident air, and planted himself before Susannah, eyeing her coldly.

He wasted no time on courtesies.

"Where were you at nine p.m. on the night Gilbert Lusk died?"

Susannah glanced uncertainly at the lawyer, who gave her a barely visible head nod which signaled, *Answer the question.*

"I was at my studio in Washington Street, painting," she said.

"What painting were you working on?" Susannah glanced helplessly toward Jack.

She'd been working on the final piece in the *Ebony David* series, a painting she considered outshone anything she'd previously done, and she didn't want to talk about it.

She'd thought the series was complete when she painted the one entered in the San Francisco show, but fresh inspiration swamped her after she'd left New York. If she talked about it, the issue of the provenance of the one in the show would immediately come into question.

Would she be adding another nail to her coffin to mention it? Jack flicked a meaningful look at Gerald, and he quickly interjected.

"I object. My client does not have to answer that on the grounds it is irrelevant to the substance of your inquiry." Susannah's face grew hot. She'd done nothing wrong, and she was being forced to act like a guilty person.

"Did you talk with Mr. Lusk at any time that night?"

She hesitated and then replied with a forthright "No."

Well, she hadn't, had she? She'd seen him, but they hadn't talked.

"What would you say if I told you I have an eyewitness who says she met Lusk on the night he died?

He addressed the question to her lawyer, who avoided catching her eye.

"Produce your witness and we'll comment then." He folded his arms across his chest and assumed a resolute stance.

"You've admitted you were once engaged to the deceased. Twice engaged, in fact. Just exactly when did the ultimate break occur?"

Susannah looked to the legal eagle for guidance, and he gave the faintest nod of assent.

"Six months ago. When I moved here. He was angry about me leaving New York, and I realized we had no future together."

"*You* realized it?" His face twisted in disbelief.

"What would you say if I suggested that Mr. Lusk broke off the engagement because he had switched his affections to another woman, and you came to San Francisco to remove yourself from an embarrassing situation?"

Susannah's stomach lurched and her mouth gaped open.

She shook her head. "That's not what happened," she said faintly.

"Furthermore, what would you say if I suggested you've not been transparent about the true nature of your relationship? You've never mentioned, for example, the child you left behind in Paris?"

Susannah stared in disbelief. "Child?" she echoed, her voice a whisper.

"That's right, Miss Carterton. A child. You left a daughter behind, and you were very upset about it. Is that correct?"

She sensed the energy sucked out of the room. Both Jack and the lawyer were staring at her, faces like rigid granite.

"I left a child with the nuns," she assented with slow moderation.

"But it was not my child. It was the child of a dear friend who died of a fever. She begged me to ensure her daughter's safety. I had to leave Athena behind when I returned to New York, and yes, it distressed me greatly to have to do that.

"But it had nothing to do with Gil. Nothing at all."

Cassidy sneered. "That's not what I've been told."

His snakish eyes turned to the lawyer.

"I'd advise you to reconsider your advice to your client, Mr. Peters. There's mounting evidence that rather than her breaking off the relationship with Lusk, she was hanging on, seeking revenge.

"She's an unmarried woman, left in Paris alone with a child. And when she returns to her home without the baby, she discovers that the father of that child has already moved on, replaced her with someone more amenable to his needs.

"A woman who did not harbor competing ambitions to rise in the world of art, and was happy to be the lifelong companion he desired."

She could feel the color draining out of her face.

So this is Mathilda's version of events. She is the only person I confided in about Athena.

Cassidy was not solely relying on the balloon toting peddler—he may have only heard of him through Mathilda—although he might still track him down to confirm his woman scorned scenario.

No. There was only one person who knew about Athena's birth, outside of the child's parents and a tight Paris circle—like the doctor who delivered her, fellow painters they'd holidayed with in Brittany, and the nuns who now cared for her.

The same person who'd entered her painting under a false name.

A wave of giddiness rolled over her. She slumped in her seat and brought her hand to her bowed head, propping her forehead in her fist.

"I feel sick," she whispered, and then she remembered nothing more.

Forty

"You were right, Jack. I've been a total fool."

Susannah gazed up at him through clouded eyes, her face deeply gouged with pain lines.

"My best friend. She's the so-called 'witness.'"

She tossed out the words, as if spitting out something foreign. A rogue hair, or a wandering fly.

"She's the one telling him about their 'true love.' Hers and Gil's."

She drew a trembling hand across her eyes, as if trying to clear her vision.

"I'd never have dreamed… It's hard to believe…"

Mad Dog Peters interrupted her.

"Miss Carterton, I need you to take me right back to the beginning. Pretend we've just heard that Lusk is dead. And this time, there'll be no secrets. No withholding of critical information. You will tell us the whole unabridged story, however sordid."

He stared down at her, his stance stern and unbending.

"If there's one thing a defense attorney hates, more even than losing, it's being caught short on his client's story. And today, I wasn't just caught short. He blew me right out of the water."

He turned aside to Jack.

"You sure delivered me a doozy here, Jack. I'll be collecting on the debt you'll owe me for years to come. That's if I get her off after the merry dance she's led us on. This folderol."

Susannah dropped her hand and raised her head.

"Forgive me. Mr. Peters. I've been exceptionally foolish. But I didn't know Athena would be considered relevant information!"

She turned to Jack, her hazel-gold eyes glittering with tears.

"There's only one person outside of a tight circle who knew about Athena. Not even Gil was in on it, partly because he despised the child's father, Ezra. Hazeltine, the Black American artist who was the model for my *Ebony David* series.

"And no, there was never anything between us except mutual respect as artists. His amour was a very dear friend of mine.

"And the only person in America who knew about them and their child is Mathilda. Gil saw the paintings in Paris, he met Ezra. But Tilly was the only one who knew about Fleur and the baby."

Jack put a consoling hand on her back. "Woah, slow down there, Susannah. Take a deep breath and start again.

"You're way ahead of us. Start right at the beginning. And if you don't tell it straight this time, we're walking away for good. You'll be on your own."

•••••••••

"I can see only one way to convince Cassidy you're not the murderer," Gerald Peters said sometime later, waggling his thick brows like a dancing bee directing fellow workers to the nectar.

"Oh?" said Jack. "And what's that?"

"We have to trap Mathilda Morgan into boasting about what she's done to Susannah. And set it up so that Captain Cassidy hears the whole thing."

Jack laughed. "Not too hard then…" He paced to the window.

"And how are you planning to achieve this feat?"

"I'm working through that in my head right now."

He gazed at Susannah through bright beady eyes, like a blackbird lining up an earthworm.

"You'd agree with our analysis so far? The most likely suspect—the only suspect for this murder is Miss Morgan herself?"

Susannah's face drained of color, but she nodded dolefully.

"I never thought it would get to this, but I agree with you. She knew about the raging argument we had the last night I saw him in New York, because I told her about it.

"I was so upset and I couldn't bother Thomas with it. He had too much else he was dealing with.

"I told her about him grabbing the knife and pulling it on me. She must have recognized I'd given her a gift as a weapon, if she'd got that far in her murderous thinking by then.

"I didn't know he'd taken it with him when he'd left. I was too upset to notice."

She shook her head. "I still can't believe she'd do it. She's had a crush on Gil for years."

"People do rash things when they're pushed to the edge," said the lawyer.

"She thought entering your painting under his name would please him. She never considered he had an ego the size of Mount Diablo.

"My educated guess is what she's done horrified him, and he came straight to you to pimp on her and insist he had nothing to do with it. Maybe he even hoped by telling tales, he'd win his way back into your affections...

"But as far as Cassidy goes... She will have already identified the knife as coming from your household. And she's told him about the fight you had with Gil and made it sound like you pulled a knife on him."

Susannah nodded silently, a lump so hard in her throat she couldn't swallow.

Gil didn't deserve this.

Forty-one
The night of the murder

The streets were empty of people as Gil wandered with a slow, aimless gait toward the building where he knew Susannah had her studio. He'd made it his business to eavesdrop on conversations at the Arts League building where Susannah's arrival in the city had caused an excited stir.

She was a minor celebrity, an artist who'd been friends with French avant-garde artists like Camille Corot and Edouard Manet. They said James McNeill Whistler, another prominent American artist in Paris, expressed admiration for her work.

When she'd kept to herself in San Francisco, moving anonymously from her lodgings with the Countess to her studio and back again without joining in on any of the local art scene, the locals felt mildly deflated.

They longed to hear stories of Paris controversies—pictures rejected by the Salon, disagreements between the old guard and the new painters coming through—but they were to be disappointed.

From reports he'd gleaned, Susannah had flitted from Elizabeth's gilded hospitality to her unobtrusive art cave and them back again like a moth drawn by light, focused only on two passions: caring for her niece and continuing her work. And that pleased him.

Maybe there's still a chance for me, he told himself. I've wasted too much time on that agent friend of hers.

She doesn't appear to have taken up with anyone else. And we worked so well together.

His way ahead felt lighter now, and he allowed himself to sway at the hips in a loose-kneed stroll, the alcohol still making itself felt in his body.

Only the occasional jingle of a passing hack disturbed the night silence. He smelt the lingering fragrance of street chestnut and popcorn stands, and his empty belly reminded him he hadn't eaten.

The streets were semi-deserted except for the occasional manager or office worker who'd worked late and was scurrying home under the gas streetlights. He stopped to watch a cat perched at the top of stone steps, eyes locked on a rubbish bin below with its heavy tin lid pushed askew.

He stood for several minutes, watching the cat watching the bin, and it wasn't long before his—and the cat's—patience was rewarded.

A sleek, dark gray rat emerged carrying a crust of bread in its front paws. The cat pounced, knocking the lid off its precarious balance and sending it rattling down the street while the cat slunk off with the rat in its jaws.

"Noisy devils, aren't they?" A young man of about sixteen, dressed in the ruffled spots of a circus clown and carrying a string of balloons in one hand, emerged from the night fog, creeping up from the harbor as the sea mist rolled in.

He stood in front of Gil's startled form, his face lit up with a best friend's kind of intimate grin. Gil couldn't suppress an answering smile.

"Which? The cats or the rats?"

"Both," said Balloon Man. "My mam told me you can't have one without the other."

"Like dogs and fleas," chimed in Gil, delighting in the diversion.

Truth was, he feared the reception he'd get at Susannah's and he was rehearsing what he was going to say. Imagining how she would take it.

"Hello Susannah. How have you been going in the last six months, since I pulled a knife on you? Sorry about that, I made a terrible mistake. Please forgive me.

"I've come to apologize. Oh, and to tell you of the biggest betrayal you're ever likely to suffer. But don't worry. I'm going to fix it."

He tried to picture her beautiful face as he said these words, but no answering picture came.

He pulled his woollen coat more closely around him. The night was still warm, but he was shivering. He'd behaved abominably the last time they'd been together, and he wasn't sure she'd ever forgive him. Not without some pretty major evidence of his repentance.

But isn't that what I'm bringing her? Telling her about Mathilda?

"Haven't I seen you at the Art Students League?" asked the balloon seller, who was still tagging along.

"You're one of those big-time artists come to town for the art show, aren't you? One of the Doc's guests?"

"That's right.," said Gil, warmed with a sense of pride at the recognition. "I'm sorry. Did we meet?"

The lad's eyes glittered from behind the white pancake mask. "You wouldn't remember me. I wasn't wearing all this muck. I'm studying with Fortunato Arriola."

Gil recognized the name as that of a prominent San Francisco artist, known for his portraits and Central American landscapes. "It's one of those situations when we all know you, but you don't know us."

"Well, I do now," said Gil with warm jocularity, thrusting out his hand. "I'm Gilbert Lusk. Visiting from New York. It's a mighty fine town you're building here."

"Pete Kosimo. My dream is to one day be good enough to enter a work in the Show. Have you got something entered?"

"Yes, I do," said Gil, before he could stop himself. "But I've discovered in the last couple of hours there are some things more important than winning competitions."

Forty-two
The Night of the Murder Part 2

Susannah woke with a jolt and opened her eyes wide. Before she'd dropped off—she'd told herself she'd just rest for a moment or two— she'd been putting the final touches to her latest work, which shone out in all its glory from the easel in the middle of her studio.

Her eyes alighted on it, and she gave a contented sigh. The work was the apple of her eye, the best art she'd ever created. She felt a fizz bubbling up from deep inside—like champagne of the spirit, she thought with a giggle—every time she looked at it.

She'd thought she'd completed the *Ebony David* cycle before she left New York. The painting she'd entrusted to Mathilda to submit for the San Francisco show had been the final one in the series till then, and she'd been more than satisfied with its completion.

But after she'd been in San Francisco a couple of months, a worm of discontent ate away at her peace of mind, like a coddling moth in an apple. You couldn't see it from the outside, but inside, dissatisfaction for things she'd left undone hollowed her out.

She'd wet her pillow with tears thinking of Athena, her darling girl with dark chestnut eyes that gazed out on the world with age-old wisdom.

As she lay in the bed at Elizabeth's, big enough for her and six Athenas, her mind churned on like the relentless hurdy-gurdy sounds she sometimes heard echoing down from the park half a block away.

Is she happy with the Sisters of St. Joseph?

Does she remember me? Miss me? Does Ezra ever visit her?

In her frantic last weeks in Paris as she packed under her brother's urgent orders to come home as fast as she could, she'd been desperate to reach out to her artist friend in Brittany and beg him to come back to Paris and Athena, to visit and cherish her after Susannah's departure, but he'd eluded her pleas for one last meeting.

He was resisting her attempts to extract a promise that he'd take his paternal responsibilities to heart. He'd already been adamant the child would be better off with someone else, and his attitude hadn't softened since.

Athena was my last chance at being a mother, and I let it slip away…

She pushed aside the rug she'd snuggled into and stood and stretched. Immediately the cool evening temperatures had her shivering, and she grabbed up the mohair shawl and slung it around her shoulders.

The painting glowed in the dim light from the street, and despite her glum mood, she smiled to herself. This work crowned everything she'd ever done. It was the work which demanded to be created, the energy that would not quietly lie down in a pile of discarded inspiration.

I've got those chestnut eyes exactly right. Penetrating and peaceful, all at the same time.

She'd titled it *Ebony Amen*, and she'd modelled it as a commentary on contemporary mother and baby pictures being produced by artists like Mary Cassatt and Berthe Morisot.

Except Athena lay in her father's arms, gazing up at him like an infant Jesus. And he returned the adoration, with a noble gentleness across his handsome features.

This was the counterpoint to the one in the show. Fine as that work was, she thought. It's captured a crossroads in life, an intersection where one way of life ends and another begins.

And it's all dreaming. A shrill little voice twittered in her head. *You know it's not true.*

She'd had time to think about it all since they'd moved to San Francisco. In the trauma of leaving her vocation in Paris, and then nursing Cordelia's mother in her last illness and comforting the child and her brother, she'd hardly had a moment to draw breath on her own behalf.

Despite the frequent and annoying disagreements with Jack about Cordelia's well-being, she'd found a spiritual home in her secret studio, and many an evening she stole off here to paint after the rest of her familial duties were complete.

Like tonight. She'd no idea if her earlier *Ebony David* picture would attract any positive comment tomorrow night at the show, but she didn't care, because she knew she'd already produced something that was so much better.

She thought back to Mathilda's odd visit the night before she and Cordelia left New York. That was the night she'd told her about Athena. About the terrible fight with Gil. And Tilly had shared her big secret.

Tilly had been bubbling to share a confidence, while swearing her to secrecy.

"You're not to tell a soul until I say it's all right," she'd told Susannah. "Promise me. Not a soul. Not even Cordelia."

"I promise," Susannah said, smothering a giggle and thinking Tilly's behavior reminded her of when they were girls.

"Gil and I are getting married," she said with a satisfied grin. "We want to keep it quiet, but we're looking at a spring wedding."

"Married?" said Susannah. "Since when?"

"Since you were stupid enough to let him fall through your fingers," said Tilly with a hint of malice. "You didn't think just because you didn't want him, no one else would?"

Susannah swallowed hard before answering. She and Gil had broken up five days ago. He wasn't wasting any time.

"Of course not, Tilly. Congratulations. Gil is a fine chap. I'm sure you'll both be thrilled."

That was the last conversation they'd had before she came West. And Mathilda had already twisted it all for her own purposes.

She drew the shawl around her shoulders and sank back down onto the sofa. She couldn't believe she'd fallen asleep on the job, and as she slumped back into the plumped-up sofa, her mind returned to her waking moments and the interrupted dream.

Even now, wide awake as she was, she remained confused about what was a dream and what was real.

A looming sense of dread had startled her awake. Her heart was beating an anxious tattoo, and her breath came in short, fast gasps. Something evil was approaching. It was almost like a drummer in the vanguard, announcing danger's arrival in simultaneous warning and rejoicing.

Shivers of anticipating fear ran up her legs, down her spine, from the back of her neck. She tried to hunker down and ignore it, tell herself it was a silly dream, but then she'd heard loud footsteps, coming this way from far down the street, growing ever louder, with the drum still beating. She could stand it no longer.

She stood, with the shawl pulled ever tighter, and tiptoed to the door. Hesitating, frightened to show herself, scared even that her shadow would give away her presence, she hung on, unable to back off.

"Be strong and of good courage…" Wasn't that what the old warrior prophet Joshua told the people? That had always been her motto.

Never let them see you're terrified.

She didn't know how long she stood there. She wasn't even sure if she'd done it, or if she was still in the dream. But then she heard hints of voices, low but unmistakeable, outside. A sharp rap on her door shot more arrows of fear right through her.

Her hand went to the door of its own volition, and she turned the knob and peered out. The first figure she saw was the balloon seller, his face a white mask, his red, white and blue balloons on strings bobbing behind him.

And then Gil stepped forward, a silly cat-like grin across his face. She could smell the whisky fumes from several feet away. He stretched out his arms, beseeching. "Tilly…. I mean Susannah. Sorry." He hiccupped without putting his hand across his mouth.

"Something's happened, and I have to explain. I don't want you to be mad at me, Susannah. But you've got to understand. I didn't mean it. I had nothing to do with it. It's all Mathilda's fault."

She put up her hand in a halt sign and took a step back.

"Go home Gil. You're drunk, and I don't care. For goodness's sake! You're free to marry whoever you want, and if you want Mathilda, then fine. Just leave me alone."

"No, but… but you don't understand. I have to talk to you." He attempted to push through the door, but a balloon man stepped out of the shadows and put a restraining hand on his shoulder.

Susannah took a deep breath, her heart pounding with the shock of his appearance. She put her hand in the center of his chest and pushed hard.

"Go away," she cried, sharp and loud, and slammed the door in his face.

She sank back into the sofa and wept for lost opportunities, for the mess her life had become, for the family she'd likely never have.

And when she woke, she couldn't tell whether Gil's late-night visit had happened, or was all part of a long and upsetting bad dream.

Forty-three

"I don't understand it, Jack. I really don't."

Jack turned away from her and took a deep breath of sea air as they barrelled along in Gerald Peters' open carriage, Gerald in the driver's seat. They were meeting Captain Cassidy at noon, and Gerald was a stickler for punctuality.

It was the sort of lovely soft autumn morning she was coming to appreciate was typical of San Francisco at this time of year, when the overnight sea mist had melted away, to be replaced by a heady sense of freedom created by the expanse of air soaring to a benign cloudless dome of crystalline blue.

How much longer will I be free to enjoy a ride like this?

She took in a deep gulp of marine salted oxygen in gratitude as Jack turned his attention back to her.

"What don't you understand, Suzie?"

Suzie? The diminutive sent a warm trickle up her spine. They'd spent so much of their time together sparring, each rejecting what the other presented. This sudden acceptance went straight to her aching heart.

She clasped her fingers together and brought them up to her chin in a thoughtful pose.

They were continuing the conversation began back at Elizabeth's, positing one key question. What led Mathilda to kill the man she loved?

"She's been crazy about Gil for years," Susannah said, dropping her hands and looking Jack squarely in the face.

"I should have seen it sooner. She was jealous when he asked me to marry him, I know, although she tried to hide it.

"But now, she'd finally got him to ask her to marry him. She was gloating about that a couple of days before I left New York. She couldn't contain herself. She had to tell me. She'd got her happy ending. So why would she turn on him and kill him?"

Jack shrugged. "The human heart has an unstable voice," he said. "Perhaps they had a fight, and he broke it off. She was frightened he was returning to you. Maybe that's why he came to visit you… to get you back?"

He gave her a tentative smile. "It sounds to me like you were the 'love of his life'—if such a thing exists." His mouth twisted in a moue of disbelief. "Can't say I've ever experienced such a thing myself."

She answered his smile with a trembling one of her own.

"We were bound by something intangible for a long time," she said, her voice faltering. "I wanted to believe I'd found a man who shared my passion for the art. Who understood my need to paint, above all else? It took me years to realize I was mistaken. "

She turned away, looking out on the passing scene, but not seeing it, lost in an internal world. She was silent for several minutes and then spoke again.

"He didn't deliberately set out to deceive me. At the beginning, we didn't understand it ourselves. We were two young artists, painting together.

"But somewhere along the line, it became about him as a man, needing female support. He didn't see us as a partnership of creative spirits, but as his place as master and mine as muse."

A tear trickled from her right eye and ran down her cheek. Jack reached out and placed a warm hand on top of the hand that rested on her thigh.

"That must have been painful for you." She tossed her head in frustration and pulled her hand away to wipe the tear clear.

"It was. My dream of two equals, each pursuing their work, while maintaining a household, with a growing family… He smashed that to pieces in Paris when he came to visit and saw the *Ebony* series.

"He hated it. He despised the idea of using Ezra as the model. I honestly think he was jealous. He saw I was onto something. I was pulling away from him into a whole new world."

She shot him another trembling smile. "He called me a 'spinster reject.' That's telling me, isn't it?" She drew out a spotless white handkerchief and dabbed her cheeks, then snuffled into it.

"Look at me," she laughed breathlessly. "I think this is the first time I've shed a tear for Gil and what might have been."

She smiled at him through shining tears. "My biggest mistake was agreeing to get back together when I came back to New York.

"I was desperate. I'd lost my Paris freedom and faced caring for a dying sister-in-law and an adopted niece I hardly knew. I'm ashamed to say I fell for the fantasy that a more conventional life might make everything more manageable. How wrong I was…"

She gave an embarrassed breathy laugh and blew her nose again.

"I think my time in Paris made him realize how much he relied on me as a pair of 'second eyes.' We always got a lot out of discussing our work… and he valued by opinions.

"I was always more fearless than him. As a woman, I had to be. I'd begun well behind the starting line. Whereas he was born to be the lion of the pride. And as the years passed, and he sensed me slipping away from him, he became more bitter. And more demanding.

"If the world wasn't yielding what he wanted by natural beneficence, he would take it by force."

Jack watched with gentle affection. "So, there was no third chance waiting for him?"

"None," she said with finality. "That knife-pulling stunt was the final straw. I got a glimpse of how he saw things that night."

"Then why do you think he came calling at your studio?"

She gazed at him intently. "Jack, he was plainly drunk. He was swaying on his feet and I could smell it on his breath. He wasn't in command of his faculties.

"Maybe he and Tilly had argued, and he was drunkenly looking for sisterly support. That was what he always expected from me. Sympathy and support. We'll never know, I guess."

The carriage slowed, and they both glanced up in surprise. They were at the big masonry police building, with its imposing columned street frontage. Gerald drew them to a halt and turned back to them.

"Here we are then." He stared at Susannah, his face stern but his eyes twinkling. "Into the lion's den, Miss Carterton. I appreciate you're a woman of spirit, used to handling things your own way.

"But here, there's one rule. Follow my cues. And do not, I emphasize, do not decide to bare your chest and tell him everything. If you follow that course, there will be no saving you.

"Do you understand?"

She nodded in docile compliance, suddenly warmed to have these two men, standing either side of her, fighting on her behalf.

Forty-four

"Can Dot come next time we got to Hugo's?"

Cordelia looked up at Jack through slanted dark lashes, and he recognized yet again how much she'd grown up the six months she'd been with him in California.

He grinned at her with fresh appreciation. "Why didn't I think of that? Of course. We must organize it soon."

His heart swelled with both pride and trepidation as he gazed at his niece, dipping her long spoon into a Neapolitan ice cream sundae with the enthusiasm of a six-year-old.

California women were developing a reputation as the most beautiful in the world, and he saw with a sudden rush Cordelia would soon be counted among them.

She paused with a serious look on her face, licking her spoon delicately. "Mmmm. I can't decide which I like best. Strawberry or vanilla?"

"Not chocolate? What's wrong with you?" He took a spoonful of his chocolate ripple and waved his spoon right back at her.

She giggled, and a wave of gratitude to the universe for the presence of this young woman in his life nearly overwhelmed him.

"Chocolate is so obvious," she said with a cheeky spark in her eye. "I prefer something a little more subtle."

He laughed out loud at that line, while he tensed inside, imagining her delivering it to the swains who would line up all too soon, hanging on her every word.

She's going to be irresistible. And I'm going to be the worst sort of protective father.

When her mother had come to California so many years ago, he'd messed up catastrophically. He still felt guilt for what had happened. Tammy had been a spirited young woman who wanted to break the chains of social restraint, and he'd let her go for it.

He'd accepted she wanted a life like he had—where she could please herself, see and do what she wanted.

If only he'd understood a free-for-all existence was not in her best interests. Not when it included an acquaintance with no-good gamblers like the man she'd married. By the time he realized the score, it was far too late to stop her eloping with him.

Dan Dandy Durkan had seemed a straight enough guy. It was only after she'd married him that Jack discovered he'd no ambition beyond living a carefree gambling life and using as much of Tammy's trust fund as he could get his hands on to do it.

And after Tammy died, he'd "sold" Cordelia to rich New Yorkers as an "arranged" adoption—a deal that was no better than child trafficking, in Jack's view.

Now that he'd miraculously got Cordelia back in his life, he wasn't going to let her wander off like he had her mother.

Susannah might be a staid matron in some respects, but he was with her on this one. They had to protect Cordelia's interests, and ensure she transitioned to adulthood with no scandals that could ruin her prospects of making a good marriage to an upstanding chap who'd look after her.

"Penny for your thoughts." He glanced up from his melting chocolate and met Cordelia's serious cornflower-blue eyes, studying him. His heart turned over. Tammy had green eyes, but the quirk at the corner of Cordelia's lips, the blonde hair that kinked slightly around her ears, was so like her mother's.

He grinned. "I was just thinking of your mother. How she'd love to see you today—all grown up and about to step out on your own path into the world."

She flashed him a wan smile. "I'd love to remember her, but I don't. Maybe a few flashes, like me sitting on her knee and we're both crying, but that's it. Nor my father either," she said.

"Your father is still alive, as far as I know," he said. "But I can't recommend him. I guess I want you to know he IS alive, just in case you run across him sometime. But I wouldn't want you seeking him out."

"Why not?"

Jack screwed his mouth up in a gesture that showed both thoughtfulness and distaste.

"You'd be disappointed. I imagine he's run to seed since I saw him last. And that was a few years ago. He was showing signs of serious wear even then. He lives hard—playing cards for a living can do that to a man. And it hasn't been successful either, so he's got a chip on his shoulder.

"He's certainly not someone your aunt Susannah would want you to have too much to do with. And his friends—if he has any? I hope you'd run a mile if he attempted to play happy families."

She gave a resigned sigh, as if he'd fully satisfied her with that explanation and she didn't feel the need to push it any further. But she still fiddled with her spoon.

"I can't believe what I'm seeing there, Princess." He tapped his spoon on the stem of her sundae glass. "Cordelia not finishing her ice cream? Unheard of," he teased. Her eyes flickered to his indulgently, like she knew when he was diverting her attention.

"What's going to happen to Aunt Susannah?" she asked, and her fingers tightened on the long-handled spoon.

"Happen? In what way?" he asked, keeping his face as neutral as he could.

"You've just said I'm not a kid anymore, Uncle Jack," she said reprovingly. "I know she's in big trouble with that policeman. Is he going to arrest her?"

Jack thought back to the scene in the police station just hours ago.

"The police are still investigating Gil's death," he said. "Mr. Peters is an excellent lawyer and we're all determined to make sure your aunt is fine."

She raised her eyebrow with such elegantly framed skepticism he had to suppress a smile.

"You know as well as I do, Uncle Jack, that having the murder weapon like they do gives them a powerful case. How are you going to explain away a monogrammed knife from our New York home? She's the obvious suspect."

"Too obvious," said Jack. "Do you honestly think your aunt would kill a man?"

She considered him gravely for a long minute.

"It depends. If her life depended on it—or if my life depended on it, then yes. You should have seen the way she wielded the candelabra that night. Gil was lucky he didn't get his brains bashed out."

Her face lit up with a cheeky glow.

"She's a great one to have on your side, is Aunt Susannah."

Jack tried to suppress a chuckle. "I'm sure she is, Cordelia. We've both experienced how resolute she can be under pressure. But this is different—and it's not a laughing matter.

"She's in serious trouble. But we're going to make sure the person who did it is arrested. Not a convenient second option. And I admit, at the moment, Susannah is still Captain Cassidy's primary suspect."

"So how can make him change his mind?" Cordelia asked.

"*We* can do nothing," said Jack with a frown. "I don't want that policeman questioning you about anything, so staying well out of his way is the best thing you can do for your aunt."

"But… but… If Susannah didn't do it, who did?" Her face glowed with indignation.

He gave an evasive shrug and said, "We're working on it."

"I don't want to lose my third mother in my short life," she exclaimed. "I'll start to think I'm the problem!"

Her eyes were blazing with a fragile defiance. He reached out and gently clasped the back of one hand and squeezed.

"Oh, Cordelia, I'm so sorry. I've been so intent on protecting you, I haven't given you credit for what you've obviously seen. We never intended to treat you as a baby."

A single tear trickled from her right eye and she took a big gulping breath to steady herself.

"You mightn't have intended to baby me." She gave the word "intended" a dry, ironic emphasis. "But you've been trying to pretend everything's normal when clearly it isn't."

He tipped his head in acceptance and looked into her fine-featured face. The face that clearly showed her to be a resilient, highly intelligent and rapidly maturing young woman.

She gently disengaged her hand, as if establishing her independent identity. "And while we're having a little adult confession session, what's going on with you and Aunt S?"

Jack felt under instant pressure. Her blue eyes locked on his, unwavering.

"Going on?" he said nervously. "What do you mean, going on?"

She laughed then, tossing her head back with an elegant freedom.

"Now, who's being the baby?" she taunted. "Going on as in, when are you finally going to admit you like her? She drives you crazy as well, yes, but you can't take your eyes off of her most of the time."

He laughed, shaking his head in uncertain denial. "That's because I'm waiting for the next candelabra to fall," he joked, his voice shaky and unconvincing. "And besides, she's made it very clear she doesn't approve of me."

Her dismissing laughter tinkled over them. A derisive shower.

"Honestly, Uncle Jack, you should know better. Even an ingenue like me can see you're both mad about each other." Her face turned serious.

"If you didn't care, why spend so much energy keeping her out of trouble?"

"Oh. That's easy. I'm doing it for you?"

"For me?" Her voice spiked with incredulity. "How do you figure that one out?"

"Well, as Susannah has made very clear, if we're going to set you up to have a good standing in society, I have to improve my ways. I mean, she's made her disapproval of what she considers my wastrel life pretty plain.

"It's just ironic that now it's her who could bring us into disrepute. The highly respectable New York matron… accused of murder. If that happens, you'll never get a decent husband."

For once, no smart retort flowed from her smart tongue.

She gazed at him, searching his face, her eyes twinkling in disbelief.

After a long silence, she spoke.

"Let me get this straight. You are spending all your time defending Aunt Susannah so I can find a decent husband? Do I understand that right? The uncle who has never married, the aunt who's never married, joining forces to ensure my respectability and sound marriage?"

She put her index finger to her temple, as if she needed a gun at her head to digest such a ridiculous proposition.

"You realize you're sounding more like Susannah every day? You've swallowed the whole caboodle. Conforming to keep others happy. Something you've never done in your whole life and neither has she…

"You see my aunt for who she really is, don't you? The Susannah who's fought her whole life for recognition as a serious artist in her own right, without having to depend on a husband?

"The Susannah who turned Gil down—a perfectly handsome, rich, respectable artist husband—because she knew he'd crush her creative life? Not once, but twice? Why is she going to turn around and kill him?"

They stared at one another across the little parlor table, their ice cream sundaes a sloshy meltdown in their glasses, his a dirty brown, hers still in rainbow stripes of pink, white and brown.

"I haven't decided what I want to do with my life yet, except I don't think I have Aunt Susannah's passion."

She ran her fingers through her blonde locks absentmindedly.

"I might like to be a fashion designer like Isla, or an artist's model like Dot."

Jack suppressed his instant disapproval at the idea of the latter with difficulty. Perhaps he *was* turning into a cookie-cutter match for Susannah. Maybe she was influencing him more than he realized. Cordelia mooned on.

"I do want to get married someday. I'm more conventional than Aunt Susannah when it comes to that, but something tells me she'd probably be happy I'm that way."

She gazed up at Jack as if taking stock. Around them, the crowded tables had thinned out as the lunchtime rush subsided. The waitress was loading dirty glassware onto a tray and wiping down the table next to them, and further away twin boys, three or four years old, perhaps, tucked into ice cream sodas.

"I want a family. A proper family," she said, glancing around her, her eyes alighting on the children. "Like them," she whispered, gazing at the twins, the longing plain in her face.

She pulled back imperceptibly, as if letting go of a familiar dream, and recalibrated.

She gestured to the melting desserts with a flick of a cheeky smile. "Sorry, I've interrupted your treat. I know you were so looking forward to it."

He gave a big, huffing laugh. "Since when did you become the adult and I the child?"

She reached out in a mirroring gesture of his earlier one and covered the back of his hand with hers. She squeezed it affectionately.

"Since someone had to point out to you something that's as plain as the eyes on your face. You and my aunt are drawn to one another in this love-hate thing. And it's getting to be more love than hate with every passing day.

"My question is, what are you going to do about it? Neither of you are getting any younger, you know."

Forty-five

Long after everyone else in Elizabeth's house—with the exception perhaps of Susannah—was deeply asleep, Jack lay, hands folded behind his head, staring at the ceiling, going over his young niece's ice cream parlor pep talk.

Ice cream parlor wisdom, he'd forevermore call it in his mind. The day a dear person he'd thought of as still a child delivered the biggest wake-up call of his life.

Bigger even than when Elizabeth cajoled him into giving up on the opium dens of Barbary Coast. Or when Cordelia was restored to him after years of loss. He'd forever remember it as the day he discovered someone knew him better than he knew himself.

All these weeks he'd been telling himself he was putting an effort into defending Susannah, for Cordelia's sake. And of course, her interests were a factor. But it was like a curtain drawn back on his heart, and he'd seen in a flash what lay there that he'd refused to recognize.

And that was a deeply held attraction for Susannah, a bone-scoring admiration for her courage and fortitude, and an undeniable desire to share her life and have a family. This was the woman he'd been waiting for, and when she'd arrived, he hadn't recognized it.

But the thing that tormented him, the doubt he couldn't confide to Cordelia but which racked his soul, was whether Susannah returned any of that emotion even in half measure.

He couldn't stand the idea that she might respond warmly to him, not out of genuine welling emotion, but in a milksop gratitude for helping her get off murder charges. Because they were going to clear her name and leave her free to follow her life in whatever way she chose.

If they were to have any chance of a life together, she had to make the choice freely, springing from a certain conviction.

What was it about her he valued the most, he asked himself in the early hours of the morning, as he rubbed his scratchy eyes and prayed to God he would fall asleep soon. He was going to be a mess in the morning if he didn't.

He was in awe of her creative talent and her determination to see it expressed. That went without saying. But most of all, what drew him like a thirsty man to water was her willingness to sacrifice her deepest desires for those she loved.

Like Cordelia. And the little baby that had emerged from the Parisian shadows. Like her dying sister-in-law. She was unequivocal. Her art was the lodestone of her life.

But repeatedly, she set it aside for others without so much as a grumble. And she'd committed her formidable energies to getting the very best for others—Cordelia, Sylvia, Athena—with the same drive she committed to her work.

He smiled in the dark as he thought back to the early days of their time in this house together. Anyone who was paying lip service to delivering Cordelia into safe hands would have stayed a couple of weeks and then run back to her own world.

Susannah, in plain discomfort, missing her work, stayed on, haranguing him about Cordelia's best interests and how he was failing her in them—and he could see now she was right.

Cordelia was the marvellously stable, wise young woman he'd seen today because of Susannah, not because she'd been "rescued" by Uncle Jack.

I've been ass headed about this whole thing. How am I going to make it up to her? And will she even bother to hear me out? Once she's free of these charges, she'll no doubt be well and truly ready to move on.

Jack rolled over yet again, willing himself to sleep. He heard the first bell-like chimes of the dawn chorus starting up in Elizabeth's garden as he finally dropped into an uneasy sleep.

Forty-six

"Susannah! Oh, my sweet girl, I've been so worried about you!" Tilly, the woman she'd once known as her best friend, encircled her shoulders with one soft arm, but Susannah could hardly bear to accept the gesture.

She held still, stiffening slightly but fighting the urge to pull away. She didn't want to hint at the suspicions building about Mathilda's role in Gil's death.

Tilly was carrying an expensive leather Chateleine purse, studded with steel and fastened with a gold clasp which Susannah recognized was very like one she owned.

"That looks like a Le Bon Marche bag," she commented with a smile. Le Bon Marche was the hugely popular department store on Paris's Left Bank.

"Yes, it is," said Mathilda with a satisfied pink flush. "Gil brought it back for me. Wasn't that nice of him?"

As Tilly gloated, Susannah caught a wave of a complex musk and ambergris, typical of the complex French perfumes which were being imported to America. Another Gil gift, she wagered.

It lay heavy and stale on her spirit. Funny. She'd always admired Tilly for the way she immaculately presented herself. Not for her the paint-stained smock and fingers.

Now she just smells of lies, Susannah thought.

Mathilda drew back and gazed at her with an expression that might have passed for concern. Unless you knew what she was up to.

"How are you, dear Susannah?" Her voice was dripping syrup.

Susannah delicately edged away from her touch.

"I'm just fine, thanks, Mathilda. How about you? It must be hard to have lost the love of your life."

Tilly looked up at her sharply, as if trying to filter out any hint of mockery, but Susannah held on to her gaze of fixed sympathy, holding her breath as she did.

"The love of my life?' Mathilda rolled the phrase in her mouth, as if tasting it.

"Funny. I always thought of him as the love of *your* life. You were together much longer than we were."

"Perhaps," said Susannah, her tone doubtful.

"Why you wouldn't think… you'd never think…" Mathilda's feathers ruffled like a threatened hen.

Does she suspect I'm suggesting they two-timed me while we were still engaged? Now I know her, it's likely she did. But that's all history now.

"Mathilda, Gil's all in our past now, isn't he? He's not here to argue over."

A sly smirk crossed Mathilda's face, a fleeting glimpse of her actual feelings.

"In my past, maybe, Susannah. Sadly, he's still very much in your present, especially where that police captain is concerned. I tried to warn you, but I'm afraid it's done no good."

"What are you getting at, Mathilda?"

The game playing suddenly irritated Susannah. "You may as well spit it out. You've been talking to him again, have you? The police captain, I mean."

"Of course I've been talking to him. I want to do anything I can to catch whoever it was who killed Gil. I would have thought you'd feel the same."

She sniffed.

"It's a villainous crime that shouldn't go unpunished. Wouldn't you agree?"

Susannah moved to a wall table where a water jug and glasses stood.

"Would you like a glass of water? I'm afraid we aren't up for coffee today—cook's gone shopping for supplies."

"Sure." Mathilda took the glass and, uninvited, moved to sit on the only sofa in the breakfast room. Susannah pulled out a chair at the dining-room table.

"So, what's Captain Cassidy got to say about it? Are they any closer to catching who did it?"

Mathilda had the grace to look sheepish. "I'm afraid he's still rather fixed on working out what was going on between you and Gil," said Mathilda. "I told him you'd do nothing to harm Gil, but he doesn't seem to believe me."

I bet you did.

Susannah fought to maintain her vague, uncommitted expression, an enormous challenge in the circumstances.

"But you would have told him Gil and I have had nothing to do with one another for the last six months, surely?" said Susannah.

Mathilda sipped her water and did not reply.

Susannah switched tack.

"There is one thing I'm curious about."

She paused. How to frame this?

"How did my painting get entered in the Bay show under Gil's name? And have you drawn Captain Cassidy's attention to that incident yet?"

Susannah took a studied sip of water to help keep her anger in check.

Mathilda did not respond. Susannah tried again.

"What happened, Tilly? I'm perplexed. You were my entrusted agent. So what gives? Who did that? You or Gil?"

Mathilda's eyes skittered away as she raised her head to answer. She couldn't bring herself to meet Susannah's direct gaze.

"I'd have thought that's the last of your worries right now, Susannah. You've got a senior police officer on the verge of arresting you for murder. He asked you about that knife and I gather you lied to him? You told him you'd never seen it before?"

In a sudden surge of confidence, she brought her eyes up to meet Susannah's.

"I'm sorry I couldn't lie for you about that one. I had to confirm you'd attacked Gil with that knife the last time you had dinner together back in New York. He told me all about it. He said he barely escaped with his life."

With a sudden upward thrust, she stood and placed the glass down on the dining table with a final bang.

"I guess you must have brought that knife West with you in case you got another chance. And the other night you got that chance, when he came knocking on your studio door. Poor fellow didn't know what was in store for him."

Her face lit up in a serpentine smile from ear to ear.

"That's what I told Seamus. The truth." She licked her lips in a satisfied smirk. "We've become quite close, Seamus and me. I guess I can be thankful for small mercies.

"Anyway, thought you should know. In case you want to skip town or something. Now, I've got to go."

She picked up the leather handbag.

"Aloysius is waiting."

Forty-seven

"Aloysius?" Jack bustled in, hindering Mathilda's exit, grinning with bald curiosity. "He's your next target, is he? After Susannah, I mean."

He blocked the doorway and Mathilda came to a sudden halt, her face dark with confusion.

"What are you talking about?" she snapped, the edges of her voice pitched sharp. Fear and uncertainty rolled into one.

"Aloysius is a professional colleague. A fellow judge. Nothing more."

Jack made a show of studied consideration.

"He wasn't in on the scandalous fraud you perpetrated, then?"

"I've had nothing to do with any fraud, and I'll thank you for remembering it. I'll vigorously defend any claims to the contrary."

She stared at Jack. She didn't bother to conceal the spite in her voice, or the malice in her eyes.

"I'd be very careful about raising it with anyone in authority, Mr. Cabot. Think how it would look for your girlfriend here. Gil submits one of her paintings under his name, and the next thing he's got a knife plunged in his chest? It's yet another motive for Susannah's arrest, if you ask me."

Susannah's voice cut in, strident, desperate sounding. "But I didn't know about the fraud when he died. I only discovered it on the night of the opening."

"Tell that one to Seamus. See if he believes you. He's got witnesses who saw you talking to Gil the night he died. They saw you two arguing. Just a hundred yards away from where he died."

She stepped forward bullishly and placed her hand in the middle of Jack's chest.

"Now are you going to move aside for me, Mr. Cabot, or will I have to lay a complaint of obstruction with my friend Captain Cassidy?"

Jack regarded her with a calculated dislike for long seconds and gently removed her hand from his ribcage.

"Your time is coming, Mathilda. Right now, I've got the nosiest private investigator in the state looking into what went on in the Portland Square area at the time of Gil's murder. It won't be long before he'll be reporting back to me about your movements that night."

He glanced from Mathilda to Susannah. "And when he does, it will be Susannah's turn to go singing to Seamus Cassidy like a canary down a mine. It's just a matter of time, so enjoy your moment of revenge."

He stepped aside. "You'll forget you ever had it when you're locked up for murder."

Forty-eight

How dare he?

Mathilda's insides quivered as she stumbled down Elizabeth Westerhoven's front steps and into the waiting hack on Pine Street. As she sank back against the leather seat and watched the Queen Anne mansion fade out of her view, she recognized the feathering quaver inside as a mix of fury and fear.

Fury that he had the arrogance to accuse her of Gil's death. And fear that he'd somehow be able to prove his wild guess was correct.

Because it is a wild guess, isn't it? Seamus would never believe it, would he?

Jack Cabot couldn't possibly know what happened that night, and even if he had his theory, he'd never be able to prove it She shook her head, as if reassuring herself.

He'll never be able to prove it.

As the hack trundled down the hill to her hotel, she pondered her situation.

Susannah looked so calm in there. She still doesn't get it, does she? She'll be lucky if she doesn't hang.

Mathilda's neck prickled with needles of irritation as she thought of her friend's calm grace.

Trust her to get to stay with a Countess. Even in San Francisco, she's got the networks to smooth her path in life.

Mathilda Morgan curled her fist into a ball and pushed it against her closed teeth in frustration. Every step of her life, Susannah Carterton had enjoyed special treatment. She'd never have attracted Gil's attention if she hadn't occupied such a cushy niche in society. He always was a slut for status.

She rubbed her eyes wearily over her brows and down her cheeks.

But her friend's run of good fortune was at an end, she told herself.

Her rich daddy and her Fifth Avenue upbringing won't be rescuing her from this one.

Not even the enticing bad boy lover with the New York trust fund will pull it off for her this time, no matter what threats he's making.

And about time. All those years, when she'd put up with hearing of Susannah's uptown woes while she lived in a downtown squat with her needy mother. The years when she'd dreamed of having Susannah's life, her career, her boyfriend, her everything.

I could have been as good an artist as she is, if I'd had the chance. Gone to Paris. Been her.

And now she was close. Closer than she'd ever been before. And she would let no one ruin it. She'd make up more whoppers to feed to Seamus Cassidy if she needed to. But she would not lose this race.

Pity about the bad boy lover, though. He'd be fun.

Forty-nine

"You were right all along, Jack."

Susannah offered him up a wan smile and sank into the capacious brown leather sofa in Elizabeth's library with a grateful sigh.

Dealing with the police captain and Mathilda in one day was more than her wrecked spirit could handle. The hour she'd spent at the police headquarters, vigorously defended by Gerald from Cassidy's accusations, had brought home her dilemma with all the reality of a baseball bat thwack on the head.

The wiry, fiery policeman was smart and utterly convinced she was guilty. In his book, all he had to do was find enough evidence to make the charges stick. With Mathilda's help, he'd have enough to bring charges soon.

And then what? Even if she was acquitted, Cordelia would be the debutante with the murdering aunt, and no respectable family would want anything to do with them.

The months she'd spent disapproving of Jack's carefree attitudes, alluding to his formerly lax lifestyle, criticizing his willingness to let Cordelia have more freedom than she approved of—all of that paled by comparison.

Aunt Susannah, the guardian of public morals and protector of her niece's virtue, was a murderer. She'd knifed the scion of an East Coast banking family, her former fiancé no less, with all the attendant scandal and speculation.

Was she a woman scorned who killed out of jealousy? Who did he dump her for? And what about that strange painting, the Black nude? Surely a respectable woman wouldn't paint that?

She shuddered and then realized Jack was speaking to her. She'd drifted off into a self-made misery cloud.

"Sorry, Jack, what was that?"

He grinned, fully aware she'd been lost in her own thoughts.

"Dreaming of fleeing to Paris to escape?" he asked teasingly. "I'm still basking in hearing you say those four precious words."

He paused for effect. "Jack, you were right." He smiled gently, to show her he was playing.

"I don't hear them very often from your lips."

He turned from the wall table, where he was filling two tumblers from a crystal decanter. He held the golden liquid up to the light, assessing he'd poured evenly.

Then he flicked his sky-blue eyes to meet hers. They still held a teasing gleam.

"In fact, I can't ever recall hearing them before, so allow me a few moments to savor the taste."

Despite herself, she smiled. One thing you could say about Jack. He didn't hold on to grievances.

"I've got a lot to apologize for," she said, taking a glass from his out-stretched hand and pausing immediately to sip.

She waited for the sense of warmth and release she knew would follow. When it came, she exhaled and sank a little deeper into the cushions.

"Oh, thank you. My goodness, I needed this."

He slipped down on the sofa end, allowing a good measure of distance between them.

"You can rely on Elizabeth to only have the finest French brandy," he said.

"But tell me, what was I right about? I want to enjoy my moment of glory longer."

"Have I been that bad?" Susannah sighed, glancing up at him.

He stayed silent, a light smile playing across his lips.

She tapped her glass. "Don't answer that. I know I've been awful. I've had my eyes firmly shut. Even after Gil died, and the police came, I couldn't believe it was happening.

"To me, of all people. It was unreal. I don't think the fact that Gil is dead has hit home yet. And that I could be arrested? Honestly, it seemed crazy. Why would I want to kill him? That was my main thought."

She put her glass down on the occasional table in front of her and steepled her fingers together.

"None of it made sense. But after today, I'm ready to believe you. Mathilda could do what you've suspected she's planned all along.

"She killed Gil, using the Carterton family knife, and then went about setting me up as pigeon pie."

She yawned into her hands and rubbed the moisture from her eyes wearily.

Jack regarded the brandy in his glass. Swirled it and leaned in and breathed in the heady fragrance.

"We're working on a lot of supposition still, but so are the cops."

It was late in the afternoon. The sun sloped to the horizon, its rays casting long shadows through the shuttered windows.

"I know Cordelia ranks high in your concerns, so I want to tell you about a conversation I had with her earlier today."

Susannah looked up in surprise. The deep calm of the man, the quiet penetration in his gaze, the benevolent lightness that played around his mouth struck her. He was more interested in knowing others than in impressing them, someone who kept his own counsel and was unaffected by the mood of the crowd.

Her eyes searched his steady face, from the broad brow above to the sapphire-blue eyes, and felt a wave of gratitude for his forgiving nature, for his ability to withstand social pressure and make his own perceptive calls.

Anyone else would have given up on me long ago.

He's a good-looking man, but he's so much more.

She felt an uncomfortable jab of self-awareness—the second she'd experienced that day—penetrate her complacency.

She'd been in denial about Mathilda and what she might do. And now, she saw, she'd vastly underestimated Jack's character. She'd labelled him a Barbary Coast wastrel without giving him a chance to prove himself, and she'd interpreted all his actions in the light of that prejudice.

Her soul quivered. A slither of recognition pierced the confidence in which she'd viewed herself and found him wanting.

You've never considered what made him fall into the slough of despair. Never given his feelings a moment's consideration. You labelled him a rake, and that was it as far as you went.

And now, your life depends on your being wrong. Again.

"Tell me, Jack," she said. "Cordelia. The one person who is precious to us both. What was she telling you? I suspect she's much more open with you than she is with me, so let me have it."

●●●●●●●●

Susannah perched on the front edge of the sofa, hunched over her brandy glass, nursing it in both hands as if it was a treasured lifeline. The green eyes that picked up every nuance were wide with questions and something else.

Jack regarded her with wary affection.

What is it she's displaying here? Self-doubt? Anxiety?

Susannah, always the model of self-assurance, certain that she was right at least 95 percent of the time, didn't know what to expect next, and she didn't feel comfortable with her vulnerability.

The paisley gold and green dress that fell softly from her shoulders emphasized the creamy pallor of her complexion, giving her a fragility she rarely admitted to. He saw she was close to the breaking point.

The protective surge that went through him as he scanned her face surprised him. On her good days, when she relaxed and forgot to run the world, she was funny and smart.

It occurred to him he'd overlooked so much about this woman, taken too much for granted, as they'd battled for territorial rights over Cordelia's future. And the child—the young woman he'd seen emerging today, like a butterfly from a chrysalis—had her own ideas about what she wanted from life.

At the mention of Cordelia's name, he sensed Susannah's heightened awareness, like a rubber band that was being stretched. Another thing he couldn't dispute.

She cared about that girl, enough to trip out here, to mess up her engagement to Gil, and disrupt her precious painting schedule.

He didn't answer immediately, considering how to phrase their reported conversation. Susannah was already sensitive that their shared charge talked more freely to him than she did to her aunt. That was what happened when people felt pressure to measure up.

Susannah reached out, as if to regain his attention. She tapped the back of his wrist, and sparks like fireflies run up his arm.

"Cordelia? Is something wrong?" Her voice took on a sharp, panicked quality. He wanted to reach out and stroke her arm to reassure her, but he held himself in check.

"Nothing at all wrong," he said. "Don't worry. Quite the opposite, I suspect. But she's turning into a young woman with her own ideas of what she wants from life, right before our eyes.

"While we've been focusing on the mess Gil's death has created, she seems suddenly to have grown from child to young woman."

He took a sip of his brandy and rolled it around in his mouth before swallowing.

"She's been changing before our eyes, and I, for one, haven't noticed. I suspect she might surprise you, too. We've had our attention diverted while she's been coming into flower."

Susannah shot him an amused look. "Enough to turn her uncle Jack poetic, it seems. Tell me about it."

"She's very aware of the danger you're in. She asked me if you were going to get arrested."

Susannah's jaw clenched, and he could see it working above her slim jaw line.

"Oh, how frustrating. You know I've been doing my best to keep her in the dark so she won't be worried. That hasn't worked?"

"No, it hasn't. And she's been doing a lot of thinking about what she wants from life, too."

"Is that so? And what does she want?"

"They're quite modest demands. No Swiss finishing school or any nonsense like that. She wants 'something interesting to do until I get married.' And yes, she's unequivocal about that. She wants to get married and have a family."

"I guess I've not been inspiring as an example of a woman on her own," Susannah said, the color in her cheeks rising.

"I wouldn't say that," said Jack. "But we need to treat her more like a young adult. If we don't include her, she's going to find her own way of getting information, including listening at keyholes. It's probably best to tackle it head-on. She's noticed far more than we can guess at."

Susannah sighed. "And you don't need to tell me I'm guilty of that far more than you. I'm too protective, but maybe I understand better than you the perils there can be for a young woman with ideas of freedom."

Jack smiled encouragingly. "Honestly, I think we can work together on that. I only need to consider what happened to her mother to appreciate the holes she could fall into. I want to do a much better job the second time round."

Susannah took a last sip of her brandy and held out the glass for a refill.

"Just an inch," she said.

"I'll take what you say about Cordelia on board. But now—can we talk about what I need to do next? And to say how grateful I am that you're still here helping me? I know it's for Cordelia's sake, but I appreciate it. I want to avoid the gallows if I can."

Her mouth quirked in a wicked smile, and Jack's heart kicked up to a faster beat.

"Not just for Cordelia," he said. "I said that to keep you in your place, but I'm not just helping for Cordelia."

"You're not?" Her voice had a high-pitched, strangled quality, as if she had trouble getting the words out.

"No Susannah, I'm not. And I won't pretend it's all about protecting the innocent, either."

He felt the color in his face brightening along with his quickening heart rate.

"That's something Cordelia was kind enough to point out to me, and it turns out she's right."

"What's that?" Susannah's eyes sparkled as they searched his face, and her whole body leaned in, as if on alert to catch his every word.

Does she have a sixth sense for what's coming?

"Rather embarrassingly, Cordelia pointed out that love or hate, we seem to be drawn to one another. She asked me when we were going to do something about it."

She gazed at him, her jaw dropped, her face blanked in shock. And then she broke into unrestrained laughter. Tears streamed down her cheeks, and she wiped them with the back of her hand as she continued to chortle.

When she regained control of herself, she skewered him with the emerald eyes he knew had pierced many an admirer's heart.

"And you're admitting to some truth in this observation?"

She was grinning wickedly, enjoying being on the offensive, relishing setting him on the back foot.

He met her teasing with an amused silence, which didn't fool either of them.

"The little ratbag," Susannah said. "She has grown up overnight. And Lord knows what we're going to do about it."

He stood, the glass she'd recently passed to him in hand, and turned toward the decanter.

"About Cordelia? Or about the question she raised?" It was his turn to skewer Susannah with embarrassment. She smiled mysteriously and shrugged.

"First priority is obviously to get this damn noose from my neck. Only then can we talk about other things."

A tentative tap on the library door interrupted them. "Come in, it's open," called Jack, and Cordelia tiptoed in, clutching a yellow cable envelope in one hand.

"This just came for you, Aunt Susannah," she said. "I think it must be urgent, so I brought it immediately."

She crossed the room to Susannah and the light-hearted banter of the last minutes disappeared like a sea mist in the morning sun.

Susannah's hand trembled as she reached out to take hold of the cable and in one sweeping hand movement opened the envelope and pulled out the message.

Her face drained to a ghostly white as she read the contents.

Then she raised haunted eyes, first to Jack, then Cordelia.

"It's Athena. The nuns say they're adopting her out immediately unless I take her. Apparently, they've got somewhere for her to go."

She doubled over in pain, clutching her chest.

"Athena. I'm losing my baby girl."

She remained bent over, fighting to regain self-control.

When she finally returned to an erect posture, she patted a place next to her for Cordelia to sit down, and told her the story of Athena, the baby girl she'd cared for after her mother's death.

"My secret dream was always to bring her back here if Ezra couldn't take her. I guess that won't be happening now. I haven't got a world I can bring her to. And I have to fight these murder charges."

She sighed.

"Life can be hard sometimes, my darling Cordelia. But Jack's been telling me how you've grown up, so you might understand that already."

Cordelia encircled her in long, skinny arms, and they embraced as Susannah buried her head in Cordelia's hair and silently wept.

Fifty

The night of Gil's death

Mathilda hadn't stopped to clean up the ruined meal. Without a backward glance at the roast chicken or the oozing soft cheese, she grabbed her overcoat and followed Gil out into the twilight.

She hovered in the shadows as he drank in a seedy waterfront tavern and then moved on to the park, where he chatted up a cheap doxy.

Gil wasn't the sort of man who paid for sex, no matter how drunk he was. So it did not surprise her after an intense conversation that the chit sidled off looking for other quarry.

Instead, she went on high alert when Gil set off down Washington Street, heading for Susannah's studio.

Neither of them had let on to the other that the first business they'd each conducted in the "Paris of the West" was to find Susannah's whereabouts. She had her contact address at Elizabeth's, but nothing more.

She'd been very discreet, keeping to herself, but word got around. An inquiry with the right person at the Students League, and you'd learn where the "great Susannah Carterton" had set up shop.

Aloysius was the one who'd told her. How Gil found out, she

didn't know, but she was certain he was carrying out his threat to tell Susannah what she'd done. Getting himself off the hook for fraud and currying favor with his former beloved.

The words he'd spat at her earlier still rang in her head.

"You'll never be Susannah…. There is no 'us.'"

We'll see about that, buddy. I'm not spending the rest of my life being your doormat, that's for sure.

Gil was bumbling along, a little unsteady on his feet, but walking with purpose. She watched as he stopped to exchange a few words with a balloon man in heavy circus makeup, making sure she kept well out of sight as they shot the breeze. That engagement might come in handy later. It would be proof he was in the vicinity.

And then, as she was loitering, trying to decide how to approach this, and what "this" was exactly, she saw they'd arrived at Susannah's door. Balloon man still hovered in the background, so she remained in hiding too.

She watched as Gil raised his hand to knock, his face suddenly transformed into a look of gooey expectation at the coming encounter.

Then she knew. He was still in love with her. She could read it in the loosening of his mouth, the softening of his lips, the renewed sparkle in his dark eyes.

He was excited to be seeing Susannah again. He was going to carry out his threat. Blacken her name with Susannah, so she'd never talk to her again. She'd warn all her influential friends off her.

Her status in the art world would collapse overnight. And it would become general knowledge she'd been engaged to Gil Lusk for five minutes and then he'd broken it off.

He's still in love with Susannah Carterton, they'd whisper. Has been for years. His whole life.

She fingered the knife she'd stuffed into her waistband as they'd moved. It was for self-protection, she'd told herself.

But now she knew why she'd brought it.

She waited with as much anticipation as Gil for Susannah to answer the door. When she did—her lush hair falling loosely around her shoulders, her eyes sleepily sexy, looking far more beautiful than a woman in midlife in a paint-spattered smock had any right to—Gil stepped confidently forward.

Susannah froze, and in his semi-drunk state Gil blundered on, unable to recognize her body language for what it was.

A loathing gripped Mathilda Morgan so deep, if she drowned in pure bleach, the hatred would still stain her.

Her darling, her sweetheart, was making a total ass of himself in front of a woman who despised him. And yet, hours ago, he'd rejected her certain ability to make life good for him.

Even she could detect from where she stood feet away that the vitriolic New York dinner had ended everything as far as Susannah was concerned. Tilly saw exactly how the land lay, but Gil ignored all the warning signs and floundered on, casting his pearls before swine.

"Susannah. My darling girl! I've got something I need to tell you." He hiccupped and half fell upon her neck, his hands intimately placed on her shoulders, leaning over her.

Quick as a flash, Susannah placed both hands flat on his chest and pushed backwards.

"No, you don't," she cried. "I told you. I never want to see you again."

The unexpected thrust, together with Gil's unsteady state, sent him sprawling backwards, his fall broken by the balloon man, who'd been watching with undisguised interest, and stepped forward to catch him.

"Woah there, fellow," he cried. "Carefully does it."

Gil was oblivious. He was protesting. "Susannah. You don't understand. I have something important to tell you. You've got to listen."

Susannah held her hands out in front of her in warning.

"Gil, I've told you already. I want nothing to do with you. Go home to Tilly and sleep it off."

"No! You don't understand…."

Arms akimbo, she stood her ground.

"I don't know how you found out where I am. And I don't care why you're here. Just go away."

She turned and flung back inside. The reverberations from the slammed door rattled on the street in the silence that followed.

Great. It couldn't have played out any better if she'd choreographed it herself.

Just bide your time. Let that buffoon of a balloon man disappear and you'll get things settled. Once and for all.

Because I'm not going down with this ship, Gil Lusk. No matter what you think of me. I've come too far to fail now.

Fifty-one

"I've someone coming I want you to meet."

Jack stood before Susannah in the library, where she'd sprawled out on the big leather sofa, hoping she could hide away and brood.

It was early in the afternoon on the day following the cable advising of the nuns' decision to relinquish Athena's care, and Susannah still felt as if she had barely enough energy to lift her head from the pillow.

If the furor over Gil's death had nearly beaten her into submission, the news about Athena was the final hammer blow to her dreams.

Her last thoughts before she fell into an exhausted sleep last night had been of desolation.

I dreamed of the world at my feet. To be a recognized artist and have a family. Now I've nothing. No career. No family. Either the gallows or death in prison. And of those two choices, I think I prefer the gallows.

And her first thought in the morning?

Athena's gone. I'll never see her again.

She understood she'd been holding out for that last hope of raising a child.

The fantasy she'd nurtured ever since Fleur's death, that she would get Athena home before the time came when the nuns would keep her no longer. She'd always known it wasn't a permanent arrangement with the Sisters of Joseph. But with imminent arrest hanging over her, she couldn't rush to Paris to rescue a baby.

She lifted her head and looked Jack in the eye.

"Please, Jack. I'm not up to seeing visitors this afternoon. Can't it wait till later?"

She'd started the sentence before she'd met his eye. When her gaze met his, something leapt within her. *Something's changed.*

Jack's usually cool, irony-laced expression was buzzing with poorly concealed excitement. His blue eyes sparkled. He clasped his hands together, as if preparing to make an announcement.

"What? Has something happened?" He gave her a wide grin. "Why?"

"Why? Because you look like the cat that's got the cream. That's not usual."

"As I said, I've someone I want you to meet. Gerry Peters will be arriving with him any minute."

"Who? Who will Gerald be arriving with?"

A pregnant pause. "Someone you thought was a waste of time."

Her stomach gave a slow flip, and her breathing sped up to an erratic cadence.

She stared at Jack's triumphant face, shaking her head in silent denial.

"I said a lot of stupid things, Jack, before I understood I needed all the help I can get. I've learnt my lesson. If this person can help me get off these awful charges, bring him—or her—on."

"Very good. Excellent."

Susannah heard the echo of the front door chimes down the hall and then the light tripping of feet to the street. Within minutes, Gerald Peters entered the library with a slight, sandy-haired man at his side.

The well-built lawyer stood head and shoulders above his companion, a slight man with hunched shoulders and a pale, unremarkable appearance.

Susannah's artist's eye saw immediately how hard times and misfortune had leached the life out of him. His threadbare suit hung off his body in a way that suggested its wearer had been ill and lost a lot of weight.

His right eye—a watery pale gray in keeping with the rest of his washed-out appearance—squinted involuntarily, closing and opening with a regularity that was hard to ignore.

"I'd like to present Sam Malarkey, the private investigator Jack got to work on your case, Susannah. Sam, meet Miss Susannah Carterton."

Sam stepped forward with his hand thrust out and when Susannah shook it, she felt immediately the determined pulse of a man with an iron will to endure. She bobbed her head in gratitude and sudden respect.

"Mr. Malarkey, I'm delighted to meet you. I will appreciate anything you can tell us, I assure you. I'm in an awful pickle and every bit helps."

Gerald gave her a broad smile of approval and gestured to Sam to sit in one of the expansive leather armchairs. Jack jumped up and embraced Sam before he sat down.

"Good to see you again, Sam. Can't say I'm surprised you've done a fantastic job for us." He turned to Susannah.

"Sam's got more than 'a little something,'" he said, his voice ringing with pleasure. "He's struck the lottery, more like."

For the first time in days, Susannah's heart leapt with hope.

"Oh my gosh, I'm all ears. But before we start, Mr. Malarkey, would you care for refreshments? Coffee, or something stronger?"

She glanced toward Jack, as if seeking guidance with the correct etiquette.

"I'm fine, thank you. Miss Carterton."

He glanced uncertainly at Peters, who slid into the chair next to him and took over the conversation.

"We've had Sam combing the inner city, looking for anyone who saw Gil on that last night. His most recent instructions were to find the balloon man."

He glanced at Sam with warm enthusiasm. "Sam's come up with two important witnesses. He's uncovered new evidence that will make the copper reconsider the line he's been taking. I'll leave Sam to tell you the rest. Go for it, Sam. First, Miss Polly. Then the balloon man."

Miss Polly? The balloon man?

Susannah had to stifle a laugh at the absurdity. Her future—her continued existence, could hang on the words of a Miss Polly and the balloon man?

She flashed Jack an apology in one glance. Then she locked her attention on Sam Malarkey. The diffident investigator glanced uncertainly at Jack before taking a big breath.

"Right. Miss Polly and the balloon man." He glanced toward Susannah. "I've interviewed two people who spoke to Mr. Lusk on that last night. First, a young woman, a 'lady of the night.'"

His head dipped in embarrassment, and he continued after clearing his throat. "A lady of the night who chatted with him in Portsmouth Square."

He cleared his throat again, nervously. "And then, Pete the balloon man. He was on the street when Mr. Lusk came to your studio door. And he has subsequent events to report, as well."

Susannah nodded, her face still hot with her own stupidity.

"As soon as the police mentioned him, it all came back to me." She nodded her affirmation. "I'm kicking myself that I didn't recall him before that."

"First, Miss Polly. She spent about half an hour chatting about life and the dead chap's hassles," Sam said.

"Mr. Lusk told her all about the fraud. He'd only just found out about it and was beside himself with rage. He had a big barney with his woman over it."

He paused, as if he anticipated the next statement might be hard for her to hear. "Polly says she told him fixing it was simple. All he had to do was go to the show's judges and withdraw the entry. He could make it all right without anyone being blamed."

A heavy silence fell over the room. Susannah was staring at Sam as the impact of his words flooded through her.

"Then why did he come to see me?" she asked. Her voice sounded thin, and she trailed off in confusion.

Pete shrugged. "Polly says he wanted to explain it wasn't his idea. She tried to tell him it would be best to leave explaining that for another time, him having been drinking and all. The important thing was to withdraw it before it was too late. I guess he decided not to listen to that bit of advice."

Susannah's heart clutched in her ribs.

Gil was trying to make a stupid decision good by protecting Tilly and reversing the falsified entry at the same time. And she had cut him off, not knowing the facts.

Her heated embarrassment of a few minutes ago drained away, replaced by a sadness so deep it left her lightheaded.

"Ohhh," she said in a long, whispering sigh… "If I'd just let him explain…"

Tears cascaded down her cheeks. "How can I ever forgive myself?"

She leaned forward and wept into her closed fists.

Jack crossed the room and perched on the arm of her chair, wrapping a consoling arm around her right shoulder.

"Susannah, you can't take responsibility for his death. That was beyond your control. Please. Listen to the rest of Sam's story before you come to any conclusions."

She snuffled in her handkerchief for a short while longer, and then sat up, breathing heavily.

"Sorry, everyone." She looked at Sam. "Please go on."

Sam cleared his throat uncomfortably. He wasn't enjoying being the bearer of upsetting news.

"You'll know what happened when Mr. Lusk came to your door. Pete was standing in the shadows and saw everything.

"He said Gil was pretty out of control. He didn't blame you for how you reacted." He glanced at Gerald Peters, as if seeking guidance, and Gerald broke in.

"If the balloon man's story began and ended there, it's a bit of a question mark if it would help you much. It confirms he knew where your studio was, and that he went there that night.

"You were probably one of the last people to see him alive, apart from his killer. But that might not help you much. It might make the cops think they've got you at the scene and further confirm their suspicions. But it's what happened just a day ago that changes things."

He looked at Sam expectantly, and the investigator gave a nervous cough and took a deep breath.

"Yesterday I saw Pete in the street again, and we stopped to chat. He told me the woman Gil accused of making the false entry—Mathilda Morgan—had approached him in the street. She offered him a bribe to go to the police with false evidence."

"She what?" Susannah's pulse jumped. He glanced up at her, his eyes jittery, but the squint kept on winking in perfect time.

"She wanted Pete to say that after you slammed the door on him, you trailed him with the knife in your hand. You called out to him, pretending you wanted to talk. But when he got close, you pulled the knife out and stabbed him."

He shook his head in disbelief. "She told Pete she knew for sure you were the one who killed him, and she wanted to make sure you got caught."

Gerald interrupted again.

"Pete told Sam he wouldn't do that. He knew for sure it wasn't what happened. Tell Susannah how he knew, Sam?"

Sam grinned. "He knew, because he followed Gil and he saw what happened."

Sam turned to Susannah. "You've got to understand, Miss Carterton. None of us street people like getting mixed up with the police. We stay as far away from them as we can. You never know when they're going to turn on you and arrest you for something you haven't done.

"If Pete admitted to them he'd seen Gil's murder, he might find himself the one arrested. They can turn the tables on you as fast as that."

Susannah nodded, the blood pounding at her temples. "Tell me, Sam. What exactly did Pete say yesterday?"

"He told me he'd seen who killed Gil, and it wasn't you. It was that woman Mathilda. And then she offered him money to lie about it. That made him so angry, he wanted to tell someone. I came along at just the right time."

Fifty-two

Susannah thought of the few days between Sam Malarkey's astounding exposé and the night of her "big reveal" as days spent living on borrowed time. They'd either be the last days she'd see of freedom—she was convinced that if she wasn't hanged she'd die in jail—or the first of a brand-new life.

Memories of her long-dead mother intruded whenever she had a moment to sink into an armchair and wring her hands with worry about whether everything was going to come together as she hoped.

Doing just that—sitting in a deep armchair wringing her hands with her brow furrowed—was an ingrained habit of Virginia Carterton's, and Susannah realized with a gulp that she was unconsciously modelling her mother's behavior, having no inkling she'd been doing it.

Together with Gil's mother, Elspeth, Virginia had been on the organizing committee for New York's biggest balls and the intense planning for that event went on for months. By comparison, the few days she had to put into organizing her big event were miniscule, but the outcome of it couldn't be more life changing.

If her audience accepted her case, she'd be free to take up her previous life, though she knew she could never go back, knowing the things she did now.

If they didn't accept her "reveal" she'd die in prison. It was as simple as that. She sent a silent prayer heavenward.

Dear Lord, never let me be so arrogant and foolish again. Let me pick up my life again with a different attitude from before.

Elizabeth Westerhoven bustled into the library, announcing her carriage was ready to take them downtown.

"I know you like walking, Susannah, but today it's different. It's important you make a statement with your arrival."

Susannah suppressed a disbelieving smile and picked up her small clutch purse and long skirts. "If you insist," she said with a gay laugh, ignoring the ever-tightening knot in her stomach.

They were scheduled to start at two p.m. in her Washington Street studio, and it was already 1:45.

"We're in plenty of time," said Elizabeth, slipping in beside her. Everyone else in the household had gone on ahead. Jack and Cordelia, Gerry Peters, Sam and Mrs. R, as well as a raft of people she had not yet seen today—Aloysius, the police captain Sean Cassidy, Mathilda, and Gil's parents Elspeth and Gilbert Snr, who'd fortuitously arrived in town the day before. They were here to retrieve his body for burial and—as they hoped—find out who killed their son.

Dot was here at Cordelia's request for a companion, and the trio Susannah thought as folk from the underground, Polly, Sam Malarkey and Pete the balloon man, were all scheduled to make appearances.

It sounds like a Charles Dickens story, thought Susannah. I just hope the people who decide things listen.

Orchestrating it all was Gerald Peters, who Susannah had got used to thinking of as Gerry, Jack's favorite nickname for him. He was a fine defense attorney and though it was some time since he'd appeared in court, he hadn't forgotten his old tricks.

As the carriage drew up outside her studio door, Elizabeth reached out and clasped the back of Susannah's hand in a warm squeeze.

"I'd wish you good luck, but you won't need it. When that police captain hears the case you're presenting, it will be 'No contest.'"

Susannah laughed freely. "Here's hoping you're right!"

••••••••

Inside her studio, two things immediately struck her. It was an expansive room. She'd hardly been aware of that before. But now that the fourteen *Ebony David* paintings hung here in their right order, the majesty of both them and the space they hung in was empowering.

She paused in the entrance and looked around her, letting the awe wash over her. It was the first time she'd truly seen them properly displayed, and the fullness of it overwhelmed her. She dashed a tear away from the corner of one eye.

These are major works, she thought. If a man had done them, they'd be acclaimed in the *New York Times'* arts pages as visionary and iconoclastic. As it is, they'd probably be remembered as scandalous artefacts by some woman implicated in a sordid murder.

Elizabeth was right at her side, standing with her in solidarity, her very presence a quiet statement that she had Susannah's back.

"I see Gerald and Jack to your right." The Countess murmured in Susannah's ear, and with a barely perceptible nudge she guided Susannah toward her attorney and the ringmaster for the event.

When she reached his side, he gave her instant concerned attention.

"I don't believe it will be necessary for you to take the stand today," he said. "And yes, I know we're not in a court of law, but old habits… you know the score." He grinned.

"I know you'd prefer to take a back seat. The others have got major evidence to present. But don't relax too much in case Cassidy has other ideas."

She nodded gratefully. "The more I can stay in the background, the better," she said. "I am so sick of being nothing more than the evil former fiancée."

Gerald searched her face with a dry wisdom in his eyes.

"Anyone just has to look around these walls to see you are far more than that."

He gave her a lopsided smile.

"Well, thanks," she said, her voice laced with irony. "Does that make me a mad genius, former evil fiancée? An even better story for the yellow press!"

He gave an appreciative guttural laugh in response. "Relax, Susannah. By the time we get through today, you'll look like Cinderella being tormented by the Ugly Stepmother. Or the Wicked Witch. I can't remember. Which one was it?"

A fluttering of attention near the door, and a subtle change in the energy in the room, announced new arrivals. Susannah glanced across and saw Aloysius and Dot had arrived, with Mathilda immediately after them.

It seemed to her, even from a distance, that Aloysius was carefully separating himself and Dot from any association with Mathilda. The last time she'd seen them together, at the opening night, Mathilda had draped herself around his neck.

Now, the freeze in the air between them was the kind that cracked and broke off glaciers. Susannah was almost on edge, waiting to hear the roar of tumbling ice.

Making no sign of noticing Tilly, Aloysius crossed the room like a ship in full sail, heading straight for Gerald. When he reached him, they exchanged soft decorous greetings, as if the portent of their business deserved respect for the dead.

They'd agreed that Gerald would give an opening address explaining the provenance of the paintings around them and advising there was one missing that was currently hanging in the exposition.

They stood, heads together—the lawyer's ginger curls bent close to the professor's long gray Bohemian locks—talking quietly, and then Gerald looked at his watch and they nodded in agreement.

Gerald clapped his hands. "Ladies and gentlemen, we've invited you all here today for special reasons which will quickly become clear. Please take your seats and we'll begin."

He gestured to Seamus Cassidy to take a seat right on the front row. Aloysius parked a briefcase on the seat next to him and gestured to Dot and Cordelia to sit next to him, which they did.

Mathilda had taken a seat in the same front row, but right at the other end was a yawning line of empty seats between where she sat and Cordelia perched.

"We have gathered you here together today in order to tease out the facts surrounding the death of Mr. Gil Lusk," Peters began. "I want to pay my respects firstly to Gil's parents, Elspeth and Gilbert Snr.

"I can appreciate how devastating this business is for you, and how your hearts must ache to discover more about the circumstances. I can assure you by the end of this afternoon you will have more information. Whether it will bring you comfort is debatable."

His face was stern and immoveable as he surveyed the room.

"Miss Susannah Carterton has had her impeccable reputation brought into serious question by the events of the last week. I believe in the interests of natural justice it is important we all hear the fresh evidence about the circumstances of Gil Lusk Junior's death.

"But before we get to that, I'd like to introduce Dr. Aloysius Mandelow, professor of fine arts and the senior judge in the Bay Gold Expo that opened a week ago.

"He will introduce the aspects relating to the art. I will leave him to explain further."

Aloysius rose and flicked the end of his black academic gown with its satin-lined hood backwards with both hands, as if to emphasize right from the outset his scholarly status.

But it quickly became clear that his love of art, and his outrage at having been landed with a fake in his inaugural exhibition, were deeply felt. In straightforward and indignant terms, he told the fraud story—of a painting being introduced like a cuckoo into the nest.

"The quality of the work was plain to see—it was the standout in the show. We were unaware it had been entered under a false name. And I hasten to add that Gilbert Lusk was also unaware of the scandal perpetrated in his name, and when he discovered it on the night of his death, it mortified him. He immediately wanted to correct the fraudulent claims."

He swept his arm around the walls. "We are in the presence of a master artist here, and the evidence is there on the walls before you."

After a furious glare in Mathilda's direction, he quietly subsided into his seat next to Dot and Cordelia and Gerald took over.

In quick succession, he called Polly and then Pete the balloon man to the front to repeat their tales of their meetings with Gil on the night of his death, and the things he'd said to them.

Looking pointedly at Seamus Cassidy, he intoned: "Neither of these people made themselves available to the police. Because of personal circumstances, they are not likely to present themselves at a police station. I understand very well why these conversations have not come to the department's attention."

Cassidy shifted uncomfortably in his seat, but nodded in appreciation.

Gerald turned and considered the room, his eyes flicking over Mathilda like an oil slick on water. "I think you can see a picture of a man with his judgement affected by too much alcohol, mortified to discover someone has perpetrated a fraud in his name. He was outraged.

"He wanted to see Miss Carterton immediately and explain he'd had nothing to do with it. But he approached it all in the wrong way.

"When he banged on her door in an inebriated state, insisting they had to talk, she did what any woman alone in her situation would do—she told him to go home and sleep it off.

"And he began on his way home, disgruntled and confused, perhaps. Unfortunately, he did not complete that journey alive. Someone, somewhere along the way, intercepted him and stabbed him to death.

"Surprisingly, because I know the police have been assiduous in their inquiries, no one has come forward to report they saw anything that night after Mr. Lusk left Miss Carterton's studio."

He gazed around the room again, his eyes seeming to alight more hawkishly on Mathilda Morgan this time.

"Until now."

Susannah, who'd been following Gerald's every nuance and gesture, saw Mathilda jump in her seat. Her face turned deathly pale.

Seamus Cassidy, too, straightened in his seat, an intense stare boring into Gerald.

"That's right. I said 'Until now.' Because someone saw what happened that night. And he has finally overcome his fear of the police to come forward and tell us his eyewitness account. Pete Kosimo, would you please return to tell us about events that occurred after the night Mr. Lusk died?"

His face sticky with fear, Pete the balloon man loped forward again.

"Can you tell me what happened the night before last, when you were returning home from your nightly balloon round. You were accosted by someone, weren't you?"

Pete looked like a frightened rabbit, but when he spoke up, his voice was strong. "Yes, sir. I was. A lady came up to me on Washington Street, near to where the chap was killed.

"She wanted me to go to the police and tell them about what I'd seen. 'Cos I did see a woman, stabbing Mr. Lusk in the chest. She said she'd pay me well if I was willing to step forward."

"And what did you do?"

"I told her I wanted nothing to do with the police."

He glanced in Seamus's direction. "Sorry sir. Mean no trouble by it. Just like to keep my nose clean."

Seamus nodded, and the ghost of a smile crossed his lips.

"But weren't you tempted to take the money? How much did she offer you?"

"One hundred dollars."

There were gasps around the room. A hundred dollars was a princely sum. It was a quarter of the Bay Gold prize money, Susannah reflected. To a hustler like Pete, living from hand to mouth on balloon sales and probably some petty crime, it was a fortune.

"A hundred dollars? That's an unbelievable amount to a man like you, isn't it, Mr. Kosimo? A gold mine."

"Yes sir, it is."

"So why didn't you take her up on it? I mean, you had truly seen what happened."

"Yes sir, but that wasn't the full story. She wanted me to say it was that lady there who stabbed him." He pointed in Susannah's direction. "The lady in the blue dress."

"Let the room be aware Mr. Kosimo is pointing at Miss Carterton." Gerald turned to Pete, his masterly command of the drama unfolding now clear to all.

It was like being in a play, Susannah thought. Her heart was pumping loudly at being accused of something she knew she hadn't done.

"Is that correct, Mr. Kosimo? You are pointing at Miss Carterton? She is the artist in the blue dress?"

"Yes. That's right, Mr. Peters."

"And what's wrong with that? You said a lady stabbed him."

"Yes, it was a lady, but not that lady. That was the howler."

"A howler, you say, Mr. Kosimo? What's that?"

Pete looked baffled at the lawyer's ignorance.

"Why a big lie, Mr. Peters. A Whizzer. Fudge. Humbug."

"Oh, I see. We get the picture. So, it was not Miss Carterton, you say? Why do you think the woman who spoke to you thought it was her?"

"I wouldn't know, sir. Because she knew for a fact, it wasn't Miss Carterton."

"That's a serious allegation, Pete. Why do you say that?"

"Because she knew who did it. She knew who killed him. She knew it wasn't Miss Carterton."

"How did she know that?"

"Because she was the one who done it. She kilt him herself."

There was a collective gasp. Gil's mother cried out. Seamus half rose from his seat.

"And how could you know that, Pete? Where did you get that notion from?"

"Because I saw her do it. I told you. I saw a woman kill that bloke, but I didn't know who she was. I had no clue. She was just a woman with reddish color hair, is what I saw. I'd never seen her before.

"But when she turned up offering to pay me to go to the police, I recognized her. It was the same one. She was the killer. And she was trying to blame someone else."

Pete looked around the room, an indignant set on his face. "Well, I couldn't go along with that, could I? Not even for one hundred dollars. It just ain't right."

Mathilda leapt from her seat and screamed. "You're not taking the word of a petty crim, are you? He's lying. It's all lies. The lot. And Polly and her heart-jerking rubbish. All lies.

"I loved Gil. We were going to get married… Why would I kill him?"

Gerald looked from her to Seamus, who had now risen fully to his feet.

"We'll leave that for Captain Cassidy to decide," said Gerald mildly.

But before Seamus could take a step forward, Mathilda sprang from her seat and advanced on Susannah.

"You don't know how much he hated always being in your shadow! Everywhere he went. People wanted to know about Susannah Carterton. Had he seen her lately? What was she working on now? Rarely did they ask him about his work. It was always all about you."

She had reached Susannah's chair, and Susannah had half risen to meet the onslaught. But she wasn't quite fast enough. With her arms on the sides of the chair, she was pushing herself to her feet when Mathilda drew a pistol from under her jacket and levelled it at her heart.

"Do you know what it does to male pride? To an artist's creativity? To always be overlooked for someone else, and a former lover at that."

Her eyes burned with long-concealed hatred.

"You never loved him." She spat out the words, loathing dripping from each one.

"You've only ever loved yourself."

She darted in on Susannah.

The power of the onslaught told her in a way that the words themselves—shocking as they were—couldn't, that the venom had been festering in Mathilda for a long time. Years.

She was far beyond the reach of any rational response.

Susannah was about to say something soothing, and affirming like "Oh, Mathilda, I'm sorry you feel that way," when the woman's fingers gripped her forearm like a steel band.

"You're coming with me," she ground out, momentarily waving the gun wildly above her head.

"If I'm going down, I'm making sure I take you with me. You're not escaping to Paris this time."

Fifty-three

"Wait, Tilly. Wait. You loved Gil. I know you did. So why did you kill him?"

Susannah pulled against Mathilda's iron grip, as she propelled her down Washington Street away from her studio.

She'd linked her right arm through Susannah's, so it looked as if they were two good friends out for an afternoon stroll. But there was a frenzied edge to all her movements, and she still held the concealed gun under her jacket.

The mechanical, relentless way her eyes roamed the street told Susannah she wouldn't hesitate to shoot her if anyone attempted to intervene.

The pedestrians they passed instinctively recognized something dangerous was happening and veered away from them, avoiding eye contact.

As the shock of the ambush faded, Susannah's mind whirred, canvassing her escape options.

Dig my toes in and refuse to take another step?

Nah. As she's said already, she's got nothing to lose. She'd kill me and run for it.

Beg for mercy?

She'd loved to hear me abasing myself, but it would probably make her hate me more. She'd feel so powerful she'd think she can kill me and get away with it.

Bargain with her?

What have you got to bargain with? She's not stupid. She knows she's going to be arrested for murder. And what is there you can offer her that matters?

In the few minutes she'd had to work down the list of decreasingly viable options, she made an instant decision.

Give her a chance to talk about herself. She won't be able to resist that.

Tilly stopped mid-stride and dug her buffed fingernails into the soft flesh of Susannah's upper arm.

"Who says I killed him, anyway?"

Susannah stared into her crazed face. "Well, Pete, the balloon man for one."

Piffle. Who'd believe him? He's a washed-up showman."

Susannah's throat was so dry she could barely speak.

"You didn't kill him? Is that what you're saying? That Pete's mistaken?"

Mathilda looked around her wildly, checking to if see Seamus or Jack were following them.

She eased the grip on Susannah's arm and for a moment Susannah glimpsed the woman she used to know, a straight talker with big ambitions.

Tilly screwed her eyes shut and then opened them wide again, like she was waking up from a bad dream.

"What happened to us, Susannah? We used to be such good friends."

Susannah shook her head, bewildered.

"Beats me, Tilly. I trusted you. I never imagined you'd put Gil's name on my work."

She gazed into Mathilda's misty eyes, focusing all her energy on breaking through to the woman she used to know.

"Why did you think you'd get away with it? Anyone who knows Gil knows it's not what he'd paint."

Tilly sighed.

"Everything you've ever wanted has come your way, Susannah, and you don't even know it. Paris academies, Gil, success in your work… Everything. While I've slaved away like some navvy, shovelling coal into a firebox that's never satisfied. It always wants more."

"What are you talking about? You were marrying Gil. I thought he was the answer to your dreams."

Mathilda gave a derisive snort

"He was only marrying me because he couldn't have you. I couldn't give him what you gave him.

"The 400-club blue blood family with entrée to all the best parties…. I didn't belong in that world. Conniving to win him a big art prize was the best I could offer, even if I had to grovel to that jerk Aloysius to get it through."

Desperation flashed in her eyes and she screwed up her face in a bitter grimace.

"But you wrecked all that."

"I wrecked it? I haven't seen either of you for six months. How could I wreck it?"

"I was over the moon when he asked me to marry him. After years of hoping, he was on the rebound after that big fight you had about coming to San Francisco.

"I thought I could get him to the altar before he changed his mind. The art prize would be a wonderful wedding present for him. It would set us up for married life.

"And then we came out here. I knew straight away he was secretly looking for you. Wanting to know what you were doing. He got more and more evasive. He didn't want to even discuss a wedding date.

"And when I finally told him about the painting—thinking he'd think it was a great lark—I've never seen him so angry.

"I knew it was the end. But I was determined. He wasn't throwing me out on the rubbish heap."

Susannah watched tears fall down Mathilda's pale cheeks, amazed at the sudden change of mood.

"Maybe after your big fight, in the heat of the moment, he genuinely planned to do it. But when he cooled down, he changed his mind. The fraud? It gave him as excuse to back out. But I have no doubts. My major sin was not being you."

"The knife…" Susannah asked. "The knife that killed him. Did he bring the knife with him?"

Mathilda's eyes flashed at the sudden change of topic. Then her face broke into a slow grin.

"That was genius, don't you think? I told that dumb policeman that you pulled the knife on Gil. And he believed me.

"I think sometimes Gil wished he'd used it on you that night. And only you, me and him, know how he got it."

"And Cordelia, Jack, Gerald. And Sam."

Mathilda stepped back, offended so many others were in on her little secret.

"Who's Sam?"

"Sam Malarkey. The private investigator who turned up all that fresh evidence the cops should have been chasing."

"Oh. Is that how you found those street down and outs?"

She began laughing, taking deep breaths and working herself into an almost hysterical lather, her shoulders shaking with mirth, drawing great gulping mouthfuls of breath.

"It doesn't make any difference. I'm not standing trial and neither are you, now."

"What do you mean, neither am I?"

"Don't be daft. Neither of us will be alive by sundown."

"Why not?"

"Because. It's the last thing I'm doing for Gil. I'm sending you to join him, and then I'm coming along too to spoil your fun. Just like I did in real life."

Fifty-four

"Stand in front of it."

"Pardon me?"

Tilly glared.

"I said, 'Stand in front of it.'"

Susannah glanced back at the third to last work in the *Ebony David* series and felt a surprising jolt of pleasure.

Here she was, about to die, and at least she could take comfort that she was leaving an unforgettable body of work behind her.

The second to last painting in the show, the one that should have carried a gold rosette and a sign that read "Best in Show"

This one is a standout. But it's not as good as the one in my studio. That's the pièce de résistance.

Susannah didn't move. She cast around in her head for another topic to divert Mathilda.

"Did you get the key to this place from Aloysius?"

"What?" Mathilda was humming to herself and looked annoyed at having her intimate communication interrupted.

"I said, did you get the key from Aloysius? You two must have got pretty close, working together on the show."

Mathilda had dragged her to the expo site and dug a door key out of her coat dress pocket while maintaining a steady pressure with the revolver in her side.

An eerie sense of being observed greeted them. Susannah guessed it must be because of the art that watched them the walls.

In contrast to the other night, when animated viewers filled the gallery, the room had a forlorn air, as if the paintings felt neglected without their admiring audience.

The only lighting came from stripes of illumination from the gas lamps in the street which shone through shuttered windows.

Susannah knew it deep in her bones: If she agreed to Mathilda's crazy demand that she stand in front of the most audacious art fraud in California's history, she'd be dead within seconds. She was using every distraction she could think of to deflect Mathilda's attention.

"Aloysius? I thought he might be an alternative to Gil, but I don't think so."

"Why not?"

Mathilda shrugged, as if he wasn't worth discussing.

"He's weak. And he's not into grown women."

"Ahhh…" Susannah didn't know what Tilly meant, but she let it go.

"You know Gil despised the David series, Tilly, don't you? He hated it."

Mathilda's face was in shadow, and Susannah couldn't read the rapid emotions that flitted across her face like clouds blown by strong winds.

"What possessed you to fake his name on that one?"

Mathilda moved toward her, the gun now pointed straight at her heart.

"Because it's unquestionably the best work you've ever done," she said, her face stony.

"Yes, but if he hated it? You know how sensitive he was. Tell me what he said when you told him you'd entered it under his name."

Mathilda stared at her, considering.

"He said it symbolized everything that had taken you away from him. Paris, your dammed insistence on your freedom… your wild ideas…"

Susannah's heart thumped in a bruised way to hear their differences stated so baldly. Marrying Gil would have obviously been a terrible idea.

"So why didn't allow him to withdraw the painting and soothe his wounded ego?"

Mathilda hesitated, and a shaft of pain flickered like lightning across her face.

"I'd given him the excuse he needed to get out of our engagement. And we had the showdown to end showdowns. There was no going back."

She jabbed the gun in Susannah's ribcage and Susannah fell back; the pain ricocheted to the soles of her feet. She'd not been expecting the sudden attack and sprawled backwards.

"You ask why didn't I back down? Because I'd had enough. I've watched you take him for granted for years. You'd pick him up when it suited you and drop him when it didn't. He'd made it clear we were over. And I wanted revenge on both of you."

She took the gun in both hands and levelled it.

"Now get over there. It's going to be my last reward. To destroy you and that painting. In one shot, if you're lucky. Otherwise, as many as it takes."

Susannah sensed a barely perceptible shift in the air in the stale, silent room. Keeping her eyes fixed on Mathilda, she listened with intense will for another shift in the current. Yes. There it was again.

"What was it like, Tilly? To dig a knife in Gil's ribs? To kill the man you say you loved?" Mathilda looked at her coldly and one side of her mouth curled in menace.

"You go on, don't you? What? Are you sad he's not around to be your plaything anymore?"

Her voice was strident and jeering.

"If gives you any satisfaction, it felt good. Super good. All the years I'd put up with being number three in a twosome. I finally got my revenge on both of you.

"Because using your family silver—it wasn't a coincidence. I planned it that way. It seemed—well, let's just say—destined. I kill him with your knife, and then you get blamed. Neat, isn't it?"

She took a step toward Susannah and waved the gun menacingly.

"Now get over there."

Susannah gave a lingering sigh and turned slowly, as if she was finally agreeing to Mathilda's orders. She took a slow step forward, then another, toward the *Ebony David*, listening with every fiber of her body for the interruption she was confident was coming.

Her foot froze in midair when it did.

"Stop! Hands in the air."

A man's gruff order, coming from somewhere close, the air finally swirling around her as he moved with power toward them.

She dove down and sideways within half a breath. The bullet that Mathilda fired in the split second after Seamus spoke whizzed over her head.

She rolled across the floor and found cover behind a wheeled cabinet which hadn't been returned to its proper place in the kitchens.

Too frightened to pop her head up to look in case Mathilda was still intent on revenge, she stayed down. She flinched at a rapid series of shots that made her ears ring.

And then the room fell silent. She heard Seamus Cassidy say, "You can come out now, Miss Carterton. You're no longer in danger."

Fifty-five

They piled into Elizabeth's Rockaway carriage—Jack and Susannah, Cordelia and Dot, on a beautiful summer's afternoon. The sort only San Francisco could turn on, Susannah thought with a contented sigh.

As they rumbled downhill to the town center, they caught glimpses of the bay, the marine blue surface mildly ruffed up by the spray of the boats that worked the wharves, a light sea breeze blowing back onto the land as it heated up and the midafternoon wind turned from offshore to onshore.

The faintest scent of salt and tar reached them, along with the comforting horsey smell from the chestnut pair drawing the coach.

Susannah could hardly believe she was a free woman. No more threat of murder charges hanging over her. She tried not to think of Mathilda, because when she did, her stomach clenched in sick waves of betrayal.

I know I'll have to forgive her sometime, but it's too soon for that now.
She was intent on sending me to the gallows.

In those crucial last minutes in the expo center, Mathilda had turned her gun on herself, but the painting remained unharmed.

With Seamus on her shoulder, she didn't have time to stage a dramatic exit in front of the disputed work and capture the attention of every yellow press rag in the country. Susannah was thankful for small mercies.

In the week since the dramatic finale, she'd gathered privacy like a comforting garment around her, allowing herself time to digest all that had happened and remember Gil at his best.

Treasured memories of golden days when they'd shared ideals and dreams and believed in their ability to change the world.

Somewhere along the way, he lost faith in his fruiting.

They'd had a private funeral for Gil with his parents and close friends, before Elspeth and Gilbert Snr. escorted his body back to New York for burial in the family crypt in Green-Wood cemetery.

Susannah had taken charge of the modest service they'd held for Mathilda, too. None of her family had the means to travel to California and so that was an especially somber occasion, with only Aloysius and their little family group present.

"Probably the best ending you could have wished for," Jack said solemnly. "I for one, would have hated to see her hung or imprisoned for life."

Today felt like a day of new beginnings. They were visiting Aloysius in a kind of post-funeral stock take to discuss how they would manage the disposition of the Expo Prize to its rightful winner.

Perhaps even more important for them, Jack was going to broach the question of Dot's indentured servant status and offer to buy her out.

"She's getting no chance for an education or anything else," he'd said to Susannah a few days before. "While we've got Aloysius in our thrall, I'd like to do something about that.

"He needs you to be gracious about the mess they made of that competition. Here's hoping he may enter some negotiation over Dot's status in return."

Susannah could see how important the issue was to him. They were both keenly aware that if the chips had fallen differently, Cordelia could have been the one who was little more than a glorified slave.

"I feel as if this is what I'm put on earth to do," Jack had said, his eyes blazing with passion, the ironic coolness he usually adopted nowhere to be seen

"I never realized what a wicked business it was until I lost Cordelia. And then found Isla. Anything I can do to ensure Dot's freedom, I'll do it."

Susannah glanced to the seat opposite her, where Dot and Cordelia sat next to each other, silk skirts rustling. Dot in a light turquoise and Cordelia in sapphire, two pretty tropical birds perched on a branch together, singing. Elizabeth and Susannah had quietly arranged for Dot's new gown.

Dot knew nothing of what they planned. Jack didn't want to get her hopes up, only to have them dashed, but the girls seemed to have picked up on the bright anticipation of the day. They giggled and pointed at scenes of interest as they rolled along.

"Look at that woman's hat! Who'd wear something like that?" From Dot. And from Cordelia: "A lemonade stand! Uncle Jack, can we stop for lemonade on the way home?"

Amazing, thought Susannah.

A couple of weeks ago, I was facing the gallows. Now I'm on my way to collect a pot of prize money, accept abject apologies for being wronged, and hopefully help free a girl from a life of servitude.

•••••••••

Aloysius' s inner sanctum at the Art Students League glowed with sun that streamed in through a large overhead dome topping the building, bathing the room in a balmy abundance.

As they filed in, Aloysius rose with a welcoming smile and advanced on the group, hand outstretched to greet them.

"Mr. Cabot, Miss Carterton, Cordelia," he paused and gave a huffing laugh, "and Dorothy, of course…" Momentarily set back by her change in social ranking, an embarrassed cloud eroded his assurance.

"Dot…You too. It's upmost in my mind to get this business sorted and to offer the Bay Gold Expo's sincerest apologies for what's happened."

Jack and Susannah shook hands cordially, and Jack muttered, "It's Jack, please, Aloysius. I think we know one another well enough to drop the formalities."

Aloysius gestured to a grouping of armchairs prepared for the meeting around a coffee table on which sat a large steaming coffee pot, a glass flask of fizzing lemonade, and a plate of pound cake sliced ready to eat.

Jack pointed at the lemonade with a delighted grin and said to Cordelia; "See, Dr. Mandelow is a mind reader. He's already got the lemonade for you."

Aloysius acted as the server, and when everyone had refreshments in front of them, he sat back like a board chairman and opened a folder before him. He rested his hands on his knees.

"Miss Carterton, this dreadful business of Lusk's death and the ridiculous attempt at fraud by the Morgan woman has sorely tested us. Everything seemed legitimate, but she conned me, and I apologize.

"She came from New York with sound credentials. But you can't account for what goes on in people's hearts and minds, can you?"

He glanced up at Susannah and then around the table.

Susannah set down her coffee cup and looked the bearded professor straight in the eye.

"Dr. Mandelow. I'm as astounded as anyone by what's occurred. I've known Tilly my whole life. At the beginning I couldn't believe it either, so please don't feel embarrassment at being caught in a sting. We all were."

"Most gracious of you, Miss Carterton." Aloysius's lips retained a wet gleam even when he wasn't talking, she noticed. She'd never liked wet lips on a man.

"I want to get straight to the point about the prize money," he continued. "The board accepts without question that the winning painting is yours. We have seen ample evidence in the rest of the series, which I believe will be one of this century's breakthrough works.

"It's a privilege for the Bay Gold Expo to have attracted a work of this caliber, and we have no problem at all in handing the prize money over to you."

He paused and took the time to sip his coffee and reach out for a piece of pound cake. He hesitated and let out a long sigh.

"You'll have probably heard that although Mathilda made a claim on it as Gil's legally affianced partner, we were waiting to be clear about the legalities. Thank goodness we did, considering what has transpired.

"We'll be happy to make this presentation as soon as we can. If it is acceptable to you, we'd like to do this publicly with an explanation as to the circumstances.

"We're resigned to the press having a field day about the surrounding events, but we can live with the notoriety if you can. It certainly has made our inaugural contest one no one will forget in a long time."

Susannah gave an understanding laugh. "Quite right, Dr. Mandelow. And after what I've been through the last few weeks, a bit more publicity can't go amiss. At least this time it will be positive, and will set the facts right."

Aloysius looked around the group with a satisfied smirk, happy the business had gone so smoothly.

"So how are you planning to spend the rest of your day?" he asked, addressing the query at the young girls.

Jack cut in. "I'm thinking Cordelia and Dorothy might like to wander the haberdashery section of the City of Paris, browsing the buttons and bows." He rose and dipped his hand into his back pocket, drawing out some loose coins and notes.

Cordelia and Dot gaped. "Shopping?" cried Cordelia. "You're letting us go shopping? By ourselves?"

"Just to the City of Paris. It's practically next door. I'm sure they've got enough pretty things to keep you interested for half a day. No further afield than there, though. I've got a small matter still to discuss with Dr. Mandelow."

He pulled out a pocket watch from the inside of his jacket. "Let's see. It's 1:30 now. Aunt Susannah and I will be outside in half an hour. At two o'clock. How about you rejoin us there, then?"

Cordelia shot Jack a look that said, *You can't fool me. I know you're discussing something you don't want us to hear.* Then she grinned broadly, merrily accepted the money he offered and left with Dot in her wake.

Aloysius looked at Jack quizzically when the young ones had departed. "There's something else you want to talk about? Please, go ahead."

"I'll come straight to the point," Jack said. "It's Dot. Dorothy. I want to make you an offer."

Aloysius's brows frowned into two deep parallel lines between his bushy brows. "Dot? Whatever about her?"

"I want to free her from her indentured service. Buy her out."

Aloysius's frown deepened.

"That seems most irregular," he said, his voice registering alarm. "There's nothing illegal about our arrangement, and she's been with me for years now. She's a good little worker."

"I'm sure she is, Dr. Mandelow. But there is something offensive to me about the whole thing, whether or not it's legal. I'm sure you've treated her well, but she's had little formal education, and there are no safeguards for these young people in service.

"The entire system urgently needs revision. Revision. or ditching entirely."

Susannah saw Aloysius's finger threaded through the handle of his coffee cup was turning white from pressure. She broke in.

"Dr. Mandelow, please understand. Jack intends no personal criticism here." She glanced at her companion. His face was glowing with righteous indignation.

"This is a topic very close to Jack's heart, because he almost lost his niece Cordelia similarly and only recently got her back. He sees Cordelia and Dot are becoming close friends, and he would like to arrange for Dot to enjoy the same opportunities Cordelia has.

"To give her the chance to aspire to something more in life than…" She paused, and then deliberately and quietly mouthed the next phrase: "benevolent enslavement."

Aloysius half rose from his seat in indignation and then sank down again. He huffed out a dissatisfied breath.

"Benevolent enslavement? That's a bit steep. Such a disagreeable way to describe a completely legal arrangement," he fussed.

"We're not disputing its legality, Dr. Mandelow. Not at all." Susannah was soothing the professor's feathers, and she could sense him settling back into his comfortable corner.

"Jack will arrange an equally legal settlement to arrange her freedom. We want to ask you one question. If Dot was your daughter, would you want to see her in indentured service?"

A pregnant silence hung in the room. Aloysius let out another irritated sigh.

"When you put it like that… No, if I had a daughter, then of course not."

"I think that answers everything we need to ask," said Jack. "Is it acceptable to you if my solicitor forwards papers to you, setting out a suitable agreement? Effective from signing?"

Aloysius's mouth quirked in one corner.

"You certainly don't waste time, do you, Jack? But in the light of everything else, I accept it's a fair arrangement.

"I feel I owe you for the generosity with which you've treated us over this other unfortunate matter. You could have made things difficult and unpleasant if you'd had a mind to."

Susannah and Jack exchanged sunny smiles and glanced back at the professor.

"We're all happy then," said Jack. "We won't say anything to Dot until we complete the papers."

"In the meantime," butted in Susannah, "could we ask if Dot can come and stay with Cordelia? As a friend's sleepover for a few nights? Like so many of the more fortunate young ladies do. Spend a few days at their best friend's house. Would that be all right?"

Aloysius's eyes shot up and his mouth dropped open.

"I hadn't expected it to happen so fast," he stuttered.

He looked at the resolute faces in front of him.

"But I suppose if it's going to happen, it may as well be without delay. I'll have to look for another young replacement."

"And if you do, may we make some suggestions for how to provide for his or her education and future training?" said Susannah with a sweet smile.

Aloysius laughed. "You're incorrigible, Miss Carterton, I'll give you that. But I suppose you have a good point. A sleepover it will be."

As they exited the studio a few minutes later, Jack threaded his arm through hers companionably. "I see I can take you anywhere, Miss Carterton," he said with a warm smile.

She laughed. "You did wonders in there," said Jack. "I was coming on too strong. I know I was, but I couldn't help myself. It never seems to occur to these fellows someone like Dot deserves education, training, preparation for a future other than being someone's slave."

She reached across and squeezed his forearm affectionately.

"I get it, Jack, and he will too, with a little help."

She gave him a big wide smile, feeling as if all the weight of the world had lifted from her shoulders.

"It's going to be wonderful. Two girls in the house to look after. What fun."

Fifty-six

Later, much later, after the girls had excitedly displayed the ribbons and bangles they'd bought at the department store, Jack and Susannah explained Aloysius had agreed for Dot to have a sleepover for a few days.

Dot's eyes filled with tears, and she was suspiciously silent for a few minutes. They'd come home to dinner and then when the girls headed to bed, still chattering like roosting starlings, Susannah and Jack retired to the library with a brandy nightcap.

Jack was reading the evening newspaper and quietly puffing on a cigar while Susannah sketched some ideas for her next series, one involving adolescent girls like Cordelia and Dot.

The silence between them was warm and companionable, until Susannah raised her head and asked lazily, "Has it ever occurred to you that Dot has got the same eyes as Isla?"

Jack looked across in surprise. Susannah continued to doodle on her sketching pad, not immediately looking up. Then she turned toward him and held up the sketching pad. There on the page, facing one another, were charcoal portraits of two young girls.

And the resemblance between them, especially around the eyes, as Susannah had remarked, was immediately discernible.

Jack's chest tightened. His breath came in quick puffs.

"What are you suggesting?" he asked, barely able to speak.

"I'm simply an artist. Following an artist's eye, noticing resonances in natural forms. Nothing more or less," said Susannah with a lightly teasing tone.

"No, you're not," said Jack with a laugh. "You're demonstrating that sixth sense all artists have for seeing below the surface to the essential form beneath."

"I wouldn't make it into anything as grand as that," said Susannah. "No sixth sense needed. It's as plain as the nose on your face. Or the eyes between finely sculpted eyebrows…"

"What is?" Jack had to ask, though he was pretty sure he knew what was coming.

"I'm tentatively suggesting something, that's all. In fact, I'm almost scared to ask the question. But do you think there's any chance Dot is Isla's lost sister?"

Fifty-seven

Isla slipped into the waiting hack alongside Jack in a fluid movement she'd executed a dozen times before, and yet today it felt different.

In that way life has of transforming from the expected to the unexpected in the blink of an eye, like when a dumpy tottering toddler turns into a well-coordinated, long-limbed child overnight, Isla had turned into a beautiful young woman while his back was turned. The cygnet was a confident swan.

He kissed her lightly on both cheeks and smiled into her glacial blue eyes.

"When did this happen?" he asked, teasing.

"When did what happen?" she replied, genuinely baffled.

"You've changed from a gawky adolescent into a lovely young woman since the last time I saw you."

"A gawky adolescent?" she said with an unladylike guffaw and all the indignation she could muster.

"Since when?"

"Since when I found you at Sophia's and bartered for your release from that place."

She smiled at him then. When he'd first met her, she was in the same situation as Dot, but in much more perilous surroundings.

Sophia Morrigan ran the semirespectable Imperial Club in the city and a string of trashy bars and brothels throughout the state.

She'd taken Isla on as a personal assistant, grooming her, Jack suspected, for a future role in running the brothels. The girl had a keen intelligence and an aloofness in her personality that deterred male attention—an attribute that had saved her until then, though Jack was uncertain how much longer it would have lasted.

Looking at her now, he exhaled an expansive sigh of relief. If Morrigan still had her in her clutches, she'd be on the block to the highest bidder within the month.

"How's Daphne?" he asked, keeping his tone light.

Isla's face lit up. "Daphne's wonderful. She's teaching me so much." Jack let his eyes run over the latest gown Isla wore—a turquoise silk edged with silver that perfectly showed off her white-blonde hair and ice-maiden beauty.

"I can see," he said. "Is that another new gown?"

Daphne Partington was an eccentric fashionista and onetime leading dressmaker to the beau monde who'd taken Isla under her wing. She protected, groomed and educated her, and when the girl showed a distinct talent for drawing and design, trained her in the arts of dress making.

"Yes!" said Isla in delight. "We made it together. It's a Dolly Varden dress." She stroked the bright pink and mauve overshirt, looped up at the edges over what looked like a white linen underskirt.

"It's named after a heroine in some old codger's books." She peered up at Jack through dark eyelashes. "Dickens or someone? It's the latest fashion and I love it! It makes me feel grown up."

"I'm sure it does," Jack said with a hint of dry irony and her eyes flashed to his, quick as lightning.

"Don't tease," she said in mock reprove.

"Tease? Me?" and they both laughed.

When they'd settled back comfortably for the rest of the ride, she asked, "Where are we going, anyway? Cordelia will be there, I hope?"

The two girls had first met during an earlier visit Jack had made to Lochie O'Riordan's studio and had hit it off.

"Yes, she will. And there's someone else I want you to meet. One of Lochie's models." He gazed out the window reflectively and then turned to look into her face.

"Sorry we've been tied up in other affairs the last few weeks. It's been pretty intense."

"Another murder." She nodded in understanding. "I've seen a bit about it in Daph's papers. All settled now, though, isn't it? And are you getting on any better with Susannah these days?"

He felt his cheeks warm, and she immediately giggled.

"Yes, I see you are. That's good. It was pretty uncomfortable for Cordelia when you were at one another's throats all the time."

"We weren't…" He let the protest die away. No point in arguing. Isla's perceptions were rapier sharp, and they had been pretty awful to be around with their sniping.

"We've sorted a lot of things out during this murder business. I've discovered she's not as bad as I thought she was."

"And who's this model of Lochie's? Not another Jasmine?"

Jasmine had been one of Sophia's soiled doves, bought, like Isla, by Sophia from the Catholic orphanage, but not as fortunate in the tasks they set her.

"Not another Jasmine. A girl called Dot, an indentured servant— a housemaid—to one of the art professors. I think you'll like her."

The cab was slowing down to pull into the Woodward Gardens, where he'd arranged to meet Susannah with Dot and Cordelia.

"There they are, waiting at the gates," said Isla, clapping her hands, suddenly a young girl again, excited to be with her friends.

"So they are," said Jack, his heart in his mouth. He felt sweat break out on his forehead and realized he was as nervous as a rabbit in a gamekeeper's sights.

Here's hoping they don't hate each other on sight.

•••••••

He jumped down ahead of Isla and guided her to the little group by the gate. His eyes went directly to Susannah, who was looking buoyant in a dress that bore striking similarities to Isla's. A red and pink flowered chintz over a deeper toned fuchsia underskirt.

As she came toward them, he noticed she was moving more freely than usual; the dress was shorter than last season's, ideal for outdoor wear. The gauntness she'd developed during the stress of the murder investigation—an ever-present pale face, dark-ringed eyes, listlessness—had vanished, replaced by a fresh ripeness. She's like a peach at its perfection, he thought.

Shut up, Jack. And get on with it...

Cordelia was bouncing up and down on tiptoes, just as excited as Isla to be meeting up again. And Dot hung back, her usually serene eyes darting uncertainly around the group, anxiously trying to follow the exchanges.

Isla and Cordelia had linked hands and were doing a merry dance of delight at meeting up again. Dot stood aside, momentarily left out of the circle.

Jack stepped in. "Girls… girls…" They paused. "You're forgetting someone."

He stood beside Dot and gently drew her closer to the rest of the group.

"Cordelia, you're already well acquainted with our visitor, Dot, but Isla, you haven't had the chance to say hello yet. Dot's staying with us at Elizabeth's for the next little while. Isla, meet Dot. Dot, meet Isla."

He stepped away quietly and a remarkable silence fell over them, like the world had paused momentarily to breathe. Like the quiet hush of early dawn before life resumes.

Isla and Dot gazed at one another, both, it seemed, at a loss for words. Isla's brow bore a puzzled pencil mark of confusion.

"Dot? Is that your real name?" The query sounded sharp. Dot shook her head, wordless.

"No… no. It's Dorothy. The people I stayed with… They called me Dot. No one's called me Dorothy for ages… for a long, time."

Isla's eyes focused on her companion. "For how long, exactly?"

Dot's shoulders shrugged. "I don't know. I don't remember."

Isla nodded, as if she'd already decided about something important. She turned to Jack.

"Are we going up the hill to the teahouse?"

He nodded. "Yes. We thought it would be nice to get out in the air and take a walk. Coffee and cake at the top." He gestured up the track. "You lead on. We'll follow you."

Isla fell in beside Dot and they started slowly up the track together.

Fifty-eight

"So…" Isla turned to Dot, dark suspicion clouding her face. "Jack says you're working for some art professor? What's that like?"

"I used to, yes. But Jack—Mr. Cabot—says I don't have to work for Professor Aloysius anymore. I'm staying with Mr. Cabot and he's going to help me get an education."

Dot glanced into Isla's face, her eyes milky with remembering.

"Aloysius was all right. He didn't beat me, so I was luckier than most. I've been working for ages now. Since I was about seven.

"Just chores, doing dishes, lighting fires. All the stuff no one else wants to do. A housemaid's job. Ever since the orphanage? I never learnt to read and write properly."

Isla grasped at her chest, as if to catch her breath. She glanced back at Jack, her eyes overflowing with meaning.

"You were in an orphanage? Do you remember which one?"

Dot shrugged. "Not really. There was this horrible old dragon lady."

She gazed up at Isla reflectively. "I had a sister who called me Dumpling. That was the only good part."

Isla's feet stopped moving. Jack halted and signalled to Susannah and Cordelia behind him.

"And what was her name?"

Dot flashed a smile, sad and bright at the same time.

"I called her Jeffer—kind of like Irish for Big Sis. Deirfiúr. I can't remember her real name."

Isla bent over, as if in sudden pain, and then rounded on Jack.

"You already knew, didn't you?"

Jack suddenly didn't know what to say or do next.

"Knew what?" His heart was thumping so hard it felt like it would jump right out of his chest.

"You knew she's my sister."

"No, no. I didn't," Jack said. He stepped forward and placed a gentle hand on the shoulder of each girl.

"I didn't know. But I—we—suspected. I admit it. Thanks to Susannah, we both wondered."

Dot was gazing from Isla to Jack, her face a whirr of conflicting emotions. Fear, confusion, flashes of wonder….

"Suspected what?" she asked of no one in particular.

Isla turned back to her, tears streaming down her face, her usual glacial composure ripped apart.

"We're sisters." The words choked out of her throat. "We're sisters," she said again, her voice stronger, the tears flowing faster and heavier.

"Your name is Cassie. And thanks to Jack, I've found you at last."

••••••••

They didn't talk again as they climbed the hill to the teahouse, arms wrapped around each other, where they all collapsed at an outside table and waited for the refreshments to arrive.

Isla and Dot held hands, gazing silently at one another, not speaking, for a very long time. The rest of the group made low-pitched general conversation about the flowers, the peacocks, the view of San

Francisco Bay, leaving the sisters to their private moments.

By the time the coffee and cakes had arrived, they'd regained some equilibrium.

"You name is Cassie," Isla repeated, in mock reprimand.

She gazed at her sister as if she couldn't believe her own eyes.

"Cassandra. Or it used to be. You'll have to decide. Do you want to be Cassie or Dot?"

"I don't know who I am at the moment," Dot said. "I'm just glad we've found each other."

"I can't believe you were right here in San Francisco and I never saw you," said Isla. She drew back and regarded her sister with a critical eye.

"Then again, I might have seen you but not recognized you. You've sure grown up!! But there was something about you. The minute I saw you, I got a funny feeling in my stomach."

She turned to Susannah. "What was it that made you think Dot was my sister, Miss Carterton? Jack mentioned you were the one who suggested it."

"Something about your eyes," said Susannah. "As soon as that blasted murder business was over and I really saw Dot, it came to me in a flash. You were from the same family. And please, I'm Susannah from now on, okay? We're all family now."

Fifty-nine

We're all family now.

Jack noted Susannah's remark to Isla, but he hadn't commented on it. He hugged it to his chest and let it warm him from the inside out.

And after dinner that evening, he found the courage to raise it. They were once again companionably relaxing in the library over a brandy nightcap. Elizabeth was out at the opera for the evening, and the girls were playing cards again.

"So, Susannah, now our lives are shaping up as almost normal again. Have you decided on your plans?"

"My plans?" Her voice was vague and far away, her eyes had a distant look, as she lifted her head from her sketching pad to gaze at him.

When she was working on anything creative, she got lost in her own world, he'd noticed.

"Yes. Will you go back to New York? Are you happy for Cordelia to stay here with me and Dot? What do you want out of life now?"

Her eyes fluttered wide, as if she was coming down to earth with a bump. He could see the gold flecks in her irises that tonight looked a deep chestnut color, offering a spark of hope for something special to come.

"What do I want out of life?"

A dart of anxiety crossed her face, as if she was frightened to say.
He remembered how she hated being vulnerable.

"It's a reasonable question, Susannah. Nothing to fear about it," he gentled. "I'm sure Cordelia would like to know, too."

"Cordelia," she said with a faraway tone again. As if she was just remembering her niece.

She shot him a wry smile. "She obviously loves it here, and the air is doing her good. I wouldn't want to drag her home."

A knot clenched in his stomach.

"Home? Is that how you still see New York?"

She seemed to wake up then. She focused directly on him and she grinned teasingly.

"Is this Twenty Questions or something, Jack?" she said. "Can I turn the tables and ask you; What do you want out of your life?"

He vacated his armchair in front of the unlit fire, and crossed to where she sat on the big leather sofa, her sketching pad open on her knee.

He leaned over, picked up the sketching pad, and placed it on the ottoman in front of her. And then he perched on the ottoman's corner and took her right hand in his.

Heightened energy instantly charged the space between them.

His heart was racing, his fingers tingling as he took her hand in his.

"I want you to stay here with us. Cordelia and me. And Dot," he added as an afterthought. "Just as you commented this afternoon. For us all to be a family."

She stared back at him, and he could sense she was holding her breath.

"If you would consent to it, I would like you to become my wife and live here in San Francisco. Will you marry me, Susannah Carterton, the most infuriating woman on earth? I can't seem to get you out of my mind or my heart."

She stared at him, her throat working, but no words emerging. There was a long silence.

"If it makes any difference, Cordelia has already given us her blessing."

At this, she burst into spontaneous laughter and reached out with her other hand to take up his, so they were sitting facing one another, hand in hand.

The heat of the connection fizzed up his arm and into his chest.

"How could I refuse such an irresistible offer?" She laughed through happy tears.

"Yes, yes, and yes." She hesitated. "Do you think we ought to call Cordelia in now and let her know? I'd hazard a guess she's probably out in the hall eavesdropping."

She'd raised her voice as she spoke, and after another few moments of hesitation there was a scratching outside the library door and Cordelia burst in, all smiles.

"How did you know?" she giggled.

"It seems to me there are hardly any secrets between you and your uncle Jack." Susannah beamed at them both. "You've both got a lot to teach me about openness. I promise. No more secrets."

Jack and Cordelia glanced at each other sheepishly. "What have I said?" Susannah asked, instantly wary again. "Is something wrong?"

Cordelia glanced at Jack, and they shared a long silent exchange

"Errr. Not wrong exactly," Cordelia said. "But we do have a confession. And we hope you won't be mad at us for interfering."

"Mad with you?" said Susannah. "Never. Especially after we've just agreed to get married."

"Okay," said Cordelia, clearly reluctant. "In that case, we want to play a little game."

She came and stood behind Susannah and gently closed both hands over her eyes.

"A kind of Blind Man's Bluff, except you sit there while Jack gets something."

Jack crossed the room and drew out from the desk the white envelope he'd hidden there for the past week. He delivered it into Susannah's upturned hands. Cordelia let go of Susannah's eyes and they both stood, watching expectantly.

Susannah cast her eyes to the envelope. "What? You want me to open this?"

"Yes. Go on. Now." Cordelia was making a poor job of suppressing her pent-up excitement.

Susannah cast a worried look toward Jack. "Everything is all right, isn't it?"

She glanced down at the thick wedge of documents on her lap.

"More than all right," he said. "Just open it and we can be sure of it."

Tentatively, she opened the envelope.

Inside, she recognized tickets. Passenger liner tickets.

She teased them out and read the stamped text.

"For a sailing. New York to Paris… in two weeks…"

"What's this?" She looked up, bewilderment in her eyes.

"You've just said you want me here, and now you're sending me away?" Cordelia trilled her laughter, and Jack swooped in and nestled beside her.

"Not sending you away. No, my dear Susannah. We're all going to Paris together. To pick up Athena. It's all arranged."

"All arranged? But the nuns…"

"I cabled the nuns. I told them you wanted to adopt Athena. They've given us extra time to get our affairs organized. I promised we'd bring Athena home by Christmas, and they've agreed."

"Oh, Jack," she cried, bursting into tears all over again. "Whatever have I done to deserve you?"

THE END

WHAT'S NEXT?

The third book in the Home At Last trilogy, (title still to be decided) will be published in the first half of 2023.

Here's what is coming
We've read Dolphie and Jack's stories in Home At Last, Books #1 and #2. In #3, adopted Senator's son Alexandro de Vile, known to readers of the Of Gold & Blood series, is grappling with his unrecognized natural father's Spanish heritage. And the woman he feels irresistibly drawn to won't take him seriously....

Like his fellow 'musketeers,' he will face adversity, right wrongs, and encounter and love feisty women who will change his life forever.

There, he'll find his way home at last.

ACKNOWLEDGMENTS

When I started *Susannah's Secret*, I didn't know Susannah would be going to Paris, but when I began to research the situation serious women artists found themselves in the mid and late nineteenth century, I discovered many of them sought tuition in Europe.

And when I got into the story, it was great fun to pursue this line of enquiry. Many of the details about Susannah's life in Paris are based on fact.

The character Ezra is based on a real-life artist, Henry Ossawa Tanner, who won acclaim for his paintings in Paris in the 1890s, admittedly a little later than the time my story is set. Born in Pittsburgh in 1859, Henry was the first of five children born to Reverend Benjamin Tucker Tanner, a future bishop in the African Methodist Episcopal Church, and Sarah Tanner, a woman who had escaped her enslavers via the Underground Railroad.

Susannah's "imagined dwelling" on the edge of Montmartre was then in apartments, and now houses the Museum of Romantic Art (the Musée de la Vie Romantique at 16 Rue Chaptal). Notables like George Sands and Frederic Chopin once frequented it, as well as celebrated artists.

The Rat Mort (Dead Rat) café was just as described—an artist's hangout which was the scene for one of Toulouse-Lautrec's famous paintings, *In A Private Booth at the Rat Mort*, now in the Courtauld Institute in London. The expatriate artist's summer community in Brittany really happened.

And the Academie Julienne was famous for its excellent tuition of artists who could not gain entry to the more formal schools. Founded in 1868, "at a time when art was about to undergo a long series of crucial mutations, the Academie Julian played host to painters and sculptors of every kind and persuasion and never tried to make them hew to any one particular line….. It nurtured some of the best artists of the day". (*The New York Times*, 1989)

As most authors agree, it takes a team to publish a book and *Susannah's Secret* is no exception. I'm thankful to the many people who helped me along the way, too numerous to name individually, though I would like to acknowledge I'm especially grateful for emergency website assistance from Nate Hoffelder.

Formatting once again handled with skill, good humor and alacrity by Marina and Jason Anderson at Polgarus Studios in Tasmania.

If you'd like to get updates by becoming a friend of Jenny's books and getting the latest news of releases and free book offers join us at:

https://www.jennywheeler.biz/free-poisoned-legacy-tangled-destiny-ebook/

Enjoy this book?
You Can Make a Difference

Reviews are the most powerful tools in my kit for getting my books noticed. Much as I'd love it, I don't have the budget of a big publisher to buy bill board ads and other national advertising. But I have the promise of something more powerful—something publishers envy. And that's a committed and loyal bunch of readers. Honest reviews of my books help them gain the attention of others who might appreciate them, too.

Post Your Susannah's Secret Reviews Here:
For Amazon: https://www.amazon.com/dp/B0BNPFNCXP
For Goodreads:
https://www.goodreads.com/book/show/63905235-susannah-s-secret
Bookbub: https://www.bookbub.com/books/susannah-s-secret-by-jenny-wheeler

ABOUT THE AUTHOR

Jenny Wheeler is the author the new Home At Last Trilogy and of the Of Gold & Blood Old California mystery series:

Poisoned Legacy #1.
Brother Betrayed #2.
Double Jeopardy #3.
Tangled Destiny (Christmas novella and Prequel.) #4.
Unbridled Vengeance #5.
Hope Redeemed, A Spanish Novella, #6.
Boxed Set/Book Bundle Of Gold & Blood, Books 1–3.
Boxed Set Book Bundle #2 Poisoned Legacy and Tangled Destiny
Tainted Fortune #7.
Book Bundle /Boxed Set #3 Book #5 Unbridled Vengeance and #6
Hope Redeemed.
Book Bundle/Boxed Set #4 Book #7 Tainted Fortune and #8
Captive Heart.
Captive Heart #8.
Three Holiday Novellas–Book Bundle/ Boxed set Books #3, #6, and #8.
Ancient Deception #9.
Dangerous Desires #10.

Home At Last
Sadie's Vow #1
Susannah's Secret #2

WHERE TO FIND JENNY

Jenny's online home is at jennywheeler.biz or email
Jenny@jennywheeler.biz

You can connect with Jenny on:
Facebook: @JennyWheeler.Biz
Twitter: @Jenny_Biz
Instagram: @jennysbingereading
Pinterest www.pinterest.nz/Jennywheelerbooks
Goodreads: goodreads.com/author/show/11371547.Jenny_Wheeler
Bookbub: www.bookbub.com/profile/jenny-wheeler

www.ingramcontent.com/pod-product-compliance
Lightning Source LLC
Chambersburg PA
CBHW051139190726
48290CB00006B/1919